C000079750

SISTER DEATH

ACID VANILLA BOOK 4

MATTHEW HATTERSLEY

BOOM BOOM PRESS

YOUR FREE BOOK

Discover how Acid Vanilla transformed from a typical London teenager into the world's deadliest female assassin.

Get the Acid Vanilla Prequel Novel:
Making a Killer available FREE at:

www.matthewhattersley.com/mak

For Suzanne and Alba

ONE

THE GIRL'S EYES WERE THE COLOUR OF DARK CHOCOLATE. So dark, one had to get up close to see where the pupil ended and the iris began. Of course, Danny Flynn had already known this before sliding onto the bar stool next to hers. Her eyes (big, oval, beautiful) were the same colour as almost every other olive-complexioned girl's here in the Spanish taberna. But pinpointing the shade, the tone, the precise hue of that brown, that was another matter altogether. And one that made all the difference.

"They're so striking," he purred, not blinking, not taking his own eyes from hers. "So rich. Like cocoa… umm, *el cacao, sí?* A deep chocolate brown."

The game was simple and arose from Danny's long-held belief that, for a ladies' man such as he, a lover of women, the eyes were not only the gateway to the soul but also to the heart, the mind, the bed. Staring into someone's eyes like this, trying to work out the exact shade, created strong, lasting eye contact, which in turn reinforced trust and likeability. He'd also read how this act of intense perusal conjured up a deep connection between two people. So the person whose eyes you were gazing into – the girl in this case (always a girl in Danny's case, and there'd been plenty) – would likely become attracted to you.

It also helped if your own eyes were the most beautiful shade of azure blue most girls had ever seen. Or so they told him, at least. Whether or not they meant it didn't matter to Danny. By that point in the proceedings, everything else was usually a foregone conclusion.

"They are just brown. I think," the girl said, with a shy titter. "Like most girls from Donasti. You are silly."

"No way," Danny went on, "they're beautiful. I'd say looking at them now, in this light, they're actually more walnut. Or chestnut. Or *raw umber*." He took his time with each description, giving the words as much sexual energy as possible.

"I do not know these things."

The girl looked away. Damn. He was losing her. *Donasti,* she'd said. Donastia. The Basque name for San Sebastian. So her family was old-school. Figured.

"Your English is great," Danny told her. "Better than my Spanish, anyway. Hell, better than my English too."

Smokey topaz? Would that have done it?
Russet?

He sometimes offered up *beaver* as a shade, test the waters that way. But with non-English speakers, the nuances of that were risky.

"Whereabouts in England are you from?" the girl asked, gazing up at him through her eyelashes.

He was wrong. *Game on.*

"I'm not actually from England," Danny chimed, with a grin to match the twinkle in his baby-blues. "I'm from Ireland. Dublin. You heard of it?"

The girl nodded. "Yes, of course. But I have not visited. I have never left my country. Never left my city."

"No way," Danny purred, as his stomach did a somersault. "I'll have to take you some time. Once we're married, of course." He held eye contact, upped the grin, delighting as the girl's light brown (*caramel?*) cheeks flushed a dusky pink.

"You are very funny," the girl told him. "What is your name?"

"Oh shite, where's me manners? I'm Danny. Danny Flynn." He held out his hand. "And you are?"

"My name is Lola." She took his hand coyly. "Pleased to meet you, Danny Flynn."

The way she said it made him think she knew his game. Knew it, but was maybe onboard all the same. These baby-blues.

"Lola, hey? Not a showgirl, are you, Lola? Or a fella?" He laughed but got nothing back, adding quickly, "Ignore me. Being daft, so I am. Can I buy you another drink?"

The girl, Lola, shifted in her seat as a nun shuffled past them and sat at a table in the corner of the small taberna. Danny watched her for a moment, stifling a sneer. A devout Catholic in his youth, he had no truck these days for any members of the cloth, man or woman. Not that he'd had any dodgy run-ins with the local priest or anything like that. But losing your dad at such a young age does have a tendency to test your faith somewhat. It seemed the good Lord didn't have his back the way he'd been told he would.

He watched on as the nun eased herself down onto a hard wooden seat. With her face hidden by the folds of the wimple and veil it was hard to tell her age, but by the way she was stooped over, Danny would have said the old dear was pushing eighty. What the blinking hell was she doing here anyway, in a bar? Trying to cockblock him?

But maybe it was a sign. God looking out for him after all. He knew he was pushing it being out in public right now. Luis

Delgado knew a lot of people in San Sebastian, and he'd be looking for him. Looking to take back what was his. Still, the way Danny saw it, if he was going to have to lie low for a few days, he may as well have some decent company

He turned his attention back to Lola, narrowing his eyes a little, enough that they creased at the sides, giving her that 'hint of a squint' that made him look so confident and sexy, and which he'd often practice in front of the mirror.

"So, a drink?" he asked.

"I am sorry, I do not think I should," she replied, flustered now. "I have to get home. I only stopped for one drink after work."

"Oh, where do you work?" Danny asked, trying to dampen any desperation in his voice.

"I am a cleaner, so I work a few places. A school. Some houses. The convent on the hill."

"Righto. I see." Danny sighed. "She give you the evil eye, did she? The old God-botherer over there?"

"I must go," Lola continued, shuffling off her seat. "My parents will be waiting for me."

"Aye, go on," Danny told her. "I'll see you around, Lola. You take care now." He turned his attention to the large barman standing at the far end of the counter with a gruff expression on his face. Danny nodded him over, raising his empty beer glass for a refill. "One more, please, mate."

"No problem."

He picked his packet of cigarettes up off the counter and stuffed them in the pocket of his off-yellow cheesecloth shirt. "I'm just away out back for a smoke," he said, gesturing at the frothy beer being poured. "Put that on my bill, will ya?"

Muttering *fecking nuns* to himself, he swaggered through the taberna and out the back door, finding himself in a small courtyard big enough for only two plastic tables and a few chairs. Danny sat on one of the chairs and pulled out a wonky cigarette from the packet. Last one. He stuffed it between his lips and lit up, before leaning back in the flimsy chair and exhaling a large plume of smoke into the night air. It was past nine, but still hot out. A warm breeze felt good against his cheeks and forehead as he closed his eyes and took another long drag of the cigarette.

What to do?

He'd already risked so much. But having only one was of no use at all. Both of them or nothing – that was the deal. Meaning he might as well not have bothered. He shook his head, his libidinous mood dropping like a lead weight onto the dusty earth.

"Fucking hell," he mouthed. "Ya stupid bastard, so y'are."

He took another long drag on the Marlboro Light, sucking until the filter was hot and his throat burned. He held the smoke in his lungs a second before exhaling thoroughly and getting to his feet. With his nicotine craving satisfied, and feeling a little dizzy, he flicked the cigarette butt into a gnarled old olive tree at the back of the courtyard and turned to go back inside.

Only someone was blocking his way.

"All right there, Sister," Danny chimed, seeing the old nun leaning against the doorframe. "You get lost looking for the bathroom? Umm... *el baño?*"

The old nun didn't answer, but slowly she raised her head to face him. Now he saw she was younger than he'd realised. Much younger. Not bad looking either. For a nun.

Danny grinned. "I don't suppose *you* fancy a drink?"

The nun still didn't speak. But as he stared open-mouthed, she lifted her hands and peeled back her veil before removing the stiff white coif covering her head. This is a bit fecking weird, Danny told himself. He'd never turned a nun before, and in all honesty he hadn't thought it'd be this easy.

She continued to stare at him in silence – which was becoming a tad disconcerting, it had to be said. He would have guessed now she was in her mid-thirties, but would have said late twenties to her face. (Always go lower). She stood about five-four, give or take, and with her swarthy complexion and dark eyes (*wenge*, he might have tried) appeared to be from the region. Her hair was thick and shoulder-length, almost black except for a long strand of white-grey that framed her face at both sides. It was these white streaks that gave the appearance she was still wearing the wimple and veil despite her flinging them, dramatically, to the ground.

"Listen, love," he told her, grin faltering a touch, holding his palms aloft. "I'm not sure what you're after here, but perhaps we should go somewhere more private. I've got a room around the corner, above the old town. We could…"

He trailed off as the nun lifted the remaining robes of the habit over her head and flung them to one side. Underneath she was dressed in all-black. Black leggings, black plimsoles, black ribbed polo-neck jumper.

"You must have been sweltering in all that," Danny said, starting to wish she'd respond in some way. Maybe she didn't speak English. "*Hablas Inglés? Estas bien?*"

Without the robes she was slim, perhaps too slim. *Nothing but skin and bone*, his old ma would have said. Danny didn't like his women too thin. Liked something to grab hold of, liked boobs and bums. Still, he wasn't going to let her lack of curves put him off.

A nun, for feck's sake.

Imagine the stories he'd get out of this.

Still not taking her eyes off his, the nun (hard to think of her as such now) reached around her back. Going for a mobile, no doubt. Back pocket. It was how it worked. He smiled, relaxing a little and putting on a show of diffidence.

My number? Well, all right then…

But the charade was short-lived as a moment later she brought her hands back around the front to reveal a long shiny blade clenched in each fist.

"What the…?" Danny gasped, stepping back, one eye on the doorway now, his only escape route. "I'm not sure what's going on but I think you've got the wrong bloke."

"No," the nun spat (though clearly she wasn't a nun, was she?) "I never get the wrong person, Danny Flynn."

His eyes were burning with how wide open they were. His mouth flapped a few times, but closed again.

Was this… Really?

"Listen, love. Whoever sent ya, we can talk about it. I don't think we need to get silly or nothing. Whatever you think I've done, I'll rectify it. Straight away. No messing. Let's be clever about this."

Despite the quiver in his voice, these sorts of exchanges were actually second nature for Danny. And not only with the many women he'd wronged over the years. As a fly-by-night antique dealer (and one who had long since cornered the market as a procurer of high-end art for the more nefarious elements of society), he was used to dealing with scary people. Though to date, he couldn't remember anyone having pulled two knives on him at the same time.

"Enough talk," the woman snarled. "Time to die."

She leapt towards him, spinning around and slashing out with the knives like some kind of deadly dervish.

With his heart filling his throat, he dodged out of the way but skidded on the dusty ground and stumbled into the high adobe wall surrounding the courtyard. No doors here. No windows either. The only escape route was back through the taberna. He got to his feet just in time as the crazy woman dived at him again and one of the blades slashed at his upper arm. Not deep, but painful all the same.

"Shite on a bike! Please. You don't have to do this." He held his hands up, walking backwards with his assailant matching him step for step around the perimeter, both with one eye on the door. "Delgado sent you, right? Tell him I'm sorry. Tell him I'll return what I took. No danger. Okay?"

The woman hurled herself forward, but this time Danny grabbed her by the wrists. He held on tight as she lurched and bobbed, jabbing the steel blades towards his chest. She snarled, spat in his face, but he wasn't letting go. Danny Flynn might be a pretty boy (*a lover not a fighter*, was what he told the ladies), but he could handle himself all right. A childhood spent in Ballyfermot, arguably one of the poorest and roughest areas of Dublin, meant he'd had to. A young man grows up fast, places like that, learns how to handle himself. Though, Danny did have principles. Despite what some might say, he wasn't a womaniser (he wasn't, he enjoyed women's company, that was all). Growing up without a father his principal role models had all been women. His ma, his aunt Sheila. He'd always enjoyed women's company far more than men's. And he certainly had never hit a woman. Up until a minute ago, even the thought of doing so would have disgusted him.

"Get to fuck," he yelled, making to knee his attacker in the stomach.

But she was too quick for him. His flailing knee found nothing but air as she dodged out of the way and the exertion meant he slackened his grip on her wrists. This, coupled with a foot to the groin, and she was able to struggle free. He staggered backwards, holding onto his old-fella and preying his lower intestine hadn't actually fallen into his arse like it felt like. His right heel touched against a raised flagstone and he stumbled against the perimeter wall. That was it. Nowhere to go.

He grimaced, waiting for the fatal blow, but it never came. Instead the woman just sneered at him and shook her head, an expression of pure disdain creasing her features.

"Look, let's talk about this." He held up his hand, the other covering his bare neck as he got to his feet. "How much is he paying you? Whatever it is, I'll double it. Triple it. I've got cash, it's not a problem."

The woman scoffed. "It's a problem for you, Danny Flynn. I have a job to do. And I will do it."

He slid his back along the wall, heading for the taberna with each unstable step. Could he make a run for it? She was fast – one swish of one of those blades and he'd be bleeding out under the stars before he knew what hit him. She stepped towards him, crossing her arms over her chest. Shite. This was it. The death strike. He pulled his own arms into his torso, shielding himself as much as possible.

"Oh sweet Jesus, no."

He screwed up his face. Waited.

I'm sorry, Ma.

"*Hey! Qué está ocurriendo?*"

He opened his eyes to see the barman standing a few feet away with his hands on his hips and a stern frown darkening his tawny features.

"*Quién eres?*" he asked.

But Danny wasn't waiting around to exchange pleasantries. Exploiting the glorious reprieve this split-second interjection provided, he rushed past the barman as fast as his trembling legs would allow. Out of the taberna and into the night, he didn't look back once as he ran through the narrow winding streets of San Sebastian's old town. Nor did he stop running until he reached his apartment building ten minutes later.

Once there, he didn't enter straight away but circled around the block a few times, scanning the busy streets for any sign of the crazy woman with the white streaks in her hair. Satisfied he'd given her the slip, he returned to the front door of his building and hurried inside.

Safety.

For now, at least.

But that didn't mean she'd give up looking. There was something about that mad nun that sent a chill down his sweaty back even now. And it wasn't only those sharp blades of hers. It was the way she'd looked at him. Like she hated him down to the soul with a deep and resounding passion. Was that what true evil looked like? He wasn't sure. But he was certain he didn't want to experience it again.

He climbed the two flights of stairs up to his room and unlocked the door. Once inside, he relocked the door and pushed a heavy chest of drawers across it before collapsing onto the bed. Barricading himself in like this did little to assuage his fears, but it was all he could think to do right now. It was quickly dawning on him that things were much more dire for old Danny Boy than he'd realised.

"Shitting, shiting hell," he screamed into his pillow. "Ya fecking eejit."

Delgado still had all his papers. Meaning he was stuck here in Spain. He rolled onto his back and checked the wound on his arm. Only a scratch, really. He'd got away with that one. Luck of the Irish and all that. Only, that luck was now running out. He stared at the ceiling and let out a deep, wavering sigh. He had some serious thinking to do. And if he was going to survive the next few days, he'd better come up with a good plan. And fast.

TWO

She stepped back from the barman as he let out a desperate wail, clenching big, calloused hands across the deep slashes that had opened up the top of both thighs, trying to hold his flesh together. His wide eyes founds hers, the brusque cocksureness he'd exhibited a few moments earlier now crumbling to dust. Yes, like all men she'd ever met, deep down he was nothing but a pitiful child.

Patético.

"*Auxilio, por favor!*" he cried out. *Somebody help me.*

They were the last words he'd ever speak. With a swish of the blades she opened up his neck, almost severing his head from his body in one violent move, like one of the huge yawning clams they sold in the Mercado de la Bretxa. She held the blades up to eye level and nodded. Good Spanish knives. Sharp. Deadly.

She stood over the barman's slumped form for a while longer, watching him die, revelling in the sight of the deep crimson as it bubbled out from the neck wound and pooled on the dry dirt beside him. He'd learnt his lesson: don't get in her way when she was working. It was a lesson hard learned, of course, and only bested by: don't become her work in the first instance.

She knelt beside the man as his last breath left him, then wiped the blades clean on the bottom of his trousers. Satisfied, she stood up and returned the knives to the sheaths hanging on the back of her belt. One last scan of the scene (mainly for her own macabre enjoyment), and she gathered up the scattered sections of the nun's habit and slipped into the bathroom to get dressed.

Once back in the black and white robes, she bustled through the busy taberna, passing the annoyed clientele waiting for service at the bar (heathens; they'd be waiting some time) and exited onto the street. It was mid-week, but the tabernas and restaurants here in San Sebastian's old town were already thriving. She cast a glance up and down the narrow lanes. She wasn't expecting to see him again, not tonight. But that was all part of her plan. Tonight wasn't about getting the hit. She wanted to size him up, get him scared enough so he'd reach out to his people.

Besides, his reaction earlier had been one of shock and confusion, and that was no fun at all. She found it much more enjoyable when there was real cold fear in their eyes, when they knew what was going to happen to them. Danny Flynn knew she was out there, coming for him. Next time he'd be ripe with terror and dread. The perfect combination.

A thin-lipped smile spread across her taut features as she headed through the town – her thoughts drifting to how she'd do it when the time came. It would be a slow and drawn-out affair, she presumed. Her speciality. Nothing like the swift way she'd disposed of the barman just now. Although, she had found some delight in the way he'd pleaded for mercy. It was in these final interactions with her quaking quarry (them helpless and afraid) where she gained something almost transcendent. As though she wasn't simply taking away their life force but absorbing it. So, yes, Danny Flynn's time would come, but not tonight. She may have lost the element of surprise, but that wasn't an issue. If anything, she'd use it to her advantage. People who were scared made mistakes, but those who were terrified couldn't think straight in the first place. Luis Delgado could wait for his pound of flesh.

She closed her eyes and took in a deep breath as she reached the edge of the town. The air here was warm and still, the cool night breeze that often came in from the ocean unable to reach her down the old labyrinthine streets. As she passed by a shop window, she caught sight of herself dressed in the full nun regalia and the vision stopped her in her tracks. It felt like another lifetime away now, but this was almost who she'd become. She'd been ready and willing to do it too. To give herself to God, to a higher calling. Although, perhaps in her own way that was what she was doing still – committing to a higher calling.

Doing God's work.

She often wondered what life would be like now if she'd gone through with her plans to join the local convent. She'd made all the arrangements. Said goodbye to her family. Was eager and ready to give up her life and surrender to her faith. But that was before the attack in the summer before she was due to move. She could still picture it when she closed her eyes.

Sometimes it was all she pictured when she closed her eyes.

Her at thirteen. Scared. Alone. The three men (boys, really, but with the brutality and lust of men) jumping out at her from the shadows, then every night after that from her dreams. That was, until she tracked them down and castrated and murdered them one by one.

Even after that she'd still considered becoming a nun. But

13

by that point the bloodlust had grown too strong. She had a new calling.

The reflection in the glass smiled at the memory.

She pressed on through the town and arrived at her destination an hour later – a small convent standing on the hillside overlooking the bay, her home whilst she was in Spain. She'd thought the idea ridiculous when it first came to her, but the more she considered it, the more it had made sense. The old stone building was much smaller than the convent she'd almost joined near her hometown. And whilst the nuns here hadn't taken a vow of silence, the convent was quiet, out of the way. The perfect place to hide out and get some peace and quiet while she carried out her work.

She kept her head down as she shuffled through the main entrance, offering a shy smile to the older nun who eyed her with suspicion as she passed but smiled back all the same. The story she'd given them was that she was an actress set to play a nun in an upcoming movie and wanted to get an authentic feel for the character – that Method Acting nonsense she'd read about. *La Madre Superiora* hadn't been too welcoming of the idea at first, especially not when she'd explained (speaking on the phone as Valentina Morales, her own Spanish agent) how the actress would want to wear the full habit. Yet funnily enough, a donation of twenty-thousand euros to the convent roof fund had changed everyone's mind rather promptly. Money, the universal easer of all problems. It never failed to both encourage and disgust her in equal measure. Whether you were good or evil, black, white or brown, as long as you had the green you could reach some sort of arrangement.

The nuns had put her up in the annex built sometime in the last hundred years, rather than the main building. There was a long corridor with rooms leading off on both sides and hers at the end. From what she could gather, the rooms adjacent to hers were empty. A little insulting perhaps, but right for her needs.

Inside, she stripped down to her underwear and grabbed her towel before walking back down the corridor to the communal shower unit. Her first time bathing here she'd expected nothing but a lukewarm trickle, so was surprised when the water burst out of the showerhead like sharp needles. Now, cocooned inside a cubicle, she closed her eyes and put her head under the water, letting the flow cascade down her face and into her open mouth. She held her hands up in the flow, the blackened blood between her fingers and under her nails turning to red and then pink before washing clean away.

Washing away her sins.

Once cleansed, she dried herself off and padded back to her room where she dressed in a modest nightshirt and pants before sitting on the edge of the bed. There was no television in the room, no books. Nothing to engage with at all, apart from a tiny window that looked out onto rough grassland and a narrow road that was no longer in use.

She closed her eyes as if in prayer. But she didn't pray. Not anymore. She hadn't done for many years. Despite everything that had happened to her, despite who she was now, despite what she did, she still hung onto her faith but she'd long ago ceased talking to God. What she was doing here was connecting with her anger and shame. Turning her rage inwards, letting the intensity of her pain and fury fuel the fire blazing in her belly. Because whilst it felt good to be back in her home country after all these years, this was not the career trajectory she had planned out for herself.

And it had been going so well…

At the age of fourteen she'd left her pathetic, simpering parents and older sisters behind and never looked back. They weren't terrible people, they were simple, god-fearing. But they'd never believed her about the attack – or maybe didn't want to – going so far as to plead with her to keep quiet about the ordeal. To save the family name, they said, and for her to remain pure in the eyes of the town.

Espíritu maligno.

They were lucky she hadn't cut their throats.

Once on the road she'd allowed her bloodlust to flourish, working freelance as a killer for hire in Spain and then Germany. And after racking up a total of fifteen hits in three years, she'd saved enough money for fake papers and a one-way plane ticket to the States. She landed in Washington DC on the eve of her eighteenth birthday and set about making a name for herself. Word of mouth mainly, with clients coast to coast, followed by a year as a fixer and cleaner for a 'legitimate' businessman with a plethora of off-the-book dealings. After that she found herself in Mexico for eighteen months as the top sicaria for the Los Continuados Cartel. It was here they gave her the nickname, *La Urraca* – Magpie – on account of the white streaks in her hair that had appeared not long after her encounter with the three men.

Then one day whilst in Vegas on a job, she ran into another assassin who was gunning for the same contract. Despite being a rival, the man was incredibly charming and they'd got on well. A little too well, it could be said, but that was another story. The rival told her how he'd been freelancing for many years but was now working for a new organisation based out of London, England. One that was fast becoming a major player in the industry. The man (calling himself Spitfire Creosote, of all things) talked of big money and a job for life. He explained how the big boss had gathered together a team of highly skilled assassins, each of them taking a new name when they joined, forced to leave their old life behind forever. Well, that suited her just fine. Spitfire went on to explain how the man in charge was a real force of nature, fancying himself as a businessman and entrepreneur as much as he did a killer. The organisation was called Annihilation Pest Control and they needed new recruits. She'd fit in perfectly, he said.

And she had. Ten years later she loved her job as much as she had that first day in London. It was a new life, along with an impenetrable new persona that she could mould however she wanted. She'd made the organisation – and herself – millions in that time, refining her already remarkable set of skills in the process. It was a magnificent life.

Until it all fell apart.

She'd always hated that wonton *puta*, but now she despised her with a passion that went beyond words. She felt it in every pore of her being. Pure, undiluted hate. She'd taken everything from her, left her without a job, without a team, without a focus. Here she was, freelancing once more. In limbo. That space between life and death, heaven and hell. A place she knew well, a place she recognised, but a place she'd vowed never to return to.

And it was all because of her.

She lay back on the bed and spread her arms wide, gazing up at the yellowing paint on the ceiling. She wasn't going to get away with it. That miserable wench Acid Vanilla was going to die. And in the most painful and protracted way possible.

THREE

Spook Horowitz pressed her forehead against the window of the number 113 bus as it crept its way along Park Road. The damp chill of the glass went some way to easing her pounding head, but the grey skies and the sea of sombre faces passing by (walking faster than the damn bus), only exacerbated the agitation in her soul. It had been another long shift at Soho Comics for Sasha Mulberry, the name she'd been using ever since Spook Horowitz was declared dead on that terrible island. Memories of what happened that terrifying weekend still made her chest tight and her skin cold. So as much as she could, she didn't think about it. Instead she busied herself with other distractions. Gaming, coding, comics. The new job helped. Going home after her shift finished, not so much.

As the bus continued to crawl alongside the sprawling greenery of Regents Park, she wondered if maybe it was time to cut her losses, move away. The last year or so had been the most messed-up period of her life so far. She'd been shot at (many times), tied up, thrown out of a plane, had a price put on her head, killed someone.

Shit… She'd actually killed someone.

The concept still sent her head spinning, and she was about to ask herself the question – *how the hell had she gone from a mild-mannered, unassuming IT nerd to a killer?* – but she already knew the answer. It was because of her. Acid Vanilla. Spook's saviour but also her curse.

As the months had elapsed since their time on the island, Spook had noticed a distinct and undesirable change in her housemate. It was as if all the drive and verve had left her, leaving nothing but a shadow of black misery. She hardly left her room now, and if she did it was only to use the bathroom (not to wash, she hadn't done that in weeks) or to shuffle downstairs, returning to the darkness of her bedroom a few minutes later with bottles clinking in her arms.

It was no secret Acid struggled with her mental health, and Spook had tried to give her leeway, but this was different. She was becoming withdrawn and nasty with it. She hadn't threatened Spook exactly, but she'd come close.

As the bus made its way across St John's Wood Road, away from the torturously slow traffic of the centre, Spook told herself that tonight was the night. She had to bite the bullet (*seize the bull by the horns* might have been a less emotive metaphor) and have it out with Acid once and for all. If nothing else, she needed to find out where her head was at, whether she was still caught up in her obsession with her ex-boss and colleagues. Her mission of vengeance had once seemed righteous, but lately had become a stick for her to beat herself with. Spook was worried about her friend. But how did you help someone who didn't want help? Or who wouldn't accept it even if they did?

Spook reached up and pressed the bell, making her way to the front of the bus as it came to a stop at Queen's Grove. From here it was a ten-minute walk along Marlborough Place to the small terraced house that she and Acid had been renting under assumed names for the last twelve months. Of course, it began to rain the second Spook stepped off the bus, so she walked at pace, head down, no stopping to look in any of the travel agent windows en route, as had been her habit recently, dreaming of another (better?) life. She got to the house in under eight minutes, a record, and once through the front door secured all three locks and slid the chain across. Coat off and straight into the kitchen, she didn't need to wonder whether Acid was home, the dull thud of bass and the twang of discordant guitars coming through the floorboards told her she was in her room. Same as always. She played her music all night and all day. It grated, but at least for Spook it proved she hadn't completely given up on life. Music was an outlet for Acid, so she didn't complain. Plus she'd invested in some heavy-duty earplugs recently.

She clicked on the kettle and threw a teabag into her mug, the one that said $C = Ek$ (P) on the side – a whimsical reference to cryptography and the simple formula that states ciphertext is the result of encrypting a plaintext with a specific key. Acid had sneered at it when Spook had shown her, mumbling something about 'hacker geeks', but it was good-natured, friendly teasing. Spook missed those interactions. Hell, right now she'd do anything for one of Acid's pointed sighs, one of her histrionic eye-rolls.

Tea made, she took the drink through into the front room (you would never call it a lounge; despite their time here, the house had few trappings associated with comfort or domesticity) and slumped down on the couch. Like always, the curtains were drawn, but she could see the orange glow of the streetlights through a crack. The nights were drawing in, getting dark early. In more ways than one.

She was sipping at her tea, wondering whether she had the

courage to go upstairs and check on Acid, when someone knocked on the front door. She sat up, heart already pounding. Apart from the odd delivery driver, they never had visitors. She scurried out the room as the knocking continued and called up the stairs, doing that stage-whispering thing – where you want to be heard, but kind of don't at the same time.

"Acid? Are you expecting anyone?"

No answer. The knocking went again. More forceful now.

"Acid?"

The music faded down a few notches and she held her breath, eyes fixed on Acid's bedroom door handle, just visible from the bottom of the stairs. But a second later the volume rose louder.

The front door went again. Heavy blows now. The bottom of a fist, it sounded like. Spook tiptoed down the short hallway. If this was someone wanting to kill them, one of Acid's old colleagues, they wouldn't knock, would they? *Would they?* It seemed reasonable to think not, logical even, but it didn't stop her shaking any less as she placed her cheek against the gloss finish of the door.

"Who is it?" she whimpered. But there was no answer.

With her stomach in knots and with a shaking hand, she turned the keys in the mortice locks, top and bottom, before sliding back the chain. Finally, she placed her hand on the latch of the Yale lock and eased open the front door.

"Oh."

She had no idea who she was expecting to see standing on the front step, but it certainly wasn't the small man in a long crimson overcoat and a dark green trilby. Rain ran along the brim of the hat and dripped onto his shoulders as he raised his head to look at her. Despite his thick white hair and heavily lined face, there was a certain youthfulness to him. But it was his piercing blue eyes that sent a shiver down her spine.

"Is Acid Vanilla here?" he rasped, in a strong Irish accent.

"She's… Well, I mean…" she stammered. "Maybe. Who are you, sorry?"

The man sniffed. "The name's Jimmy O'Rourke. But you might have heard of me by my old name – The Dullahan." He nodded, smiling joylessly at the recognition he must have seen in Spook's eyes. "That's right. So, ya understand, I need to speak to Acid. I need her help. Urgently."

FOUR

The Dullahan glared at the girl – who he already knew to be Spook – as another droplet of rainwater ran down his back. Acid's friend or not, he'd had one shitter of a day and if she didn't invite him inside soon, things weren't going to go well for her.

"Am I coming in then, or what?"

"Uh, sorry," she stammered, as he bustled past her. "I'm just shocked to see you here. I mean, I know who you are. Acid's told me all about you."

"Aye, well I won't ask if it was all good stuff, because I doubt it was." The words were lost on her. He waited for her to lock up the front door and tried again. "So, is our mutual friend home?"

"Yeah, she is. Well, sort of," she replied, taking the offered trilby and overcoat and holding them in front of her like they were a bomb about to go off. "Why don't you come through?"

She scampered past him and through a door that led off from the narrow hallway. The Dullahan glanced up the stairs, hearing music drifting down from the door on the landing, before following on behind.

"This is where Acid Vanilla has been living for the last year? Jesus, Mary and Joseph." He scanned the room, taking in the net curtains, the dirty magnolia paint on the walls and ceiling, the threadbare carpet. "What the feck is she playing at?"

"We didn't plan on being here that long," Spook mumbled. "But any plans we had have gone to hell recently."

"I see."

"Have a seat." She nodded eagerly at a choice of grimy sofa or grimy armchair. "Do you want a drink of anything?"

"Oh, aye, cup of tea would be grand," he said, opting for the armchair. "Milk and two."

Spook stared at him for a moment before spinning on her heels and darting out the room, still clutching his coat and hat. He waited a moment, getting to his feet and walking over to the window to peer through the curtains, already cursing himself for having his driver, Mickey, set off back to Manchester so soon. He'd actually wanted to stay parked up, just in case, but The Dullahan had insisted. Acid was a friend (these days, at least) and she owed him. His plan was to stay here tonight, explain what he needed from her, and then catch a train back sometime tomorrow. But something already felt off and he wondered if he might regret not having the extra muscle a big lad like Mickey provided.

"Here we go." Spook again, shuffling in holding two mugs of hot drink. "Two sugars, yeah?"

"Aye. So where is Acid?" he asked, cutting down any more small talk. "Like I say, I need to speak to her, urgently." He watched the kid as she did everything she could to avoid eye contact. "What is it?"

"She's upstairs," she said softly. "But I'm not sure how much sense you'll get out of her."

"How's that?"

"Umm…" Spook stared into the mugs of tea. "She's not been well. To put it mildly. Here."

She handed him one of the mugs and he took it in two hands, twisting it around until he found the handle. The mug was red-hot, but his old hands, covered as they were in calluses and scar tissue, hardly felt it. "So what is it? Serious?"

"Not physically. Depression, I'd say. She's in a real pit. Nothing seems to be able to get through to her. All she's done for the last month is stay in her room."

He sat down. This was not what he'd been expecting. Not what he needed. He chewed on the inside of his cheek, exhaling noisily down his nose as he considered this new information. "Maybe I can snap her out of it," he said.

"I don't know… sir," Spook mumbled. "It doesn't really work like that."

"Well, what way does it work?"

"I don't—"

"Let me try." He put his mug down and marched out of the room. *Fecking depression.* He didn't have time for this shite. He ascended the steep staircase, gripping hold of the bannister to pull himself up quicker, sprightly despite his age. "This one is it?" he called down, already knocking on the first door on the landing. He listened at the wood. The music coming from inside was metallic and brittle, like someone throwing a drawer of cutlery down the stairs to a staccato backbeat. He knocked again, harder this time. "Acid. It's The Dullahan. Open this door."

He heard movement, the sound of breaking glass. Then muffled voices. The music dipped in volume and a second later the door creaked open.

"Fecking hell." He put his hand up over his mouth and nose as a potent wave of toxic air hit him in the face. Made his eyes water. "You got a three-week-old corpse in there with ya?"

Acid Vanilla loomed out of the darkness and leaned against the doorframe. She shrugged. "Something like that."

All she was wearing was a faded black t-shirt (sleeves and collar cut off, *Richard Hell and The Voidoids* written in bright pink across the chest), but which was (thank Christ) oversized enough to cover most of her body. Her thick black hair was greasy and pointing in all directions, with the odd lank strand stuck to her face. To say she looked a real bloody mess would be an understatement, but it was her face that gave him most concern. Not the copious amounts of smeared mascara and lipstick, he'd seen her like that many times over the years, but more so the look in her eyes. Those striking eyes of hers, one blue, one brown, always so fierce, so alert, were now glassy and dull, the fire in them quenched.

"Wha' ya want?" she slurred.

"Jesus, Acid. The state of you. What's going on?"

"Huh?"

"And turn that fecking racket off. I'm not surprised you're depressed, listening to that shite."

She rolled her head around her shoulders, looking all the while like a petulant kid. "It's Teenage Jesus and the Jerks," she told him. "They're amazing."

"Is that right? And what are you doing in there, apart from listening to terrible music?"

She sniffed and rubbed her eye with a thumb. "Chilling, thrilling, spilling. I needed a little 'me' time, what can I tell you." She narrowed her eyes at him and snorted loudly. "Oh it's you! Shit, Dullahan, you should have said. What the bloody hell are you doing here? Woah. Nice suit. Is that your..."

"Aye," he spat. "It is. So you know I mean business."

The Dullahan had only ever owned three suits. The first was a charcoal number he'd bought second-hand in the mid-seventies, when he was still a foot-soldier in the Irish mafia up in Manchester and had a few court dates he needed to attend. The second one was a dark blue affair, navy you might call it but darker than that. It was the suit he'd worn when he married Sheila, the love of his life and the woman who had eventually convinced him to step away from his life as an assassin. Unfortunately the main way she'd managed to convince him was by becoming sick. The third suit was the one he was wearing. Jet black, with emerald flecks dotted through the cotton. This was the suit he'd always worn whilst at work, a uniform of sorts, his killing suit.

Acid stuck her bottom lip out, looking him up and down. "You here to kill me?"

He tensed, a way of holding back his rage. "No, of course not. But I'm here on important business. I need to call in that favour you owe me."

"Pfft. Wow. Okay… Oh, you getting off, sweetie?" She stepped aside as a young man with dark stubble and messy black hair shuffled out of the room. Fully dressed, thankfully. He smiled sheepishly at The Dullahan before slinking past and heading down the stairs. Acid watched him go, a wretched smirk playing across her face, before turning back to The Dullahan. "Hey, how are you?"

He lifted his chin, fighting the urge to grab the insolent girl's head and smash it into the doorframe. "Did you hear what I said? I need that favour."

She hit him with a big grin, ear to ear. "Fine. What do you want me to do?"

He shook his head. "Not like this. Put some clothes on and we'll talk downstairs."

"Aw, do I have to? I like it in here. It's nice and warm." She stretched and her t-shirt rose up over her stomach.

The Dullahan looked away in time. "Get dressed. Now. I'll ask Spook to get a pot of coffee on for ya as well, hey?"

"I don't want coffee."

"Acid Vanilla. Remember who you're talking to. Don't you push me."

"Or what?" she sneered, shoving her face at him. "What will you do? Kill me? Give me another good scar?" She held up her forearm, the long red welt running from wrist to elbow still visible in the light from the dim bulb overhead. "Well go on then. Do it. Kill me. Put me out of my misery. I'd really appreciate it."

"Now listen here, Acid, I…"

He trailed off as the door opened a little wider and a girl snuck around the side. She was a couple of inches shorter than Acid and a few years younger, with platinum blonde hair and false eyelashes. Good-looking in a trashy kind of way. She was also naked but for a grubby towel wrapped around her waist and a bundle of clothes clutched over her chest. "Sorry, I need to use the bathroom," she squeaked, before Acid grabbed her by the face and stuck her tongue down her throat. The girl kissed her back, the sordid display going on for an uncomfortable amount of time as The Dullahan seethed silently.

Finally the girl pulled away. "Let me go, my shift starts in half an hour, I need to have a shower."

Acid stepped to one side and smacked the girl on the arse as she hurried away giggling to herself. Once the girl was locked in the bathroom, Acid glared back at The Dullahan, her eyes wide but still with no light in them.

"You got anybody else in there?" he asked her.

She held a finger up to him, stifling a burp as she peered into the dark room. "I don't think so. Not sure."

The Dullahan seethed some more. "What the feck is going on with you?"

"Nothing going on with me." She held her hands up. "I am fucking brilliant, mate. Don't know what you're talking about."

He stepped towards her, his eyes blazing with ferocity as he employed that infamous stare of his, the one that had made hundreds of grown men shrivel up in fear over the years, from Manchester to Mongolia to Mumbai. Once he'd been the best in his field, the deadliest, the most feared. He was The Dullahan for Christ's sake. The Dark Man. Despite his senior years and his body not being what it was, he still had a demon inside of him.

"Listen here, missy," he snarled, keeping his voice low and under control. "I came here because I've got a pressing issue that needs sorting out. And unfortunately for me, and you, you're the only person I know who can help. So I suggest you take five minutes, get dressed, get your fecking act together, and I'll see you downstairs. Okay?"

Acid looked him up and down, nodding along with some thought she was having. Then as her eyes met his, she grinned. "Yeah, don't fancy that. See ya."

"Acid—" The Dullahan started, but the door had already been slammed in his face.

FIVE

"INTERFERING OLD BASTARD." ACID WALKED OVER TO THE stereo and switched it off before slumping down on the edge of her bed and casting her eyes around the room. A neighbour's security system cast long shards of yellow light through the gaps in the curtains and along the walls, illuminating the piles of empty bottles and dirty clothes, the screwed-up tissues and condom wrappers. Like Tracey Emin's bed rolled out into an entire room.

She closed her eyes, listening to the rain beating hard against the windows, but unsure whether the sound was actually an extension of the invisible bat wings fluttering across her nervous system.

Because right now, the bats – the enlivened way Acid referred to the manic aspects of her condition (Cyclothymia, a rare form of bipolar) – were out of control. Which in itself she could have coped with, having long since learned how to hone this skewed part of her psychology into an almost valuable trait. Yet, she'd become aware of a different kind of beast now fighting for space alongside the bats. One more vile and unmanageable. The gross manatee of depression, which had weighed heavily on her chest and shoulders for the last few weeks, leaving her unable to move, to breathe. To be.

Not lifting her feet from the floor, she moved over to the wardrobe, kicking at bottles as she went. A bottle of cheap vodka caught her eye and she snatched it up, draining it of the last few drops of loony juice. It didn't even touch the sides. She needed more. Needed out of this place. This life. It was too dark. She'd made a mistake. She was useless here. No point to any of it. To anything. No feelings. No fun. No fun at all.

She opened up the wardrobe to reveal the seven shiny bullets on the top shelf. Each with a name scraped into the metal casing and representing a member of her old team. Symbols of her rage. Her kill list. Five of the rounds were laid down on their side. Already taken care of. But two remained. As the bats screeched across her synapses, Acid reached in and picked up the one marked 'Caesar'.

"Where the bloody hell are you?" she slurred, over curled lips.

A vision flashed across her pre-frontal cortex. Berlin, Germany. Nearly eighteen months earlier. She'd had a clear shot at him, but she'd hesitated, effectively letting him escape. So what the hell was that all about?

"Sorry, mum," she whispered, as salty tears ran into the corners of her mouth. "I don't know what I'm doing. I don't know anything anymore."

She'd been hunting Caesar ever since, but after their last encounter on the island where he had sent her and Spook to be killed, the trail had gone cold. Maybe that was a sign. Leave it alone. Move on. But if she did that, what else did she have? If darkness was an absence of light, what did an absence of darkness look like?

She placed the round back on the shelf, making sure it remained upright. That was important, for some reason. Then she shut the wardrobe and grabbed at a pair of knickers hanging from the door handle.

Let's see what the old fucker wants.

SIX

SPOOK WAS SITTING AT THE KITCHEN TABLE FIDDLING WITH AN empty glass when The Dullahan appeared in the doorway.

"You weren't kidding about her being in a pit, were ya?" he said, shuffling into the room.

"No I wasn't," she replied. "I take it you didn't get through to her."

"Not yet. But I will. Mark my words." He scraped a chair out from under the table and sat opposite. "What is it you lot call it – when you get onto a fella with a drink problem?"

"You lot?"

"Aye, the Yanks. It's some sort of hippie bullshit. Intermediary or something."

"Oh, an intervention. You think she'd go for that?"

"She might. If we lean on her hard enough."

She removed her glasses and rubbed them on her t-shirt. "I don't know. You saw her just now. She's in a bad way." She placed the glasses back in time to see The Dullahan loosening his tie knot.

"What's caused this change in her?" he asked.

"I have my theories. She's been an assassin all her adult life, and before that she was in a home for psychologically dangerous girls or whatever it was called. I think she's been completely institutionalised. She doesn't know how to be – or who to be – in the real world."

"The real world?" The Dullahan sneered. "What's that?"

"You know what I mean. The outside world, then. I think she's finding it difficult to fit in as a civilian, as she calls it. She's bored. Depressed."

Spook sat up when the sound of slow, deliberate clapping echoed around the room as Acid entered.

"Interesting theory, kid," she said. "Can't say I disagree." She walked over to the fridge and yanked it open, running her tongue around her lips as she squinted at the contents.

"I thought I said get dressed," The Dullahan snarled.

"I put some knickers on, calm down." Still peering into the fridge, she lifted the back of her t-shirt to reveal a pair of black lace pants, wiggling her arse at him. "Have we got anything decent to drink?"

"There's water in the faucet," Spook said, and sniffed.

Acid slammed the fridge door and shuffled over to the sink, repeating Spook's words back in a high-pitched whiney voice as she filled a glass with water. She drank it noisily, letting half of it run over her chin. Once the glass was empty, she filled it again and plonked herself down on the remaining chair, sitting in between Spook and The Dullahan.

"Jesus Christ, when did you last have a wash?" The Dullahan gasped. "I thought your room smelt bad."

Acid lifted her arm and snorted her pit. "I can't smell anything."

"Aye, well, take it from me, you smell like the inside of a dog's arse. Forget getting dressed, a shower's your first port of call."

"All right, Dad, calm down. So anyway," she said, clapping

her hands together, "are we actually having an intervention? What fun."

"Less of the lip, lassie. Spook here is worried about you," The Dullahan snarled. "We both are. I need you to straighten up. I have work for you."

"Yeah, you said that already." Turning her back on him, she looked Spook dead in the eyes. "So you think I'm institutionalised. Do go on."

Spook leaned back in her chair. "What's more to say? I keep telling you, there's so much you can do with your life but you don't seem to be able to see it. I think if you gave it a chance you might—"

"Tell me then, Dr Ruth," Acid snapped, serious now to the point of angry. "If I can't cope with civilian life, if I can't fit in, what does that say about me? That the only way I can be happy is as a killer?"

"Were you happy as a killer?"

"I've never been happy," she yelled, spraying spittle across the table.

It was the first time Spook had seen Acid lose her cool. It was unsettling.

"But at least I had some sort of purpose," she went on. "What good am I now? I'm losing my edge. Lost it. Everyone says so. I'm soft and useless and I'm so... fucking... tired. I'm never going to get justice for my mum."

"You've had a lot to deal with the last few years," Spook replied, feeling braver. "I wonder if maybe you've got..." She trailed off, suddenly feeling less brave as Acid eyeballed her.

"What?"

"Well, I was going to say... maybe you've got... PTSD?"

"Oh, don't be so bloody ridiculous."

"Okay, so jumping at any loud noise, lunging at shadows, what would you call that?"

"I'd call it survival," Acid replied. "I'd call it my life! My job! The way I've had to be since I was eighteen years old. Tell her, Dullahan, we have to be on our guard. Keeps us alive, right?"

"I can't argue with her there," he said with a sigh. "You relax in this game, you die."

Spook ignored the old man. He was clearly no help. "But it doesn't have to be that way. Not anymore."

Acid looked at the wall. "How else can it be? I am who I am."

"But that's not true," Spook cried, frustration trumping her nerves momentarily. "You're bright, funny, clever as hell, when you want to be. You can do anything you want, but first you have to make peace with the fact that you aren't your past. Step out of the shadow of being an assassin, and I promise, who you are will still be there." She shut up, pleased with her speech, and allowing the words to hang in the air.

In turn, Acid stared at her with her lips parted, as though considering the idea. Then she let out a loud scoff. "What a load of bloody piffle," she sneered. Then again with the whiney voice. "*Ooh, step out of the shadows. You aren't your past.* Pfft! You watch too many movies, sweetie."

"Acid," The Dullahan barked. "Can we please talk about why I'm here?"

She took a big gulp of water and turned her attention to the old man. "Fine. Why are you here?"

The Dullahan looked at the ceiling, muttering to himself, before locking those steely and determined eyes with Acid's. "You still owe me, right?"

She shrugged. "I guess so."

"You know you do, and I'm cashing in. I need you to go to Spain. As soon as possible."

"Spain? What's in Spain?"

"Not what, who. Sheila's sister's boy, Danny. He's got himself in a whole lot of trouble, so he has. I've not yet got the full story but my sources tell me he's taken something he shouldn't have from a man called Luis Delgado. I'd never heard of the fella before a few days ago, but by all intents and purposes he isn't someone you want to get on the wrong side of."

"And?" Acid asked. "Why doesn't he get out of there?"

The Dullahan put his hands together and leaned forward. "Not as easy as that. The lad's a bit of a wheeler dealer, an antiques expert. From what I heard the stupid eejit handed his passport and visa to Delgado as insurance whilst he brokered some sort of big art deal."

"That was stupid of him."

"Aye. It gets worse," The Dullahan continued. "This Delgado is a bigger, meaner cat than Danny realised. He wants the lad dead. Has put a contract out on him. Fifty-thousand euros."

Spook had been listening hard, trying to take it all in. "Can't you help?" she asked. "Being who you are and all?"

The Dullahan sighed. "I'm retired. Don't have the sway I once did in the industry. Although I did hear a couple of older guys turned the job down, out of respect for me. And fear too, I like to think. But no. I've no authority any longer. Especially not in Spain. Plus, I'm an old man, what am I going to do?"

Acid put the glass down. "What are you asking me?"

"I've got him a new passport and papers in my coat pocket," The Dullahan replied. "All you have to do is find the boy, and bring him home. That's it. No mess. But here's why it might interest you. The person who got the job is a freelancer. Calls herself *La Hermana Muerte*. Sister Death."

The Dullahan took out a piece of paper from the inside of his jacket pocket and slid it across the table to Acid.

"Everything I know is on there. Danny's last known whereabouts, that sort of thing."

Acid stared at the note but didn't pick it up.

"Sister Death," Spook mouthed the name to herself. "Who is she?"

"That's the thing," The Dullahan went on. "I did a little digging, turns out she's Spanish by birth but spent the last ten years or so in the UK working under another name. Magpie Stiletto."

Spook gasped, flicking her attention to Acid. But her face, awash with eyeliner and fatigue, didn't flinch.

"And you're certain it's her?" she asked.

"I'm certain."

Spook knew the name well. Had seen it too, scratched on the side of a bullet casing on Acid's shelf. One of the two still standing.

A silence fell over the room as Spook glanced from Acid to The Dullahan and back again, fighting the urge to say something herself. Acid stared unblinking at the tabletop in front of her, as if searching the faded laminate for an answer. If she got one, it was unclear.

"I'm sorry," she said, before screeching her chair back and getting to her feet. "I can't help you."

"What the feck?" He was on his feet in a second, moving around the table so he was standing less than six inches from her. Toe to toe. "Remember who you're talking to, lassie. You owe me, for Christ's sake."

"Look at me," she hissed, tears forming in her eyes. "I'm useless. I can't help you."

The Dullahan glared back, the two of them fixed in a battle of wills. "Get a good night's sleep. We'll talk in the morning," he said, calmer.

But Acid shook her head. "You're wasting your time. I

can't. I'm sorry. I'm not cut out for it. For anything. You can stay here tonight, but first thing tomorrow I want you gone."

"You owe me, damnit! Don't be stupid."

She pushed passed him. "Well I am stupid," she called back. "And I'm breaking the code. So you do what you need to do, Jimmy boy. I'll see you around."

Spook leaned around the side of the door and watched as she staggered down the hallway and made her way erratically up the stairs. She looked up at The Dullahan. His face was ashen, a cocktail of rage and frustration turning down his mouth and creasing his already well-lined forehead.

She shrugged meekly at him, smiled her best smile. This despite the pulse points in her neck throbbing intensely. "You can sleep on the couch," she told him "Wait here, I'll fetch you some bedding."

SEVEN

DANNY'S HANDS WERE TREMBLING AS HE UNZIPPED THE BLACK leather holdall and began stuffing his clothes inside. Normally a neat man, on a different day, in different circumstances, he'd have taken his time to properly fold each item, packing his t-shirts separately from his jeans, from his dress shirts, and balling up his underwear to create more space. But not today. Today his clothes were grabbed up with wild abandon and stuffed in the bag as fast as he could – although, as was often the case in life, the stress shaking at his limbs and tightening his throat meant everything took twice as long. Once his clothes were packed, he went to the small en suite bathroom and gathered up his electric stubble trimmer and toothbrush, ignoring the array of shampoo and body wash on the shelf below the mirror.

Still shaking, he threw the toothbrush and trimmer on top of his clothes and moved to the dresser under the window where he slid open the drawer and removed the five-inch by five-inch wooden box inside. Despite feeling like he was drowning, he took a moment to lift the lid and, with the concentration of a brain surgeon, examine the contents. It was still there. Still perfect in every way. He closed the lid and stuffed the box under the first few layers of clothes before zipping the holdall shut. Next he hurried over to the bedside table and grabbed the roll of euros from out of the drawer. A little more than six grand. Enough to procure a fake passport if one of his local contacts came good. If not, who knew? But why was his uncle not answering his bleeding phone?

Cursing himself for every stupid mistake he'd ever made, as well as his own recent bad luck, he peeled off a couple of hundred euros and laid the notes out on the dresser top. Then he stuffed the money in his back pocket, slung the holdall onto his back and left the room behind.

He'd made it down the creaky old stairwell and along the dark corridor towards the building's main entrance when he heard her door open.

"Señor Flynn? Danny? You are leaving?"

He stopped, closing his eyes for a second in silent dismay, before turning around to see the kind face of Camila staring up at him. A look of confusion had crumpled her usual affable demeanour. Despite the hour she was fully dressed, wearing a flowing flower-patterned dress and her trademark black shawl.

"Sorry, yeah, something unexpected has come up," he told her, trying to sound upbeat. "I need to get off. I've left this month's rent in my room, plus a little extra for your troubles. Sorry about sneaking off like some thief in the night, didn't want to disturb ya."

The old lady's face dropped. "*Vaya. Vaya.* Is a shame. You will be okay, Danny?"

Up to this point he'd been bouncing from foot to foot, eager to make his leave but now he paused and gave the woman his full attention. "Aye, don't you worry about me. And thank you so much for your hospitality. You're a fine lady, Camila."

She beamed at him, her eyes sparkling in spite of her years. He knew her own son (Raoul, was it?) had died a decade or so earlier. Drugs. Heroin, to be exact, but wasn't it always? She'd confided all this to Danny one night over a glass of local wine after he'd arrived home to find her sitting alone in the dark of the TV room with the box switched off. Since then they'd shared a few more nights like that, a few more glasses of wine, and had been company for each other. If only she knew the shitstorm coming his way she'd be heartbroken. A kind woman, she'd probably try and help. Not that she could.

No one could.

And that was one of the reasons why he had to leave right away. If that mad nun was still out there, his staying here put Camila in danger, and he wouldn't do that. The old lady had been like a mother to him these last months. Cooked for him. Even did his laundry. It made leaving so abruptly all the more heart-wrenching.

"Tell you what," he told her, forcing a smile. "When I get to where I'm going, I'll drop you a line. Maybe we could write to each other? Or something…" He trailed off, feeling ridiculous.

"You be careful, *peque*," she said, reaching up and holding his cheek. "*Dios te bendiga.*"

He closed his eyes, leaning his face into her soft hand. Time to go. With a straight back and puffed out chest he gave her an assertive nod, but with her looking at him now with a suspicious eye. Fair enough, she wasn't stupid. And she could handle herself. If the nun came here looking for him she'd tell her he was long gone, no forwarding address, and that would be the end of it. No reprisals. He had to believe that.

Without another word he turned and marched towards the end of the corridor. One last glance back at the old woman, and then he yanked open the stiff wooden door and stepped out into the cool night air.

EIGHT

BACK IN LONDON ACID VANILLA AWOKE WITH A START. A
cursory examination of her surroundings told her she was in
her own bed. That was something at least. A good sign. She
ran her tongue around her mouth and lips, trying to piece
together the last twenty-four hours. Hell, the last forty-eight,
the last two-hundred. The days and nights all swam together
like a terrible psychedelic dream. The parts she remembered,
anyway. As reality hits, the insanity grows.

She peered out into the darkness of her room as swirls of
grey morphed grossly into the vision of her poor mother. Her
eyes were open like they had been that night. Empty and
lifeless. But unlike that night she was surrounded by a cauldron
of demons, laughing, chattering, baring their teeth, morphing
now into more human forms. Davros, Spitfire, Magpie. All of
them laughing at her, at her mother's rotting form, mocking
her. Raaz Terabyte there too now, and the Sinister Sisters, but
all of them engulfed by the bulk of him – her nemesis and
mentor, Beowulf Caesar. She reached out, hands clawing at the
manifestation of her pain. Another blink, a cry, and the scene
faded to grey.

She shook her head. Fully awake now. Casting out an exploratory arm, she was surprised and relieved to find she'd had the foresight to bring a pint of water to bed with her. Rolling onto her side she drank it down in one go, spilling some of it onto the grubby bed clothes but caring little. In truth she was still trying to work out what had happened prior to her being here. Was there something she should remember? If she closed her eyes, focused her attention, she sensed the shadow of a recollection, hovering there on the cusp of her awareness like the memory of a forgotten film. And why the hell was she awake at this hour?

She flung the hot duvet aside and swung her legs off the bed, listening intently now. There it was again. Footsteps, for sure. Someone moving around. She closed her eyes to better focus on her hearing and get a locality on the steps moving from the front room and along the hallway towards the stairs. She heard the creak of wood second step from the bottom. It always did it, and Spook had wanted to rip it up, but Acid told her no. She knew the value of an early warning system. For moments exactly like now.

Whoever this was, they were half-way up the stairs now. She rocked onto the balls of her feet and crept on unsteady legs to the bedroom door. Her head was banging and her mouth tasted like she'd been licking battery acid, but she was certain now she wasn't dreaming, wasn't in the midst of some alcohol-induced narcosis. This was happening. It was real.

Another vision flashed across her recall. Some seedy bar somewhere. Buying drinks for someone. Had she brought them home? Was this them? She couldn't remember names, or faces, or even genders, only a sense of hot, sweaty flesh next to hers. A brief moment of shuddering, shaking distraction, before succumbing once more to the incessant numbness of her existence.

Could be anyone…

She gasped. "Oh, shit."

The Dullahan.

He was here. In the house. She screwed her eyes shut in a vain attempt to pull more memories from her troubled mind. He'd asked her for help, wanted her to do something, be somewhere. She groaned, a flicker of a conversation coming back to her. She'd been rude to him. Disrespectful.

Not cool.

Not a good idea, either.

The Dullahan might be past his peak but he was still a fierce customer. Still the only person to have ever bested her. She ran her finger down the deep scar on her forearm, remembering their first encounter. Back when she was the new killer on the block and he was still top dog.

Another creaking floorboard told her he'd reached the landing. Was he coming for her? Pissed off she wouldn't help him, that she – oh bugger, now she remembered – shook her arse in his face.

She pressed her cheek to the door, talking in a gruff whisper. "Hey, Dullahan. Listen, I'm sorry about earlier. It was the booze talking. My head's not in a good place. I'm sure you guessed that. But I'm very, *very* sorry."

She listened.

No answer.

But she could sense the presence standing outside her door, could hear heavy breathing.

"The bathroom's at the far end," she offered. "Follow the landing around."

The Dullahan sniffed and the footsteps shuffled past her room. He was half-asleep himself, she presumed. Nothing to worry about. In the morning she'd explain herself properly, apologise profusely, fall on her sword sort of thing. But her answer would be the same – whatever it was he needed, she couldn't help him. She was in no fit state to help anyone, physically, mentally or spiritually. She knew that much. Her heart and sense of self had been splintered into a million tiny pieces. She was lost. Unfixable.

Satisfied The Dullahan had moved on, she slunk back into bed, pulling the duvet over her and laying her head on the soft pillow. With her eyes closed and her breathing slowing, the benign embrace of sleep was already close. So much so that when her door handle clicked open and a shaft of light speared across the bed, she hardly stirred.

"Wrong room," she mumbled. "I'll see you in the morning. We'll talk properly."

She kept her eyes closed but could sense he was still there at the door, looming above her. What the bloody hell was he playing at? One eye flickered open, then the other, both wider now, a lot wider, realising the dark presence standing over her was far too broad to be her old rival. She made to cry out, to move, but before she had a chance he was on top of her and with a large, rough-skinned hand over her mouth.

The bats screeched across her nervous system as she wriggled to free herself, raising her legs and scissoring them around this neck. With a lurch she pushed herself upright and kicked out, pushing him off her. She followed this up with a foot to the face that did little to stop him but meant she had time to slide off the bed and get her back to the wall. In the darkness of the room it was difficult to make out the man's face, but his body was taut with muscle and malice. He clambered across the bed towards her, snorting heavily with each breath.

Despite her head screaming for her to move, to get the hell out of his way, she remained still. Because the bats had other ideas. She sucked back a sharp breath as a rush of adrenaline parted the fog in her mind. Then, as the man lunged at her, she shifted to one side, and with a hand on the back of his bald head, drove his face into the wall with a satisfying crunch. She followed up with a sharp knee to his kidneys and a heavy hammer blow down on the nape of his neck, the muscle memory from sixteen years living on her wits taking full control. She leapt back as the man stumbled against the side of the bed.

"Oh, come on," she gasped, as he immediately righted himself and turned to face her. Now illuminated by the light coming in through the windows, she could see the determination on his face. A face that was covered in scars and pockmarks with a grotesque boxer's nose spread across the centre – to truly emphasise he was a man not to mess with. He eyed her in readiness, his tongue greedily licking at the blood gushing from his nose.

"Time to die, bitch," he snarled, before rushing forward and pummelling her in the chest with a heavy fist that sent her tumbling into the wall.

A sinewy forearm wrapped around her throat, pushing down on her windpipe as she fought for air. She clawed at his skin, digging her nails in as far as they'd go and scraping them down his flesh, but he held on tight. An elbow to his ribs did nothing either, nor did an overhead punch which only found empty air. She gasped, fading fast. One last chance. She sprung her legs off the floor, finding purchase with the wall and pushing against it with all her might. The room spun, falling over on itself as the two of them toppled across the bed and landed on the floor with a heavy thud, Acid on top. From this vantage point she delivered a swift double elbow which loosened his grip on her and, with renewed vigour, smashed her head back into his already broken nose. She rolled off him and stumbled for the bedroom door, gasping in disbelief as her attacker got to his feet, using the bed as support. Once more he bounded towards her, grabbing hold of her wrist as she backed out onto the landing.

"Go to hell," she yelled, before another big fist found its target and knocked her into the wall. He kept hold of her wrist, punching wildly at her with his other arm. This time however she managed to swerve out of the way and the force of the swing knocked him off balance.

It was the opening she'd been looking for.

A swift knee to the balls and a sharp elbow in his face had him teetering on the edge of the top stair. She followed this up with a knee to the stomach she hoped would be the final blow, but what she hadn't counted on as he fell backwards was him hanging on to her wrist for dear life.

"Shitting hell."

With a cry she was dragged down the stairwell on top of him, but managing to position herself on his chest and riding him like a toboggan to the bottom.

"What the fecking hell is going on?" The hall light flashed on to reveal The Dullahan standing in the doorway to the front room.

"He… attacked me… was in my room." She got to her feet, trying to catch her breath as a flash of anger burst across her awareness. In the bright light of the hallway she could see her attacker wasn't actually made of much. There wasn't an ounce of fat on him, he was small-framed, wiry. She pushed two fingers into the flesh of her stomach, disgusted at how out of shape she was, how she'd let herself get like this. In her prime she'd have handled a guy like this in a fast second. But it was over, at least. The man had landed badly, his head twisted to one side.

"Feck me. Mickey? No." The Dullahan stepped over, shaking his head.

"You know him?"

"Aye, he calls himself Mickey Mad. He drove me down here. A tough fella, but I've known him a few years. I thought he was on the right side of wrong. Knew the code. Feck."

She straightened herself, checking for wounds or anything broken. Apart from a banging headache she seemed unscathed. Sometimes the looseness of semi-drunkenness had its advantages.

She stepped over Mickey's fallen body as Spook appeared on the stairs wearing a pair of blue pyjamas with a neon pink dinosaur pattern. "Who's that guy?" she asked sleepily. "What's he doing?"

"Not a lot, now," Acid told her. "Come down, I need to get my head around this." She closed her eyes, easier to think that way.

"I'm sorry, Acid," she heard The Dullahan say. "Stupid fecking coot I am. Should have been more careful. Getting sloppy in my old age."

"Why is he trying to kill me?" she asked, eyes still closed. "There's no hit on me on the open market, is there?"

"No. Why would Caesar put one out now?"

Acid opened her eyes to see Spook standing next to her, staring at Mickey with her head on one side. She tugged at the kid's sleeve, guiding her down the hallway towards the kitchen – away from the distraction – nodding at The Dullahan to follow.

"All right," she snapped. "Tell me everything you know about this guy. And why the hell are you here?"

The Dullahan stared at her. "Are you serious? You don't remember?"

"I've had a messy few weeks."

"Aye. So ya have. Well firstly, I don't know why the hell Mickey is trying to kill ya. Like I say, I thought he was a decent fella. And there's never been an open contract on ya. Caesar was adamant he wanted to keep it in-house. Hmm. I guess that's hard when you've almost wiped out his entire workforce. This has to be him. I'm sorry, love."

She turned away, every fibre of her being telling her to go the cupboard and grab a bottle of something to drown out the pain and confusion. Because The Dullahan was correct. This had to be Caesar. Despite him going dark, he was still out there. Him and Magpie Stiletto.

Ah shit… Magpie.

That was why the old man was here. She lifted her head, about to tell him once more he'd had a wasted trip, but as she turned Spook screamed and pushed her against the wall. A loud crack of gunfire reverberated through the hallway.

What? Shit. When?

She righted herself in time to see Mickey's grinning face over the top of a revolver. He closed one eye over the sight, but before he had a chance to pull the trigger there was an ear-shredding crack and his brains splattered up the wall.

Acid lurched around in a disorientated stupor, seeing The Dullahan standing in the living room doorway with his arm outstretched and a Walther PPK gripped in his bony, liver-spotted hand. Her head was spinning and her ears ringing. She opened her mouth to speak but no words appeared – the weeks of self-abuse combining with intense stress levels had finally bested her. As she slid down the wall, she saw Spook standing in the kitchen doorway. Her face was white. Her mouth open. She met Acid's gaze, before their eyes simultaneously drifted downwards, to the dark red stain spreading out across the lower half of Spook's pyjama top.

"Acid," she mouthed, looking up with an expression of pure horror, just able to get behind her breath. "Help me."

NINE

THE MANIC ENERGY COURSING THROUGH ACID'S VEINS SENT her dizzy as Spook slumped to the floor. She was by her side in an instant, placing a hand under her neck and lifting her head up onto her lap.

"Don't you fucking dare," she whispered, before tentatively lifting the kid's top and sucking in a sharp breath. "Ah, no, Spook."

The bullet had gone in an inch below her navel, a small hole, a .22 by the looks of it. Blood was already bubbling out of the wound. She reached around Spook's back, poking around at her flesh. She glanced over to The Dullahan who was checking Mickey's pockets.

He caught her eye. "No exit wound?"

She shook her head. "What can we do?"

The Dullahan got to his feet, holding a mobile phone and squinting at the screen. "Looks like we were right, Caesar got to him. The fat prick."

"Let me see."

The Dullahan tossed her the phone, the screen showing a facial recognition app. It had been updated since the last time she'd had cause to use it (In-Field Verification, they called it – proof for the client), but the interface was recognisable as the one Raaz Terabyte had created, linked to Annihilation Pest Control's dark web portal.

"That lousy bastard," she slurred, tossing the phone to one side and getting her weight under Spook's shoulders, lifting her up. "Come on, help me get her onto the table. She's bleeding out, she needs help."

"Aye, but she needs more than I can help with," The Dullahan replied, coming to assist her. "Besides, I don't have any of my equipment with me."

Acid chewed on her bottom lip. Taking her to hospital wasn't an option. All records said Spook Horowitz was dead, there'd be too many questions. But with the bullet still somewhere inside of her, she needed attention, proper attention, and fast. They got her to her feet and dragged her into the kitchen where they placed her gently on a chair. She was barely conscious with the shock of it all, mumbling something Acid couldn't make out.

"Do you know anyone?" she asked, turning to The Dullahan.

"Maybe I do," he said, getting out his own phone and jabbing at the screen. "He's an old contact, but I believe he's still around. It'll cost though."

"Anything," she spat. "Make the call."

FIFTEEN MINUTES LATER AND THEY WERE IN THE BACK OF A Hackney carriage, speeding through the rainy streets towards Chinatown. They'd patched Spook up as much as they could before getting in the car, stuffing her wound with some Radial gauze to contain the bleeding a little. Acid gripped the handrail above the window tight, willing the car to drive faster, for Spook to survive, propping her upright as her head lolled from side to side with each turn. When they passed by Tottenham Court Road tube station she mumbled something weird, about cats and jumpers, but that was a good thing. If she was conscious, even a little bit, it meant her vitals hadn't dropped too far off the scale.

Acid watched the driver's eyes in the rear-view mirror as they flicked from the road ahead to the back seat. It was hard to determine demeanour from an inch of face, but every cell in her body told her he was suspicious and growing more so.

"She's diabetic," she told him. "We ran out of insulin and she's gone into shock. Don't worry, if she vomits we'll pay double. Triple. Okay?"

He didn't reply, but nodded as if satisfied. Acid leaned across Spook's wilting form, addressing The Dullahan who was peering out the window.

"We nearly there?" she asked.

"Aye, around this next bend." He leaned forward, speaking to the driver. "Drop us on the corner here, that'd be grand. By the red car, there. Good lad."

The cab driver did as instructed and didn't even turn around as Acid threw a fifty at him.

"Over there," The Dullahan told her, as she dragged Spook out into the cold night air. "Above the bookies."

They took an arm each, walking Spook over to the nondescript door next to the betting shop as she mumbled groggily and rolled her head back. Once there, Acid took most of her weight so The Dullahan could push the buzzer. They waited in silence, nodding pointlessly at each other the way people do in tense situations, smiling tight smiles.

Hurry the fuck up.

Finally the intercom crackled and a voice barked, "Who is it?"

"It's me. The Dullahan. Open up."

Another crackle of static. "Say password."

The Dullahan raised his eyebrows and sighed. "I am the Walrus," he said, shaking his head. Then to Acid, "Beatles fan."

The Dullahan's contact was a small Chinese man with a round but stern face and a bowl cut reminiscent of George Harrison's circa *Rubber Soul*. He introduced himself as Song Shi and led them into his establishment (by day a herbalists specialising in Chinese medicine) and through a hidden door behind a screen, where a full operating room was set up – gurney, lights, even a heart rate monitor. The disparity between the dark wood of the main space, with its lanterns and Chinese wall-hangings, and this stark, sterile room of chrome and steel was jolting to say the least. Acid hadn't been anywhere this bright in a long while. The lights hurt her eyes.

Song Shi signalled for them to place Spook on the gurney, where they removed her coat and the thick cardigan they'd wrapped around her.

"What are we dealing with?" he asked, his voice clipped and clinical.

Acid moved around to the far side of the operating table and lifted Spook's top. The wound looked even worse under the halogen bulbs. The gauze was sticky with blood and plasma and the skin around the sides of the wound had turned a dark purple.

"I see," Song Shi muttered, pulling on a surgical glove. "When did this happen?"

"Half an hour ago," Acid replied. "But there's no exit wound."

Spook groaned as Song Shi felt around the wound with two

fingers. He glanced at Acid. "I need to operate. Right now," he said. "Dullahan, you assist me, please."

Acid leaned in. "What can I do?"

"You can give me space," was the sharp reply. "Room is small as it is. Don't need an audience."

She nodded, taking in The Dullahan. "I'm going to wait outside. I need some air."

"Aye. I'll come find ya when we're done."

"But you can save her?" she asked the doctor.

He snorted back a nostril-full of something nasty. "I don't know until I open her up." He scowled at her. "You have payment?"

She didn't. They'd left in too much of a hurry. She threw a pleading look The Dullahan's way.

"We'll sort something out," he growled.

"Fine. Now go," Song Shi snapped. "We're losing time. If you want your friend to live, let me do my work."

TEN

IT WAS GONE THREE IN THE MORNING WHEN SONG SHI FINISHED stitching Spook up. He'd sliced the poor kid up good too, with a long incision down the middle of her abdomen that would leave a tasty scar. But it had meant he could open all four quadrants and catch all the damage caused by the .22 as it blossomed inside her belly. The procedure had taken more than four hours, but he'd performed a full exploratory laparotomy on her – the works – and from what The Dullahan could tell, she'd been lucky. A few pieces of shrapnel had clipped her lower intestine but only superficially, and it was easy enough to patch up once Song Shi had stemmed the bleeding and located the injury. The rest of the shrapnel had lodged itself in her lower rib on the left side. Both Song Shi and The Dullahan were covered in her blood, and she'd almost arrested once, but she was through the worst of it.

"You think she'll make it?" The Dullahan asked, grabbing up a bunch of wet wipes and cleaning the blood from his face and hands as Song Shi laid a large piece of padded gauze over the kid's stomach.

"I'm good at what I do," he replied, sticking down the

dressing with surgical tape along the sides. "But with these sorts of injuries she'll need follow-up care if she's to survive. Now I need to monitor her blood culture for sepsis."

"Meaning it's a few nights' stay yet?"

Song Shi nodded. "A week, at least."

"That's going to cost, I imagine."

Another nod. "That going to be a problem?"

"I'll go speak to her now," he said, pulling a poseable mirror attached to the wall towards himself and checking his face for blood. "That's Acid Vanilla, ya know. One of Beowulf Caesar's lot, only she's not with Annihilation any longer."

"Yes. I heard. I also heard no one was with Annihilation Pest Control any longer thanks to her."

He grinned. "Aye. She's hot-headed is the lass. But she's got her reasons. I'll go speak to her now and be back."

He grabbed his overcoat and trilby before making his way down the dark stairwell to the front door. With each step he began to decompress from the intensity of Shi's operating room, but as he got to the foot of the stairs he realised his heart was beating far too fast. He removed a bottle of Tenormin pills from his coat pocket and knocked two out into his hand, swallowing them down dry. Gripping hold of the door handle he took a moment to compose himself, then yanked the door open and stepped outside.

The cool night air felt good on his face and he welcomed it after the stifled confines inside. Yet there was no sign of Acid. Letting the door close behind him he made his way up the street, checking in the window of every bar and fast-food joint as he passed by. But nothing. He'd almost given up when he reached an alleyway that ran down between two Chinese restaurants and squinted into the gloom. Despite his eyesight not being what it was, especially at night, he'd noticed a familiar-looking silhouette slouched against a fire escape. As he watched, the figure raised a cigarette to their lips and inhaled. The glow of the ash lit up their face momentarily.

"There ya are," he said, shuffling into the dark alley. "I thought you'd buggered off, for a minute."

She jumped at his words. Then seeing it was him, asked, "Is she okay?"

"Aye, she will be."

As he got closer and his eyes grew more accustomed to the darkness, he could see the glass bottle in her hand. Only a lager, from the looks of it. She raised it to her lips and slurped down the last dregs before chucking it petulantly into the alleyway. It didn't even smash. Poor lass couldn't catch a break.

"You certain she's going to live?"

"I'm certain."

"That's good," she said, her voice now hoarse with fatigue and emotion. She sniffed back. "That bullet was for me." She kicked out at something in the dark but missed, slumping pathetically against the side of the building and sliding to the floor with a grunt.

"Calm down, girl. Getting worked up won't help anyone. You know that." He moved closer. "Spook's going to be fine, so she is. But yer man upstairs wants to keep her here for a few days to monitor her for sepsis and the like."

He waited for a response. None came.

"You got money to pay for this?" he asked, but Acid just took another long drag of the cigarette and shrugged. "I don't remember you smoking."

She sneered, but still didn't look at him. "I used to. I still do when I'm feeling especially shitty about everything." She took another long drag before flicking the spent stub against the building opposite. "And yes. I have got the money. I think so, anyway. Sort of."

"Sort of? What does that mean? Because Song Shi is a

good man but I've seen him turn nasty. Don't let the mop-top Chinaman act fool ya. He'll want paying."

Acid was silent for a long time. She pulled out another cigarette but held it between her fingers without lighting it. "It's just… my savings have been somewhat… depleted over the last year or so. You know how it is. No revenue coming in. Plus trips to Berlin, Hanoi, New York. I know, I know: should have started living to my means, budgeted, or whatever normal people do. But it's hard to change after more than a decade living in the best hotels, paying for premium everywhere you go."

The Dullahan smiled into the darkness. "That luxury lifestyle never stretched to your wardrobe though, did it?"

"How do you mean?"

"I mean you dress like a moody teenager."

"What can I say, I'm a fucking enigma." She peered up at him through her fringe. "Anyway, that's only the clothes you've seen."

"Oh, I see. So you wear expensive dresses in your downtime?"

"No. I mean, old man, that my underwear costs more than your entire outfit."

He looked away. That sort of talk made his blood boil. Very disrespectful, so it was. But Acid knew that too. She gave it a beat, then mumbled something about being sorry, wouldn't happen again.

"How much is Spook's treatment going to put me back?" she asked.

He sucked his teeth over his gums. "How much can you get your hands on in the next week or so?"

"Fifty grand. At a push."

He grimaced. "More than that."

"Jesus. Who is this guy?"

"He's the best. He saved your lassie's life, and off-the-record as well. Costs a lot these days for that sort of job. Done well, at least."

Acid blew out a long sigh, her head rocking back and forth like one of those nodding dogs you see in the backs of cars. "I don't suppose... you could you help me out?"

"I might be able to."

She blew out another dramatic sigh.

"Come on then," she told him, raising her hand and clicking her fingers impatiently. "Give it."

Gracefully, and without a hint of conceit, he reached into his inside pocket and pulled out the slip of paper. He handed it over and watched Acid as she squinted at the contents.

"Fine." She clambered to her feet and cricked her neck to one side before turning to face him. "It looks like I'm bloody well going to Spain, doesn't it?"

ELEVEN

Danny woke up confused and unsure where he was. Normally when this happened there was a warm body lying next to his, a pleasant reminder of the previous evening and why he wasn't in his own bed. But this morning, not so much. Through the fog of sleep he stretched out with his hand and felt something hard, his fingers opening out and sending whatever it was scuttling noisily across the floor. Sounded like a glass bottle. He sat upright and groaned, his neck sore where he'd been lying awkwardly on the cold, stone floor of... what... some sort of chapel?

He groaned again as it all came hurtling back. His remembrance of the last twenty-four hours hitting him in the guts like a prize fighter.

"Fecking hell, laddo," he muttered to himself. "This is the mother of all messes right here."

He got himself upright and stretched an arm across his chest, at the same time working the thumb and forefinger of his other hand into his trapezius muscle. It was painful as hell. Felt like a trapped nerve. His eyes fell on the empty wine bottle lying a few feet away, some cheap local plonk. That explained why his mouth tasted like a donkey's backside. *An ass's ass.*

He continued to work on his shoulder, sensing a dull throbbing pain at his temples too. Well, that was damn stupid, wasn't it, necking back a full bottle of wine when you were up to your eyeballs in it? Situations like this, you were supposed to stay alert, keep your mind sharp. Although, in his defence, the alcohol had helped him sleep, taken his mind off his problems for a few hours.

"Oh, shite. No."

His heart almost stopped, then jumped into his throat as he remembered how he'd left in a hurry. He glanced around the chapel, praying he hadn't been so stupid. Surely he'd brought it with him. Because what the hell was all this about if not? He spotted the black holdall stuffed underneath an old pew and hurried over to it. Forgetting briefly about his crushing hangover he wrenched out the bag and, falling to his knees, unzipped it. Without taking a breath he rummaged through the pile of clothes, his unease swelling until, mercifully, his fingers touched on the wooden box.

"Ah, thank Christ. Ya little belter."

He lifted it out and shifted so he was sitting with his back against the stone wall of the chapel and the box on his lap. Carefully he lifted the lid to reveal the contents. Wow. Even now – running for his life and with his head in bits – he couldn't help but feel a surge of good emotions, being in the presence of such a magnificent piece. Truly breathtaking. This was the first time he'd had a proper chance to examine it since stealing it from Luis Delgado's office, and seeing it up close he knew his instincts had been correct. It was the genuine article all right. *The Cherub with Chariot Egg.* One of the six rare Fabergé eggs many thought had been lost forever. This piece in particular was from a series of fifty-two jewelled eggs made by

Fabergé himself for Alexander III of Russia. It was so rare, so lost to antiquity, that only a single photograph existed of it – and even then it was only a blurred image, reflected on the side of an adjacent piece.

He held it closer, squinting at the detail of an angel pulling a chariot studded with a tasteful abundance of sapphires and diamonds. All intact. A precious and exquisite work of beauty. Perfect in every way.

Or so it seemed. Because as Danny tilted the egg upside down to examine the base, he heard something loose inside. He gave it a gentle shake. Yes. Something was rattling. Not what he wanted to hear.

Like many of his eggs, Fabergé had built a surprise inside of the *Cherub* for the owner to delight in finding. In this case it was a tiny clock face, which although hadn't told the right time in years was still a wonderful addition. He clicked the latch and felt the excitement rise in his guts once more as he lifted the top to see the miniature clock gazing back at him, encased as it was with more diamonds and the promise of a better life. But the clock was fixed in place, not the cause of the rattling. Instead a small black plastic rectangle, about the size of his thumbnail, was loose in the bottom. It must have been hidden behind the dial on previous inspections and had now come free from the mechanism. He tilted the egg and shook it. With another rattle the object came loose and fell out onto the palm of his hand. He could see now it was a USB drive. He shunted it down his palm and pinched it between his thumb and forefinger.

"What's all this then?"

He considered his new find. There were no clues on it to what was contained within, but something told him this USB drive could be his ticket out of trouble. Or, more than likely, the cause of it. But either way, he had to know what was on it.

Once the egg was safely packed up inside his holdall, he

shuffled over to the door of the chapel and eased it open. The bright morning sun sliced into his groggy retinas as he scanned the horizon for threats. But there was no one in sight. One of the reasons, he imagined, his drunken alter ego had picked this hideout was its remoteness, and the fact it hadn't been in use for the last fifty years. He'd discovered it whilst on a walk on his first week in San Sebastian and had brought girls up here a few times – local girls, who seemed to get off on the idea of being ravished in an abandoned chapel. It was a dangerous and incredibly blasphemous experience, and all the more exciting because of it.

By his reckoning it had to be early morning still, not yet nine, but the low sun was already burning hot. Even its reflection was dazzling as it rippled across the deep blue of the Bay of Biscay and the North Atlantic beyond. Danny's thoughts now drifted to food. He was starving, and if he was to think his way out of this mess he needed sustenance, as well as fluids that didn't have a percentage by vol. After that he needed an internet café, somewhere he could plug in this cursed device and understand what he was dealing with. He'd try emailing his uncle too, seeing as he wasn't answering his phone and the battery on his own had died some hours earlier. The old man could still be a lifeline. Knowing that kept him going. He gave the chapel a last nod, then headed down the path into town. It was a risky move, of course, with the mad nun still out there, but he needed answers. And right now all he had were a whole bunch of unanswerable questions.

TWELVE

Whilst Danny Flynn was getting to grips with his predicament, across the other side of the bay, Magpie Stiletto – *Hermana Muerte*, Sister Death – was already up and dressed (civilian attire today, a light pair of linen trousers in cream and a crisp white t-shirt), and walking along the coastal path that led down to the eastern side of the sprawling beachfront. She'd slept well though briefly from midnight until four, but had woken with a start, her mind already racing with dark memories and a prickliness in her veins.

On reaching the seafront, she stayed on the high ground rather than venture onto the sand, walking along the paved esplanade that curved along the length of the bay. While she walked she took in the foamy unsettled sea, pondering what today might bring, and whether she might finally fulfil her promise to herself. She was considering this, her mind wandering in murky but inspiring contemplation, when her phone vibrated irritatingly in her pocket. She thought about ignoring the call, but that was not her way, never had been. In her experience, those who ran from things found themselves running for the rest of their lives.

She pulled out the burner phone and answered.

"Is it done?" a voice asked.

She waited a beat before answering. "I told you not to call me again. No further contact."

"And I told you I want to be kept informed of what's going on. I have paid a lot of money for this job. For you to return my property." Luis Delgado sounded different today. His voice was less assured and higher-pitched, his words more hurried.

"I told you how I worked. When I've done the job and retrieved the items, I'll contact you via a secure server to arrange delivery and final payment."

Delgado was silent, though she could hear him swallowing back a mouthful of frustration. But this was the way it was. Even powerful people had to sit in patience sometimes, understand the value of fortitude. All being well, neither of them would have to wait too much longer.

"If what he stole from me falls into the wrong hands, I'm finished. You understand me?"

"Please don't raise your voice."

"Are you kidding me? Do you know who you're dealing with? Who this implicates? Believe me, you wouldn't be so calm if you did. If you fail this, we're both dead."

She reached the edge of the bridge that crossed over into the old town and stopped to gaze out over the ocean. The waves were high today. "Are you threatening me, Mr Delgado?"

A part of her wished he was. It was the part of her she pushed down inside herself, a reckless angry part of her psyche that was always there, bubbling away under the surface, and which she kept a handle on. As a young woman it had almost risen up and consumed her, but now it stayed hidden – like an evil twin locked in the attic of her mind lest it escape and take her down with it. These days she valued how controlled and serene she could be, even in high-stress situations. Life was all about control. But death even more so.

Delgado sighed. "It is not a threat. But I'm eager that we get this done. Soon."

She set off walking again, curling her lip at a group of teenage girls dressed in tiny shorts and vest tops. "Patience, Mr Delgado. You have hired the best and I will get the job done. But on my terms."

"When? Tell me."

She went into her head, doing a quick calculation. The mark would no doubt have reached out yesterday or first thing today. Another day for her to make arrangements...

"Tomorrow," she told him.

"You can promise?"

"I don't make promises. But it will be done. Don't contact me again."

She hung up before he could answer and shook her head at the phone before slipping it back into her trouser pocket and continuing her journey towards San Sebastian's old town. Once there, she made her way down the Calle Mayor to where the Basilica of Santa María del Coro stood grandly at the end of the street. She peered up at the stunning eighteenth-century church, knowing she should find enjoyment in its beauty. Or at least feel something. Be impressed by the craftmanship, for instance. But like always when encountering things of inherent beauty or worth, she felt nothing. Above the church stood Mount Urgull, awash with dense and vibrant green-leaved trees swaying gently in the morning sun. She shrugged. Still nothing.

But so what? She wasn't here to feel good. Wasn't here to sightsee or make merry. She was here for work and she was here for revenge.

There was an internet café a few streets away which she'd

used the day she arrived in the city. She made her way there and slipped ten euros to the boy behind the counter who sniffed and mumbled "*Número catorce*" at her without looking up from his iPhone.

Perfecto.

Screen fourteen was at the back of the long room, with the screen facing the wall and nothing else behind it. She already knew the connection wasn't fast, but she only needed a few minutes. Being late morning there weren't many other customers in the café – just an old man with his back to her who was scrolling frantically through someone's Facebook photos, and a young Asian girl near the door playing an online game.

Magpie logged in and went straight to the *DuckDuckG*o browser – not as secure as a Tor browser would be, but there was nothing that could tie her here. Once the site loaded, she input a series of seemingly random digits and was taken to another site, which to anyone glancing over her shoulder appeared to be a basic online forum for Bitcoin trading, but was in truth the new go-to place for the killing industry. A place to find jobs, post hits and send secure messages.

She signed in and scanned the message boards, hoping she might see some indication that her plan was working, but there was nothing she could decipher. No matter. It didn't mean all was lost. She had faith in the people involved to do what she expected of them. Whilst here, she sent a message to a contact in the Middle East, asking them if they'd heard anything from or about Beowulf Caesar. She also left a post on one of the forums, heavily coded, asking him to contact her if he saw it. It reeked a little of desperation, and was perhaps a pointless exercise – the boss was in the wind, a shadow – but she still held onto the belief Annihilation Pest Control would rise again. It had to. It was all she had.

She was about to leave when she noticed a new customer had come in. A tall man with long, wavy dark hair and a few days of stubble growth. He was standing at the counter, bouncing from foot to foot and glancing nervously around him. Normally the sight of someone like this, with his louche appearance and cheesecloth shirt open to his navel, would have made her blood boil. But today she ducked in front of her screen to hide the trace of a smile as it parted her cruel lips. It was him. The Irishman. Her mark.

Ahí está.

She stayed low, busying herself on her computer but with one eye on the Irishman as he made his way down the rows of terminals on the left of the café and sat at a screen a few metres away. He hadn't seen her, didn't even glance her way before pulling out the plastic chair and hunching over the keyboard to log in. He looked sicklier than she remembered, more nervous too, and that lascivious twinkle in his eyes had been dampened somewhat. She smiled to herself for the second time that day. Being on the run from an international assassin would do that to a person. She'd seen it many times over the years. Grown men, strong men, reduced to quivering babies with the realisation of their fate.

Patético.

Keeping a careful watch on the mark, she reached down into the canvas bag at her feet and removed a raffia straw hat and a pair of Gucci sunglasses. A few clicks of the mouse and she brought up the computer's webcam, her face and shoulders now on the screen. Using the image as a makeshift mirror she placed the hat on her head, before tucking her hair behind her ears first and concealing the tell-tale white streaks up inside of it. Once done, she slipped on the sunglasses and logged off.

Moving slowly, with an air of forced nonchalance, she edged down the café towards him, keeping her face forward but with both eyes – hidden behind the dark glasses – focused on his screen. As she got closer she paused and sighed dramatically as though she'd forgotten something and made a show of searching through her bag. The mark didn't even turn around. He was on some sort of secure messaging sight, with rows of text already on the screen. A conversation between himself – *DannyBoy69* – and username *D1950*. She narrowed her eyes at the screen. D for Dullahan?

The mark had a USB drive connected to the terminal which looked very much like the item she was meant to retrieve. She tensed. It would be so easy right now for her to finish this. She'd walk up behind him, break his neck, grab the USB and be on her way before anyone knew what the hell was going on. She remained where she was. There'd be time enough for her to do what Luis Delgado wanted, but first this Irish fool was going to work for her.

She scanned the first few lines of his conversation, him asking someone for help, telling them he was desperate, stuck, with no passport and someone out to kill him.

This was it. The plan was working.

Danny Flynn's leg jigged up and down as he waited for the reply, and she stepped back a few steps lest his growing agitation have him glance around. But he didn't take his eyes off the flashing cursor on the screen. They waited. Both as tense as each other. Then, ten, fifteen seconds later, the screen flashed and a reply appeared. It was staccato in its prose but lucid.

D1950: Heard about the hit. All under control. If you need to speak to me, ring the secure line. Not the house phone! Don't tell me your whereabouts here. I've sent someone to help you.

The Irishman read the words a few times, shaking his head before banging back a reply.

DannyBoy69: Someone to help? What do you mean? Where are they?

Once more the cursor flashed for a stomach-clenching amount of time before the reply came. The Dullahan no doubt sizing up his communications, making sure he was talking to the real Danny. The words flashed up on screen

D1950: On their way. A woman. She'll find you. Bring you home. I'll call later with location. Keep head down until then.

And there it was.

A woman.

The mark was back on the keyboard, asking more questions, but she'd seen enough. There was only one woman The Dullahan could be referring to. Only one woman the old fool would trust to help his pathetic nephew. And she was on her way to Spain. Coming for the mark.

Magpie straightened, and with an air of quiet satisfaction sashayed out of the internet café onto the busy Constitución Plaza. The sun was rising higher in the sky, its searing presence hot on her skin. She took in a deep breath of salty air. Today was a good day. Her plan was working. She was still going to kill the Irishman, of course, and retrieve the items for Delgado, but this way she would get so much more. Things no amount of money could buy.

Revenge.

Vindication.

The vanquishing of her enemy.

That miserable *perra* Acid Vanilla had no idea what awaited her in this glorious city. But she was going to die. Magpie Stiletto, Sister Death, would make sure of that.

THIRTEEN

THE FLIGHT ATTENDANT SMILED SUGGESTIVELY AT ACID AS SHE handed her another chilled grapefruit juice. "Is there anything else I can do for you?"

Acid shook her head, ignoring the come-on. It really wasn't the time. "No. Thank you," she said, in a voice full of subtext. *Leave me the hell alone.*

The attendant glided off up the aisle, and Acid picked up the plastic beaker to sip at the bitter pink juice. It was her third of the flight and it didn't taste any better than the previous two. She returned the beaker to the lap tray and let her head loll back against the headrest. Next to her an old woman slept with her temple pressed to the window, purring softly. There was, however, still enough window on view for Acid to notice land over on the horizon. Jersey, most likely, then France, then straight on to Spain and the San Sebastian airport.

She took another sip of the murky juice, noticing her arm was shaking, her legs too, fidgeting with a mixture of nervous energy, apprehension, and a healthy dose of delirium tremors. Not pleasant, but she was on the right path, ready for what came next.

Since leaving Spook at the Chinese doctors, she'd had a good wash, had even straightened her thick mane and shaved her relevant body hair. This, coupled with a depressing juice cleanse and some serious sweating out of toxins (a couple of 10K runs around the local park) and physically, outwardly, she was back in business. Inwardly? Well, that was anyone's guess.

She tried to close her eyes, join the old woman in a little nap, but it was useless. Despite the health drive, she hadn't been able to sleep the last two nights, which she knew was down to numerous reasons: worrying about Spook, the fact she was no longer existing in a drunken stupor, and because (like always when the drinking stopped) the bats had returned in force. She could physically feel the intensity of her moods flowing through her body, like hot needles in her skin. It was this same energy that kept her eyes propped open, her jaw tense and her muscles aching for exertion. Alongside the physical issues, her mind was now on overdrive, a million chaotic thoughts colliding together, fighting for control. She took a couple of deep conscious breaths that helped a little, but not much.

Like always when she was working, she'd packed minimal luggage and carried it on with her. She reached under her seat, retrieved her iPod from the canvas overnight bag and stuffed the earphones in her ears without bothering to untangle them. If sleep was out of the question, she had the next best thing: spiky, snotty music, played as loud as possible – the exact opposite of relaxation for most people but for her it was the perfect way to get out of her head for a little while.

She opened up the music player and scrolled through the albums on offer, settling on the Misfits' *Static Age*. As the heavy droning guitar of the title track burst forth, she settled back in her seat and slipped an eye mask over her head. Time until arrival: one hour, fifteen minutes. She'd been toying with ordering a drink – a real drink – but with the music filling her world she was able to put the thought out of her head. Better this way. From the sound of things, The Dullahan's nephew was in it up to his neck, and with Magpie on his tail time wasn't on their side. This despite the fact she had little information to go on, other than the nephew – Danny Flynn – was s*omewhere* in the city. *Great, thanks for that. Big help.* So, like always, she had no idea what she was walking into.

Once off the plane and safely through customs, Acid (or rather, Joselyn Mulberry, the name on her passport) headed for the nearest taxi rank. The queue was moving fast, but she had enough time while she waited to check her accommodation details, having booked herself into the Hotel Maria Cristina for four nights – a luxurious five-star hotel with views overlooking the Cantabrian Sea and Urumea River. Any longer than that and Danny Flynn wouldn't need saving. He'd be dead.

She twisted her mouth to one side as she read from the confirmation print-out. The Maria Cristina wasn't the most expensive hotel in San Sebastian but it wasn't far off, and would put her back the best part of a grand for the stay. Perhaps not the savviest of decisions considering her current cash flow issues, and the fact she now owed a Chinese doctor (and, by proxy, The Dullahan) a whole tonne of money, but she'd figure something out. She always did. Well, apart from all the times she hadn't, but who was counting? It was important to stay positive and all that shit.

At the front of the queue Acid jumped in the next cab and gave the driver the name of the hotel. Considering her in the rear-view mirror, the man shifted around in his seat, a wide grin creasing his tanned face, ready to say something smart or lewd, or both. A hard stare over the top of her shades cut that idea in two. Instead the man nodded meekly in agreement and pulled the car away.

Out from the cover of the taxi concourse the sun was blazing hot, and as they left the airport behind Acid wound down the window, enjoying the warm breeze on her face. Fresh sea air. You couldn't beat it. (You couldn't beat a dark smoky bar either, but she wasn't thinking about that). The road from the airport was long and narrow and snaked up high into the mountains, whilst all the while the deep azure of the ocean was visible down below. As they drove along, she closed her eyes and worked on shifting her mindset back into work-mode. Into kill mode. It wasn't always a pleasant experience, and she always felt she lost a part of herself when she went through this act of consciously stepping into a colder, inhuman persona, but it was needed. If she was to survive the next few days and complete her mission, then it was most definitely needed. In her mind's eye she pictured Magpie Stiletto, pictured herself slicing her scrawny neck open. The same way Magpie had to her poor mother.

Yes.

She could still do it.

She could do it in an instant.

It had been no secret to anyone at Annihilation Pest Control that Acid and Magpie hadn't got on. Although, really, that was the understatement of the decade. Absolutely fucking despised each other was closer to the truth. Acid had tried her best though, especially in the early days – both of them young and full of energy, the only female operatives in a group of men. They should have been allies. But Magpie had made it clear from the start she viewed Acid as a lesser assassin and, as became clear, a lesser person. Then the whole messy affair between Acid and Spitfire happened and that was the final nail in the coffin. After that Magpie would do everything she could to get at her, undermining her whenever possible to Caesar and her colleagues. Yet the unwarranted vitriol only made Acid want to prove herself more. She'd thrown herself into her training, took on as many jobs as she could get, gaining more and more experience, striving all the while to be the best, to be better than Magpie. So really she should thank her. The hatred she'd received had only made her who she was.

Yes. She'd thank the wizened old sow. Right before she put a bullet between those badly plucked eyebrows.

"We are here, Señorita. Maria Cristina." The driver pulled up outside a huge, fortress-like structure, reminiscent of a government building in Whitehall.

"That's wonderful, thank you." She grabbed up her bag and shuffled over to the kerb-side door to exit the cab. "How much do I owe you?"

"Give me… twenty euros." He said it like he was doing her a favour.

She went into her back pocket and found a couple of crumpled notes. "Here's thirty, keep the change." She shoved the notes into the small plastic tray and was out the door before he could reply.

Outside the air-conditioned cab the sun felt even hotter, and not for the first time in her life she felt her trademark black jeans and leather jacket weren't the best choice of attire for the situation. She rolled her neck around her shoulders.

Damnit. Haven't packed for the sun.

Apart from a handful of clothes, clean underwear and some deodorant, she'd only packed money, her own passport, a new one for Danny, and that was it.

She pulled out her phone: 11.15 a.m. local time. She was due to meet Sonny Botha (the South African gun-runner she'd met in Hanoi) in a couple of hours, so she had time for a little shopping, and to get acquainted with her surroundings. It was her first time in San Sebastian, but it seemed like her kind of city. Not too big but buzzing with life, and with plenty of side streets and alleyways in which to disappear – although not so easy if you were dressed as the only goth in Sunshine Town. So, first port of call had to be a new outfit, something that said *tourist* rather than *torturer*.

After dropping her bag off in the hotel room (very grand, done out in cream and gold, and overlooking the river) she set off towards the shops. Although thirty minutes later, looking around the bespoke independent boutiques in the old town, she'd conceded that her concession to holiday attire stopped short of flowery dresses and brightly coloured t-shirts. She'd tried on a few items (a white linen shirtdress, a matching shorts and top combo in pastel blue) but she couldn't do it, couldn't bring herself to wear these hideous clothes. In the end she opted for a pair of black denim shorts and a plain black t-shirt. It was close enough, and she did enjoy the sun on her bare legs as she exited the shop and strolled through the winding back streets until she reached the beachfront. From here it was another thirty minutes' walk up the hillside to the rendezvous point. She reached into the small canvas shoulder bag she'd bought to complete the look (black, of course) and checked the time on her phone. She had wondered about having a swift beer before she set off, only a small frosty one, from one of the many inviting tabernas she'd seen dotted around the place. But no. It was time to meet Sonny and after that she was to make contact with The Dullahan. So with the blistering sun overhead, and the soft, salty air licking at her skin, she headed to meet the gun-dealer. The beer would have to wait. It was time for Acid Vanilla to get back to work.

FOURTEEN

"THERE SHE IS. I ALMOST DIDN'T RECOGNISE YA WITHOUT THAT damned jacket!"

Acid dropped her shoulders and smiled up through her fringe at the leathery rogue who looked even more weather-worn than he had in Vietnam, standing there in a black Stones t-shirt with the sleeves cut off and tiny red shorts. His thin, sinewy arms hung heavy with a stack of bracelets around each wrist and a thick silver ring adorning each finger. On their first meeting, Acid had taken an instant liking to the old bugger, and seeing him again now buoyed her spirits a little. Although to be fair to the man, the 'old' descriptor might have been a little harsh. It was difficult to pinpoint his exact age, but she'd guess somewhere between mid-forties and late sixties. It was the UV rays that did it, and Sonny looked like he hadn't spent a day indoors in his life.

"Nice to see you too," she told him. "You're looking well."

"Ya bloody liar. But I feel well. Always do." He glanced over her shoulder as she got closer, his watery blue eyes wide with intensity for a moment before they relaxed back into their usual hooded sleepiness. "You want to do this here?"

79

She glanced around. They were up on the headland alongside a giant stylised sculpture of a bird that looked out over the sea. The piece (called the *Paloma de la Paz* – the Bird of Peace – according to the guidebook she'd flicked through on the plane) symbolised the city's commitment to peace, freedom and coexistence. Considering why she was here, it seemed fitting in its irony. Other than the imposing winged structure there was no one else around. Still, these things were best out of the open.

"You got a van or anything nearby?"

"Sure do. Follow me." He gestured to a dirt road, where an old VW campervan in red and white was parked on its own.

"This your accommodation, too?" she asked, as they walked towards the van. "You know, I did actually have you pegged as a bit of a surf bum."

"Get to fuck," Sonny sneered. "It's cover, is what it is. Don't let my rock and roll appearance fool ya, miss, I like the high life as much as anyone."

She couldn't help but smile grimly at the statement. She knew exactly what he meant.

"So what are you after?" he asked, as they neared the campervan. "I'm afraid my stocks have been depleted of late. Been driving across Europe from Russia for the past few months, and everyone seems to be starting a war right now."

"I'm not starting a war," she told him. "I'm finishing one. But to be honest, I only need a small piece and some ammo."

"I see. You couldn't have got that from a local dealer?" They stopped at the side of the van and he pulled a key from the pocket of his shorts. "Hell, you've got fake papers, right? You might have even got one from a legitimate dealer if ya fluttered your eyelashes the right way."

She sucked back a deep breath but let it go. "Yes, well,

thank you. But I was hoping you might be able to give me some intel as well."

Sonny laughed to himself as he unlocked the door and slid it open to reveal a huge industrial cargo box made from reinforced steel. "Is that so?" He heaved the box to the edge of the van and worked on the combination lock. "Go on then, spit it out."

Acid removed her sunglasses and leaned forward as he lifted the box lid, the usual tingle of excitement running down her arms at the sight of all that firepower. A veritable treasure chest of guns and rifles and stabbing weapons. "You heard of a man called Luis Delgado?" she asked, squinting up at him. "I think he's based around here. Some sort of art dealer."

Sonny straightened his back. "Yeah, I know him. Dealt with him once. Not a very nice dude. To call him an art dealer would be like saying Al Capone was only a casino boss."

"That's what I figured. So who is he?"

"Most people know him as a local-boy-made-good, a friend of the region. He's bought himself a good reputation over the years, despite being a total shit and having his crooked fingers in many pies behind the scenes." He put his fist in his other palm and cracked the knuckles. "This about The Dullahan's lad?"

Acid sniffed. "Nephew. So you've heard?"

"I keep my eye on things. Pays to know what your clients are up to. You know me Acid, I stay impartial. Anything else is bad for business." He leaned closer, his gravelly voice even rougher as he lowered it to a harsh whisper. "But I take it you also know who's here, who took the job?"

She nodded. "Do you know where she is?"

"No. And that's the truth. I sold her a few items going through in the other direction a month or so ago. She's been in Spain a while, from the sounds of it."

"I like to think she's been hiding from me." The way she said it, it sounded like a joke, but she really hoped it was true.

"You here to kill her?"

She looked out across the ocean. "I'm here for the boy. But if she gets in my way that would be a nice bonus."

"I had wondered whether you might have let the old vendetta go, after everything…"

"No. Not a chance." She huffed bitterly to herself. "Those bastards betrayed me, killed my mother. They deserve to die, all of them, only…" She trailed off.

"You don't want to get yourself killed in the process?"

She wrinkled her nose. "Maybe. Let's just say I'm working through a few things."

"Well, I'd hate to lose a customer."

"Don't write me off yet," she told him. "I always finish what I've started."

He nodded and ran his tongue across his top teeth. "I'm surprised Magpie Stiletto took the job, to be honest. Kind of domestic for her. But I guess she was bored since Caesar disappeared."

"Have you heard anything of him?"

He laughed. Back to his jovial self again. "Come on, love. You know better than to ask me that. Bad for business, like I say. Speaking of which…" He waved his hand over the box of guns. "What can I do for you?"

She held his gaze a moment longer, before turning her attention back to the guns. "What do you suggest?"

"I've got a nice Russian piece, an MP-446 Viking." He reached into the box and pulled it out, handed it to her. "It's a variant of the Rook, used by the Russian police. Not as powerful as its counterpart, but lighter. 9mm. Eighteen in the mag. Clean and unused, like always."

Acid held the gun at arm's length, feeling the weight in her grip. "Do you have any Glocks?"

"Only a 21, I'm afraid. As I say, they've been flying off the shelves lately."

"No. I don't want a forty-five." She shoved the Viking down the back of her shorts and let her t-shirt fall over the top. "I'll take the nine and four mags' worth of ammo. That should do me."

"An excellent choice," Sonny beamed, reaching into the box and stuffing four magazines into a small zip-up bag. "For you, my dear, I'll do the lot for two thousand euros."

He handed her the ammo and she slipped it in her bag, before pulling out a roll of notes – a loan from The Dullahan – and handing it over. "Here you go, that's two thousand exactly."

"Wonderful. I won't bother counting it. I trust ya."

"I'm glad."

"I also know where to find ya," he rasped, over a phlegmy laugh. He held up the roll of euros. "Great doing business with you again and sorry I couldn't be more help. You ask me though, Acid, both Delgado and Stiletto should be approached with caution. Before you say it, I know you can handle yourself, but still, don't get cocky. You hear me?"

"I won't," she told him. "And thank you."

There was an awkward moment where she almost gave him a hug but pulled herself back at the last moment.

Jesus.

"I'll see you around then," she mumbled, already returning back towards the centre. As she reached the main road, she heard Sonny shouting something after her. She didn't turn around, but it sounded like he was saying good luck and be careful. Be very careful indeed.

FIFTEEN

Leaving the Dove of Peace behind her, Acid drifted down a side street that led to the main part of the city before crossing the bridge back into the old town. A particularly authentic-looking taberna had caught her eye on the way to meet Sonny and she was now drawn there. Just the one drink. To level her nerves a little.

An air of excitement hung over the streets as she passed by chattering groups of locals. Everyone seemed to be gearing up for some kind of festival. Stalls were being set up, a stage too, with colourful flags stretching from building to building, whilst off in the distance a hidden sound system blasted out bass-heavy electronica. This could go either way, she thought, as a man with a large papier-mâché devil head approached her. Crowds were often useful, especially in her old line of work where the goal was often to slip away unseen, but they also meant finding The Dullahan's nephew would be trickier.

Luckily, she found the taberna easily enough (a compact but tasteful establishment called Paco Bueno), and the second she stepped foot inside, her stomach was grumbling. The enforced juice cleanse of the last few days might have done her good but now it was real sustenance she needed. Something hot and salted and garlicky. And a beer, or two, why not? When in Rome and all that... The stout man behind the counter greeted her with a large smile as she entered.

"*Hola, quieres algo de comer?*"

Acid slid her sunglasses onto her head. "*Sí, por favor,*" she replied. Her Spanish was ropey after years of disuse, but she liked to try. "*Qué es bueno?*"

"Ah, you are English?" the man boomed. "I sorry, you look Spanish, no?"

She allowed him a sweet smile. As sweet as she ever got, at least. "My mother was Italian. I guess that's it."

"Ah, *bueno*. What can I get you, Miss Italy?"

She was already scouring the range of inviting dishes on display under the glass counter. Porcelain bowls of huge, shiny olives, cubes of Manchego cheese and unctuous tortilla, still moist in the centre, as it should be. Her eyes settled on a tray of massive pink prawns swimming in garlic oil. Sold.

"Those *gambas* look amazing," she said. "And some bread?"

"*No hay problema.* And to drink?"

"*Cerveza*, please. *Grande.*" The words had left her lips before she even had a chance to ask herself whether she should. Screw it. She had to stay sharp, but one wouldn't hurt.

The owner gestured for her to sit and she moved over to the side of the room, choosing a high stool next to a shelf that ran around the side of the taberna. Once settled, she pulled out her phone and swiped through her contacts to find The Dullahan's secure line. He answered in two rings.

"It's me," she told him. "I'm in Spain."

"Good lass."

"How's the kid?" She tensed, not sure she wanted to know the answer.

"She's doing fine. She'll live."

"You sure?"

"Aye, I told you yer man was the best in the business. She's awake. Sitting up. Making shite jokes. Song Shi wants to observe her a few more days but then she'll be home." He trailed off and an awkward silence fell over the line. Acid wiped the smile off her face, she knew what was coming. "And then he'll want payment, of course."

"I know. I'm working on it. Can you help, until…"

"I told you I would. Did you meet with Sonny?"

"Yes. Got a decent piece but not much info other than what we already know. The guy who ordered the job, Delgado, he's bad news. I still don't understand why he outsourced the hit though. Some guy steals from you, you get a couple of goons to sort it. Not someone like Magpie." She shifted on the stool, scoping out the taberna, but there was no one sitting nearby, no one paying any interest to her.

"I'm still wondering what the full story is myself," The Dullahan said, and sighed. "I've touched base with the boy over the internet, and he rang me on this line a few minutes ago. Says he's fine, for now, though he had a narrow escape from a mad nun carrying two large knives, who I assume was Stiletto. I didn't want him on the line long, but I told him you'd meet him at six tonight. By the carousel in Alderdi Eder Park. Will ya find it all right?"

"I'm nearby," she told him. Then, as the barman appeared by her table. "Thank you, just there."

She shifted back as he placed a sizzling bowl of prawns in front of her, followed by a basket of thick white bread and a chilled bottle of San Miguel with droplets of condensation running down its neck.

"Who ya talking to?" The Dullahan snapped.

"Relax," Acid told him, slugging back a mouthful of beer. "I'm in a bar, having some food. That okay with you?"

"All right, but don't get complacent, Acid. You know what can happen."

"Yes, I do know, and I won't. Six tonight, at the carousel. Got it. Shit—" She snapped her attention to the door, one hand on the gun under her t-shirt as a loud crack echoed through the taberna. "What the fuck?"

A few metres away, the bar owner was smiling as he wiped down a table. "Don't worry, Miss Italy," he sang. "Is not someone trying to kill you. Is the cannon fire from Alderdi Eder. It is a good thing. Signals the start of the *Semana Grande.* Our summer festival."

Acid chewed her bottom lip. "A festival? I thought as much."

"Yes. You eat, you drink, you dance. We have fireworks and music and of course the *gigantes y cabezudos* parade. How is it… umm… *Giants and fat-heads.* You will love it. Is very much fun. All over the city. Today it starts in the park. Lots of people."

"I see. How long does it last?"

Another big grin. "Is all week."

"All week," she said. "Lots of people. You hear that, Dullahan?"

"Aye, is it going to be a problem?"

"Not one I can't handle."

"Okay. Ring me when you get a chance. But for now, focus on finding Danny and then the two of you getting the hell out of there. Speak to you soon."

He hung up and she stuffed the phone back in her bag before turning her attention to her food, grabbing up a fat prawn, pulling its head off and slurping the garlicky tail into her mouth. It tasted so damn good. Exactly what she needed. For now at least the bats were at bay, but she wasn't stupid. These moments of relative calm were fleeting. Another three hours and she'd meet Danny. Whether it was as easy as The

Dullahan had made it sound, she wasn't sure. But it felt good to be busy again, to have purpose. And whatever happened next, she was ready.

SIXTEEN

THREE MINUTES TO SIX.

Danny had checked the time on his new burner phone twenty times in as many minutes. But he was nearly there. Safety. Soon this hell would be over. That hadn't quenched his urge to call his uncle back in every one of those twenty minutes – get some more information on whoever was coming to meet him – but he'd refrained, stayed strong as told. In their last conversation the old man had expressly told him to get off the burner phone and stop talking *so fecking much*. The less information passed over communication networks – even seemingly secure ones – the better. All he knew was a woman, someone his uncle vouched for, was about to deliver to him a new passport and then help him get out of the country.

Easy as pie, right?

But despite his reservations and trepidations, Danny wasn't about to go against his uncle's authority or experience on these matters. Growing up, he'd always admired his uncle Jimmy – who'd been a father figure to him, of sorts, after his old man was killed when he was only two years old. For the young Daniel Flynn (small for his age, not many friends), Uncle

Jimmy was funny, relatable, but with a real edge to him, which meant you knew never to talk back or overstep the mark. Of course, as Danny got older he began to hear the stories, the whispered asides whenever Jimmy stepped into a room. But it was the fear he saw in people's eyes that sold it. So he knew what Jimmy was, what he had been, and for that reason – at least in a situation such as this – he trusted him completely. Trusted him with his life.

Shite, what other option did he have?

"Come on, where are ya?" he muttered to himself, squinting his eyes into the hordes of people on this side of the park. Families with young kids mainly, all chattering and whooping excitedly at the huge-headed figures on display, their excitement audible even over the loud music pumping from the speaker-stacks dotted around the area.

Another check on his phone told him it was six.

So where was this woman? Was she even coming?

He began to cautiously move around the side of the large carousel when it started up, walking in the opposite direction as the painted horses rose and fell to the music, ridden by loud, highly strung children, chuckling gleefully at the archaic ride. It surprised him that, notwithstanding the fear knotting his stomach, he could still smile at the sight. Nice to see a little ray of innocence shining through the poisonous shitstorm he'd created for himself.

As he walked around the carousel, his attention veered from female face to female face. Not an unusual occurrence for Danny, but today it was for a very different reason.

Was that her?

Was that?

He made eye contact as he passed by them, smiled a slight half-smile, but received no flicker of recognition in return. In his imagination he was looking for an older woman, possibly a local. Although, he quicky realised that was because in his mind's eye he was picturing Camila, the kind-faced old dear from his guest house.

But if this woman was anything like the vision in his head, it meant he couldn't rely on her to be anything other than a mere conduit for the new passport his uncle was sending. From the moment Uncle Jimmy had told him it was a woman coming to help, Danny had misgivings. How the hell was one person (and a woman, at that) going to be any use at all against that killer nun and the combined force of Delgado's mob? He hadn't said any of this, of course, because his uncle was adamant. A woman was on her way to Spain, an old friend, who would help Danny get home. End of story.

As he circled the carousel, he came across a long line of food vans and saw a woman standing next to one with a steaming pan of paella on the counter. She was wearing large dark glasses that obscured most of her face but appeared to be looking straight at him. When she smiled and held up her hand, he did the same.

"I was thinking you weren't going to show," he gasped, as he got nearer. "Thank fuck you're here tho—" He shut up as she hurried straight past him and flung her arms around a young woman with short blonde hair wearing a tie-dye tube dress. "I see," he muttered. "Back to the drawing board."

On a good day, he'd think the smells coming off the food stalls was glorious and would definitely have stopped to indulge. Exciting-looking delicacies bubbled in hot oil that was bright orange with paprika and rich with garlic and herbs, sweet and spice all rolled into one, a feast for the nose as well as the eyes. But Danny had no appetite. In fact, if anything, the smells made him feel nauseous as he completed another futile circuit of the fairground ride.

The phone screen read ten past six now and his next

thought was to again call his uncle, tell him his plan had failed and that this woman, whoever she was, wasn't coming. But as he cast his gaze over the crowds one last time his heart stopped and his breath froze in his throat. Standing by a small group of trees, shaded from the late afternoon sun as it made its descent over the horizon, another woman was staring at him. A woman he recognised. The habit was gone, the headdress too, but Danny would know that face anywhere. The brutal sneer, the heavy eyebrows twisted into a deep scowl had been burnt into his memory, labelled by his threat response network as *Danger* – as *Get the hell out of here!*

The woman stepped out from the cover of the trees and walked towards him, weaving slowly through the swarms of revellers as Danny began to back away. A perimeter fence had been set up around the edge of the park for the festival – mainly as a structure from which to hang advertising boards, rather than to keep people enclosed – but nevertheless his means of escape were now limited. He scurried around the carousel, pushing past people as he went, skipping around groups of children and almost falling over a small dog, all the while glancing back over his shoulder. She was still trailing him, moving methodically but without haste, her eyes fixed, her face without expression. It only made her seem more sinister.

Around the other side of the carousel, Danny hurried along a long strip of fencing that led towards the south side of the park. The festivities hadn't yet spread this far, which meant he was leaving the relative safety of the crowds, but he could now get some speed up, put distance between him and the sadistic killer nun.

But not so. As he opened up into a sprint, a cursive look over his shoulder told him she was matching his pace, step by step. Gulping for air, he swerved over to the centre of the park, stumbling through a tree-lined passage that opened out into an exotic garden with a huge ornamental fountain standing in the middle. It was quieter still here, with only a handful of people sitting peacefully on the benches that surrounded the fountain. None of them looked up as he hurried past them, desperately searching for an escape, a place to hide, anything.

For a stomach-leaping moment he thought he'd given his pursuer the slip, yet as he ran through the gardens, heading back towards the far side of the park, she stepped onto a raised flower bed a few metres in front of him and slipped her hand into the pocket of her jacket.

"Shite."

Before she had a chance to pull out the weapon (a gun most likely, but with her it just as well could be a fecking samurai sword) he ducked behind a large flowering bush and made for a path running alongside the main road. Over the top of the perimeter fence he could see banners and flags being waved around to the sounds of upbeat electronica. He kept going, running now as fast as his weary limbs would take him and looking over his shoulder every second or two to see if she was near. Because if that was a gun she'd pulled from her pocket – and a glint of sun reflecting off metal told him it was – he'd like to be ready for it. They say you never hear the bullet that kills you, and maybe that was for the best, but his ego wanted to know, to be prepared, to look his killer in the eyes in his last moments.

But all this meant Danny's focus was away from the path in front of him as it curved around a small patch of Spanish carnations, and he ran full speed into someone. The impact knocked him off his feet and he scraped his knee against the gravel path trying to keep momentum. The nausea almost came to fruition as he staggered to right himself and get away, but he couldn't move. Something was holding him back. Something physical. A hand on his arm.

No. Please. Move. Have to move.

Have to get away.

Danger.

"Wait," a voice rasped in his face, husky but well-spoken. "Come with me."

He shot his attention to the figure gripping his arm. A woman. Dressed in black and standing about five-five in her battered Converse trainers. She was wearing sunglasses and had dark, almost black hair, but no white streaks. Not the nun. Not his killer.

"Are you—? Did my uncle—?"

The woman's face was stern, and her full lips were pressed into a determined pout. "It's Danny, yes?"

He nodded. Gasped for air. "S'right."

She peered over his shoulder and he was certain he saw the hint of a smirk twisting the corner of her mouth. "We need to get out of here. This way."

The woman kept hold of his arm, leading him through the ornamental gardens and along a wide path that led out of the park where the road was flanked on both sides by cheering crowds. Danny risked another glance over his shoulder and spotted the now-familiar white streaks as the nun appeared at the gate and glared his way.

"She's still coming," he cried, while they shoved through lines of people and onto the main street. "Woah, fecking hell…"

A procession of dancers was heading down the road towards them, each of them wearing huge papier mâché heads. Monsters, farmyard animals and grotesque caricatures of (what he imagined were) Spanish government officials made

up most of the ensemble, as well as one guy dressed as Jesus
Christ and carrying a bright pink inflatable guitar.

"Get a move on, will you?" the woman snarled, almost
yanking him off his feet as they wound their way around the
dancers, both of them peering back the way they'd come.

"You see her?" he asked.

The woman halted, straining her neck. "No. But that
doesn't mean we can relax." She let go of his arm, before
launching herself through the crowds on the other side of the
street without an *excuse me* or an apology or anything. Danny
watched on incredulously for a moment and then quickly
followed on behind, distorting his face into an apologetic
grimace as he pushed his way through.

"Hey, you," he called out as they got through the mass of
spectators and the woman made for an alleyway that ran
between two apartment complexes. "Do you know where the
hell you're going?"

She spun around but didn't stop, walking backwards whilst
facing him. "Somewhere away from that crazy bitch for
starters."

"Then what?" Danny asked. "You got a plan?"

The woman shrugged and grinned manically. "Not really.
But I'm sure I'll think of something." With that she turned and
ran down the side of the buildings, took a left, and
disappeared.

SEVENTEEN

Acid was already regretting taking the job as she got to the end of the alleyway and stepped up into an unused doorway to wait for Danny. What the hell was he playing at, trotting along like there wasn't someone chasing him ready to put a bullet in his skull?

Not cool. Not what she needed. At all. Soon as they were safe, she'd ring The Dullahan and tell him she couldn't do the job. She'd have to pay him back some other way because it was too much to take on and she wasn't ready. Not for this. Not for anything. She had assumed (hoped) that seeing Magpie again would have conjured up a renewed energy inside of her. That experiencing the vile woman – and all she represented – would have spurred her on to complete what she'd started. As it was, she just felt… Well, she didn't like to think about what she felt, or what that meant. But her lack of impetus wasn't the only thing plaguing her thoughts as she huddled in the doorway.

She'd been watching Danny as he paced around the carousel in the park, convinced she had the wrong person. He was nothing like his uncle at all. The Dullahan was small and wiry, with intense eyes and a ferocity you could sense from a hundred metres away. In contrast this man was at least six-two and broad-shouldered, with warm eyes and an easy cheeriness to his demeanour that, given the situation, meant he was either stupid or didn't understand how much trouble he was in. Either way, it wasn't a good look, not someone she wanted to get involved with. In fact, she'd pretty much convinced herself that this lolloping oaf with his tan and pretty-boy looks couldn't possibly be her guy, when Magpie had showed up to prove otherwise.

Which was the other thing bothering her. How the hell did the sour-faced witch know they'd be there?

"Wait a minute, will ya?" It was Danny, standing a few doors down with his hands on his hips, gasping for air. "Talk to me."

"We haven't got time," she yelled. "We'll talk later."

"No. Wait."

She'd already turned to set off again but the fierceness in his voice had her stop. Maybe he wasn't so dissimilar to his uncle after all.

"Fine." She sighed as he caught up with her. "Talk."

Danny scowled. "Well, firstly, who the hell are ya? And how do I know I can trust ya?"

"My name is Acid Vanilla, okay? I'm a friend of The Dullahan. He sent me."

"The... what?"

She rolled her eyes at him. They really didn't have time for this. "Your uncle Jimmy. He asked me to come and get you. Bring you home. Okay? So we're good?"

She made to set off once more but Danny grabbed at her shoulder. "Hang on, you said your name was *Acid Vanilla*?" He said it like it was the most ridiculous concept in the world, and maybe it was. She had no clue anymore. No semblance of right or wrong, up and down, good or bad. "You're pulling my leg, right?"

She removed her sunglasses and hung them over the collar of her t-shirt before fixing him dead in the eye. "No, sweetie. I'm deadly serious. I'm here to save your arse. So shut up and follow me or you'll get us both killed."

As if to highlight this point beautifully, a gunshot echoed down the alley and pinged off the brickwork a few feet from Danny's head.

"Shit. She's here."

With the bats screeching songs of mistrust across her already fraught nervous system, she dragged Danny onwards, cutting through an adjacent alleyway where enormous metal refuse bins had been placed at intervals along each side. The chicane effect provided them cover as they zig-zagged around the tall bins with bullets thudding into the thick metal behind them.

The end of the alley opened out into a wide road mercifully awash with people, most of them seemingly locals, this being the business district of the city. They took a left, mingling in with the crowds as best they could and continuing down the street until they reached a busy crossroads. Without waiting, Acid continued across the road, winding around slow-moving, overheating cars whose owners blasted on the horns in annoyance and ignoring Danny's bleating protestations over her shoulder.

Seriously, what the hell did this idiot think was happening right now?

Once across the other side, she leapt up into the recessed doorway of a bank and pulled Danny in beside her. She gave it a beat before peering around the doorframe and throwing her bristling awareness over the scene, at the sea of faces and bodies, ebbing and flowing in the early evening sun. But no sign of Magpie. She gave it a few more seconds, casting her gaze a little wider. But for the moment it seemed they were safe.

"All right," she said, keeping her eyes on the street. "My hotel's about three blocks away. If we can get there without being seen, we can lie low. Work out our next move."

When Danny didn't respond she turned around, catching him suppressing a sly smile.

"Your hotel?" he said, bright blue eyes even bluer in the sunlight. "If you say so."

Acid threw up an eyebrow. "Seriously? That's your first thought?"

"Can't blame a fella for being optimistic."

"Optimistic?" she spat, stepping down from the doorway and edging her way around the side of the bank. "You'll need more than optimism, son. Try a miracle. Now if you want to live past this evening, I suggest you follow me, keep your head down and your mouth shut."

"Ah, come now, I was only messing. Trying to lighten the mood a little."

"Yes, well we don't need the mood lightening, thank you." She moved steadily along the street, eyes flitting around and scoping out every angle, every face. "Optimism gets you killed. Expect the worst and everything else is a bonus."

"Jesus, I bet you're fun at parties."

"I'm fabulous, actually. But I'm even better at not getting myself killed." She glanced up at Danny. "And what did I tell you about keeping your mouth shut?"

EIGHTEEN

"Woah, would ya look at this place?" Danny spun around on the spot, holding out his arms as he took in the luxury. "It's like a palace. Must cost a fair bit to stay here."

Acid pulled the Viking pistol from out of her shorts and placed it on the chest of drawers facing the bed, making sure Danny clocked it. "What can I say, I have expensive taste."

"You must earn a fair bit."

"Used to. Not so much lately." She smiled, joylessly. "One of the reasons I'm doing this job from your uncle. I owe him."

"I see, so you and Uncle Jimmy..." He placed his bag down and sat in the Regency-style chair opposite the bed. "How do you know each other exactly?"

She lowered her chin. Clearly the boy fancied himself as a bit of an Irish rogue, god's gift and all that, and to be fair he'd probably had plenty of evidence from facile young girls to back up that theory. He was handsome enough in a certain light, she'd give him that, but cocky and annoying with it. A bad combination. Plus she was in no mood for games. "We've got a long history," she replied, holding up her forearm to reveal the raised scar along its length. "First time I encountered him, he gave me that."

"So… you're in the same line of work?"

"What line of work might that be, Daniel?"

"Daniel? Wow." He sat forward in the chair. "Are you flirting with me, Acid Vanilla?"

She sighed dramatically before marching over to the large chest of drawers standing alongside the bed and yanking at the middle drawer. Once open, she slid her hand to the back, feeling around until her fingers touched on what she was after.

"Here," she said, flinging the new passport at him. "This is what I'm here to do. There. Job done."

He fumbled the catch but laughed it off, not taking his eyes off her as he reached down and scooped it up. "Thanks a lot."

"Don't mention it. So for the next twenty-four hours, or however long it takes us to get out of here, you'll answer to Seamus O'Neill."

He scoffed, opening up the passport to check. "Seamus O'Neill? Fecking hell, could you not think of something more Irish? Eamonn Shamrock, perhaps? Darragh Luckycharms?"

She turned from him, fighting a smile. A sharp cough sorted her out. "Your uncle arranged it, blame him. Besides, I'd say Danny Flynn sounds like a cliched Irish name in itself, especially combined with this cheeky chappy routine you've got going on."

"Cheeky chappy? Geez. But yeah, it'll do. Thank you." He flung it on top of his holdall and looked at her, his face widening. "Speaking of names, you were having me on before, weren't ya? You're not really called Acid Vanilla?"

She sat on the edge of the bed facing him. "Yes. That's my name."

"Yer mammy name you that?"

"That's not what I said. But that's who I am now."

He nodded in acknowledgement. "So that's... what, a codename? An alias?" She didn't respond. "So you are in the same line of work as old Jimmy? What was it you called him again?"

"The Dullahan. I'm not sure he'd appreciate *Old Jimmy*."

"*The Dullahan,*" Danny repeated, rolling it around his mouth. "Je-sus. Isn't that a demon from Irish folklore or something? Aye, I remember from school. Something about if he called yer name you'd drop down dead."

Acid stuck out her bottom lip. Sounded about right. "You never heard him called that?"

"He was always Uncle Jimmy to me. His wife is my ma's sis. Though I've not seen him since Auntie Sheila passed away. Poor old cow."

A flicker of humanity washed over him, muting the twinkle in his eyes for a moment, but a second later he was back and grinning at her. "And you're somewhat of a bad-ass, is that right? Ya come here to protect me?"

"I'm here to give you that passport. That's all." She stood up and walked into the bathroom, leaving the door open and talking as she splashed water on her face. "If I remember correct, the next flight back to London is in three hours. You can stay here until then."

She grabbed a towel from the heated rail and patted her face dry before leaning around the door. Danny was waiting for her, his face a picture of confusion. "What about the woman trying to kill me?"

"Not your problem anymore."

"What do you mean?"

She cracked her knuckles, realising she'd had her hand gripped in a tight first. "I mean, I'll take care of it. All you've got to do is toddle off home. Simple."

"Why?"

"Why what?"

"Why will you take care of it? Who asked ya to? Uncle Jimmy?"

She sighed and sat on the bed, leaning back against the headboard. "For heaven's sake, I can't decide if you're stupid or trying to wind me up. You must have been a nightmare as a kid. But, no, all right? This is nothing to do with your uncle. You don't need to concern yourself with all that. We just need to get you safely out of the country."

Danny was silent now. He stood up and paced around the room, his roguish facade replaced by intense concentration.

It didn't make her feel any more comfortable. "What is it?" she asked him.

"What if I helped you find her, help you kill her. That is what ya mean to do, isn't?" He sat beside her on the bed. "Then you can help me with something."

"Absolutely not."

Danny baulked. "That's it? *No*? You don't want to hear what I have in mind?"

"I can guarantee it won't be worth my trouble."

"Is your trouble worth ten million dollars? Perhaps more?"

Her face remained neutral (okay, on the sneery side of neutral), but the words had landed in her lap like a tonne of gold bullion. Ten million dollars. A lot of money in anyone's book. And money that she was in dire need of. At present, Acid didn't have the first clue how she was going to pay for Spook's care.

"You said yourself money was tight," Danny said, leaning in, as if he already knew how to push her buttons. "Ten million dollars. Think about that. All for you."

And she was thinking about it. But the bats weren't happy. This was not part of the plan, they told her. Tread careful.

Screw it.

Now she really needed a drink. A proper one. Something strong and spicy to dilute –or better still, drown – the growing unease in her stomach. Without a word she slipped off the bed and walked over to the minibar where a selection of drinks and extortionately priced snacks were on offer. She grabbed two Jack Daniels miniatures and held them up for Danny to see.

"Oh go on then," he said. "Ya twisted my arm."

Thankfully the minibar also had proper tumblers, made of glass (an absolute must), and once the drinks had been decanted she carried the tumblers over and handed one to Danny. *Cheers.* She resumed her place on the bed and held the glass to her lips, letting the spicy fumes envelop her senses before taking a long and delicious sip.

"Okay, let's say, hypothetically, that I'm interested…" she said, as the bats screeched their disquiet.

Stop this.

Stop this now.

She knew full well that even entertaining this joker was a massive red flag. She could already sense herself spiralling, the brittle craziness at the base of her soul swelling into her consciousness. She was thinking too laterally, was too eager to take risks, but also right now she didn't care. Because wasn't this always the double-edged sword of being who she was, of thinking the way she did? A part of her knew she was heading for the cliff-edge, but another part relished that fact, lived for the *fuck it, let's see what happens*-ness of it all. Plus, she told herself, if the money was real, it could be the lifeline she needed.

She glanced at Danny. "How do we get our hands on this money?"

"That's the spirit," he said, raising his glass. "Although to be honest with you, Acid, I don't think you're going to like what I've got planned."

NINETEEN

DANNY GULPED BACK A MOUTHFUL OF JACK DANIELS, HOPING, praying, that the strong liquor might provide him some instant courage. As it was, it only made him feel more nauseous and no less wary of this strange, scary, enigmatic woman sitting in front of him. It was safe to say Danny Flynn wasn't used to strong women. Not ones he found so damned attractive, anyway. There was his ma, of course, Aunt Sheila too. Both strong as all hell, mentally at least. But this Acid Vanilla was like no woman he'd ever met. She was sexy, strong, and with a fierce tongue on her that made him not want to speak ever again. He certainly had reservations about telling her his plan. Because really it wasn't a plan at all, was it? A vague notion at best. A sketch of an idea he was pretty much making up on the spot. He shuddered, the whisky passing his throat as Acid nodding eagerly at him, gesturing that he get on with it. He fixed her in the eyes, at the exact moment that everything he was preparing to say fell out of his head.

"Woah, there," he spluttered. "I've only this second noticed your eyes. Would ya look at that, they're different colours. Never seen that before. They're... beautiful."

Those same beautiful eyes (one dark turquoise, one light umber – although he might have gone with *rich caramel*) rolled back in annoyance. "Quit stalling, Romeo," she told him. "Tell me your plan."

But for once it wasn't a line. Danny was transfixed. Those eyes, together with her striking bone structure and full, natural lips had him entranced. And she was still staring at him. Waiting. Her impatience growing.

"Enough stalling," she said. "Spill or I'm out of here."

"All right, here goes." He stood up and hit himself on the chest a couple of times with the heel of his fist. "So… The man who hired the man, he's called Luis Delgado. A local businessman and art dealer."

"Yes. I'm aware of him. And the mad nun? She goes by the name Sister Death. Also Magpie. And she's no nun."

"Right. Well that's reassuring – for a minute there I thought she was here to make me atone for my sins. Anyway, if you know Delgado, you'll know he's big news here in the Basque Country. Although, I didn't realise just how big until yesterday. See, I've been working with him – or rather, for him – for the last few months. Brokering a deal on a few pieces. Fine art, mainly. He invited to me to his house on a couple of occasions. We ate together, drank. I felt like he was looking after me." He shook his head, took another gulp of Jack. "Then Billy Big Balls here goes and fucks it all up. Like he always does."

"What the hell did you do, Danny?" Acid asked. "I'm still struggling to understand why someone like Delgado – who I imagine has plenty of goons on his payroll – outsources to an international killer like Magpie. That's a big price to pay, and for what?"

Danny slid off the bed and walked over to his holdall.

"This," he said, removing the egg from its box and holding it up. "I stole it from him."

Acid squinted at the piece. "Fabergé?"

"You have a good eye," he told her, returning to his position on the bed. "But this one's been missing for decades. Super rare. Like, only a handful of people have ever even seen it. I've no idea how it came into Delgado's possession but it's pretty much priceless."

"Okay, so I'm still not understanding where this all fits in with Magpie. Why hire her in particular?"

"I don't know, but it was fecking stupid of me to take it, I know that. But I saw the opportunity and here we are. I was blinded by how much it could bring and what I could do with that sort of money. Plus, I figured by the time he realised it was missing I'd already be in the wind. He'd never see me again. Only in the excitement I left my passport and papers at his place. Stupid fecking eejit."

"That's pretty much what your uncle said as well."

"Aye, fair enough." He smiled grimly, his eyes on the egg, over which he ran his thumb. "You see, even then I didn't worry too much. Delgado's worth close to a billion euros. Losing one little egg wouldn't have been such an issue for him. Only I stole more than the egg."

"How do you mean?"

Danny shook the egg so they could both hear it rattle. "After escaping from your Magpie, I started to wonder, like you are, why is he sending professionals after me? He's got men to do that sort of thing. A guy called Hugo and a few others. Big mean dudes. They'd have handled a cocky Irish tinker like me in a second. Anyway I got away, as you know, and was hiding out in a wee abandoned chapel on the headland when I found this." He opened up the egg and shook out the USB drive, holding it up for her to see.

"Wonderful," she said, with a sigh and a mighty eye-roll. "I should have known."

He frowned. "Sorry?"

"It's nothing. Do you know what's on it?"

"Aye, I found an internet café and opened it up and, well, fuck me, turns out Luis Delgado is way more than a local businessman and art dealer. *Way more*." He shook his head, still not quite believing it. "Amongst other things held on this little piece of plastic, are his books for the last three years. His real books I mean, not what you'd give to the tax man. We all do it in the antiques world, but nothing like this."

"So it's incriminating?" she asked, holding her hand out.

"Oh, I'd say that's an understatement." He handed the drive over, not taking his eyes off it as she held it to the light. "But that's not to say Delgado isn't a legitimate businessman. He can cite two art galleries, three restaurants, a studio catering company and a massive vineyard as part of his empire. All this I knew, of course, which was why I made a beeline for him when I arrived in the region. But as his books show, the main purpose of those businesses is to launder more than ninety million euros a year, generated from drugs, hijackings, as well as shipping stolen cars and guns into Europe and the Far East. People, too. Young girls."

"Sex trafficking?" The emotion was clear in her voice.

"Aye, he's a real piece of shit, so he is." He held out his hand and she placed the USB back in his palm. "This little drive is basically a Who's Who of European and Russian crime lords. Traffickers. Arms dealers. It's fecking crazy. So yes, I'd say it's pretty incriminating."

Acid leaned forward, her face twisted in thought. "Fine. That's the background. Where does the ten million come in?"

Danny took his time placing the USB drive back inside the

egg, wondering if he should go on. "There's another egg," he told her.

"O-kay."

"Aye, somehow Delgado has also gotten his hands on the *Hen with Sapphire Pendant*, which, if anything, is even rarer than the *Cherub* here." He held his breath, but she didn't respond. "Both eggs together are worth at least thirty million."

"Oh, and I'm only getting a third of that?"

He walked the egg over to his holdall and zipped it safely inside before returning to the bed. "We can talk about the cut later. Thing is, I've already got a buyer for both eggs. A guy in London called Petre Kaminski."

"And who's he?" she asked with a frown.

"A Polish businessman. Aye, I know, another one, but he's the sort who doesn't care how the eggs came to be in my possession." He locked eyes with her, feeling the energy bristling between them. She was considering it. He went on, "I've known him for years, sold him a few nice pieces, and we both know not to ask too many questions about the other. But what I do know for certain, he's not someone you want to let down."

"And what," Acid said, "without the second egg there's no deal?"

"No kneecaps for me either, I expect. So hopefully it won't come to that. From him or Delgado. You see, once I sell those eggs I'm gone. Forever. I won't have to worry about dodgy businessmen ever again." He took a deep breath, his gaze drifting off into the middle distance. "I've got my eye on a place in Antigua. Right on the beach. I'll be happy to lie low there for the rest of my days. No one will ever find me."

She looked down, but he noticed she was hiding a smile. "You like to make trouble for yourself, don't you?"

He leaned in closer. "What's life without a bit of trouble?"

She stuck out her bottom lip in agreement. "I'm assuming you want me to help you steal this second egg?"

"You've got to have had experience with this sort of thing, a bad-ass like you?"

"A *bad-ass*?"

"Sure," he replied. "A bad-ass with a good ass."

"Wow." She shook her head, but he noticed a glimmer of mischief in her eyes. "That is lame as shit."

"I can do better."

"Can you?"

"Sure can…"

"Woah… Danny." She pulled away, wiping at her mouth. "What the fuck?"

"Sorry," he gasped, sitting upright, the room swimming back into focus. Their lips had touched for a mere moment, but it felt like heaven. "I thought you wanted me to."

She swung her legs off the bed and marched over to the window. "I was intrigued, that's all," she told him. "Trying to get my head around your ridiculous story."

"I really thought you wanted me to."

"Well, I didn't. You'd know if I did. Jesus."

"Fine. I was only—"

"Leave it, all right? It doesn't matter. But this is bullshit, Danny." She spun around and glared at him. "How do you expect to get to the egg? Delgado's not going to just open his house up for us, is he? And then there's the little matter of Magpie. She's not going to go away. She's still out for your blood. Mine too now probably."

Still a little dazed, he picked at a cream appliqué rose sewn onto the bedspread. "I don't know. I'm thinking on the trot, like always. Sorry, love. I—"

"Enough," she snapped, holding her hand up. "And if you

want me to kill you, keep on calling me *love*. I mean it. I'll—" A loud knock on the bedroom door shut her up.

The two of them stared at each other.

"Who is it?" Acid called out.

No answer.

She moved over to the dresser and grabbed her gun. "Who's there?"

"*Servicio a la habitación*," a woman's voice replied. She sounded old, speaking with a heavy accent. "Is room service. You order Champagne?"

With a hard scowl creasing her features, Acid glided to the door. "No, wrong room," she said through the door. "Not for here."

There was a pause. Then, "Oh, I sorry."

It felt like Danny's heart might burst through his chest. He went to speak but Acid held one finger up, still listening at the door.

The room went silent, before a scuffling noise could be heard, coming from the corridor, followed by the sound of a key card being shoved in a lock and the high-pitched beep as it opened.

"Hey, what's going—"

Before he had chance to finish the sentence Acid flew into the bedroom and tackled him over the far side of the bed.

"Get down," she yelled. "Now."

TWENTY

ACID AND DANNY TUMBLED OVER THE SIDE OF THE BED AS THE door slammed open and Magpie Stiletto burst into the room, firing as she went. Bullets pounded into the duvet, sending feathers spiralling into the air. Acid returned fire, forcing her old colleague along the wall and into an alcove obscured from the main bedroom by a partition wall. She fired a few more shots into the plasterboard, hoping she might get lucky, but the angle meant Magpie was out of range.

"I was ready for you, bitch," she called out. "How do you like that?" She kept her aim high, finger tight on the trigger.

"*Maldito perro*," came the hissed reply. "You may have been ready, but there's no way out for you. Not this time."

Acid ducked for cover as Magpie leaned around the side of the wall, firing a string of bullets that thudded into the headboard. She held her nerve, turning to Danny and giving him what she hoped was a reassuring look. Times like this, worry got you killed as fast as a bullet. She put a hand over the side of the bed and fired back a couple more shots in retaliation, driving the bitch back into the alcove.

"Think you can get over there and grab the bags if I cover

you?" she asked, as another bullet whizzed overhead. Danny looked at her with wide, worried eyes. His mouth flapped. "The bags, Danny." She gestured at her travel bag and his holdall, lying next to each other on the opposite side of the room. Normally she'd have left them there (in her line of work it was usual to abandon her possessions at the drop of a bullet casing), but their passports were inside, not to mention the Fabergé egg.

He swallowed. "What are you going to do?"

"I'll keep her back. Once you've got the bags, we're going through the window." She glanced behind her as more bullets studded the wall and into the mattress too, so close she could smell the scorched material.

Danny eyed the window cautiously. "Bit of a drop, isn't it?"

"There's a terrace a few feet below."

"A *few* feet?"

"Okay, it's a drop, but it's our only way out," she said. "We don't know how much ammo she's packing. I can't hold her off forever."

"Fine. I'll do it."

Acid gripped the Viking pistol to her chest. "Straight over there and then out the window. On three. One… two…" She knelt upright, taking aim at the lip of the partition wall. "Three. Go."

As Danny scrambled across the bed, she fired off a flurry of shots, splintering the wooden frame of the wall and sending plaster dust flying into the room. With one eye on her old nemesis and the other on Danny, she got to her feet, squeezing off a couple more rounds as she moved to the sash window which was already half open. She was able to keep her aim high whilst lacing her other hand under the frame and sliding it all the way up. Danny slid back across to this side of the bed with the bags held tightly to him.

"All right, go," she yelled, covering him with another hurl of bullets as Magpie appeared around the side. They exchanged fire, shooting wildly and without prejudice, but Acid was almost out. She glanced at the window to see Danny straddling the frame, making a big deal of it. *Bloody hell.* Another second and Magpie would have the upper hand, if she didn't already. With a yell, she hurled herself at Danny, grabbing him around the waist and propelling them both out into the warm evening sun as bullets shattered the glass.

They were only one floor up but they seemed to be falling forever. Enough time for Acid to position herself for impact, twisting her hips and grabbing the two bags from Danny to cushion their fall. A second later they crashed onto a small wooden table that was standing in the centre of the terrace. A sharp pain burnt up her side as the table legs gave way and they hit the concrete with a muffled thud. On her back, she pointed the Viking at the window, firing off the last of her rounds at the shadowy figure taking aim from the room.

The gun crack echoed around the open space and Magpie stumbled backwards as if she'd been hit. Not waiting to find out, Acid clambered to her feet, pulling Danny with her.

"Come on," she told him. "This way."

They hurried over to a set of patio doors left partially open and slipped into a vast suite much grander than hers. Passing through the room swiftly and without words, they got to the front door, which Acid pulled open cautiously. They'd escaped but by only one floor. If Magpie had survived that shot, she'd already be on her way down.

A glance up and down the corridor told her they were clear. For now, at least. She gave Danny a nod and they slipped out into the dimly lit corridor. The air here was still, almost dead, with not a soul around.

"There," Danny whispered, pointing at a gold sign that

read *Ascensor.* "This way."

Acid halted. They were six flights up, but the elevator wouldn't be her first choice, or even her second or third. Often where there was an elevator, there were stairs nearby. Stairs she imagined Magpie was currently traversing two at a time.

"Too dangerous," she replied. "We need to find the emergency exit."

Experience told her these were often positioned on the corner of a building away from the more centralised elevator. She led them down the long corridor, the room numbers rising as they passed, before they turned a corner and found a white door with a green sign in front of them. *Salida de Emergencia.*

"Bingo."

She ushered Danny past her, walking backwards in his wake and aiming the 9mm back the way they'd come. Over her shoulder she heard a scuffle, Danny trying to get the door open. She glanced around to see it was a push-bar lock.

So push the damn bar, dummy.

The anxiety was getting to him. He might think himself a plucky Irish rogue, able to talk himself out of any situation, but he was still a civilian, not cut out for these situations. Keeping the gun pointed down the corridor she sidled nearer, ready to help him. Her hand was on the bar when she heard voices, and snapping her attention over the barrel of the gun she saw an elderly couple vacating their room a few doors away. The old man was doddery but tall, with a white comb-over that was struggling to make much impact on his visible cranium. In contrast his wife was small and round with a healthy glow to her cheeks and a deep throaty laugh that burst out of her. Acid concealed the pistol behind her just in time as the couple looked their way and smiled breezily and conspiringly, the way people do when they're on holiday and free from the stresses and worries of everyday life.

Or so they thought.

Because behind them, at the far end of the corridor, Magpie had appeared.

Shit.

The energy in the corridor was suddenly electric as the two former colleagues faced each other. Acid gripped the handle of the Viking tight, holding it concealed behind her upper thigh at arm's length. On seeing the old couple, Magpie immediately slipped her own pistol into the pocket of her jacket, which was good to see. It meant she was still adhering to some semblance of the code. Staying in the shadows. Keeping civilians out of it.

"She won't do anything in front of witnesses," she whispered to Danny. "Keep your head."

Time slowed to a halt as Magpie strode towards them, stopping in front of the couple and wrinkling her nose in disgust as the old woman placed a huge canvas beach bag in her path and bent over.

Acid shoved the Viking in the back of her shorts and had her hand on the push-lock, ready to wave her old colleague a sassy goodbye, when the old man stepped backwards and stumbled into Magpie. The next thing she heard was the recognisable *phut phut* sound, of bullets travelling along the internal baffles of a suppressor, and blood splattered up the wall and ceiling.

Acid felt Danny freeze beside her as the old couple slumped to the floor. With the bats screeching decibels of rage and panic, she flung herself at the door bar and fell through into the stairwell. As she righted herself, she glanced back to see Magpie stepping over the fallen couple and raising her gun.

"This way," she yelled, grabbing Danny's arm and yanking him down the stone steps as a bullet zipped past his ear. "We need to get out of here. Fast."

TWENTY-ONE

DANNY DIDN'T NEED TELLING TWICE. HE RAN DOWN THE emergency stairwell faster than he'd ever gone in his entire life, taking the steps two, three at a time and using the paint-chipped railing to haul himself around the corner towards the next level.

He heard the mad nun jump down the first two levels before stopping to fire a few shots their way, bullets pinging violently off the metal railing mere inches from his hand. Too close. She was getting far too close.

"Keep going," Acid snarled, returning fire. "Two more levels and we're at the lobby. She won't try anything there."

"You sure of that?" he spluttered. "Cos I'm not sure ya poor old couple up there would agree with that logic. No witnesses though, you were right about that."

He copied Acid in leaping down the next flight of stairs, keeping a tight hold of the bags as they took the last landing. One flight to go. The door to the lobby was in sight. Another bullet pinged off the concrete wall behind him as he jumped the final four steps and Acid pulled him, stumbling, through the door.

Now, the young Danny Flynn had always been partial to a certain type of movie genre – action-comedy, you might call – the sort of movie that was cheesy and serious in equal measures, with snappy dialogue and rising tension towards the finale. Usually made in the eighties (think *Ghostbusters, Beverly Hills Cop*), there was always a scene in these sorts of movies where the hapless hero, on the run or in a panic, would fall chaotically and noisily into a quiet room (a posh restaurant, for instance, or a church service), and the atmosphere would be so at odds with their current predicament you couldn't help but laugh… So when he fell through the door at the bottom of the emergency stairwell and looked up at a serene palatial lobby and a sea of confused faces all staring his way, he couldn't help but think he was living out one of those movie scenes. Although in real life, as it turns out, it wasn't half as funny.

"Shite, sorry," he mouthed, to the expectant guests and hotel staff as he scrambled to his feet. "I tripped."

"Get up," a now-familiar voice snarled in his ear. "She's almost here."

Message received and understood, he hurried after Acid as she headed for the exit, gripping tightly to the bags slung across each shoulder. He did, however, risk a furtive glance behind him to see their pursuer framed in the stairwell doorway, her gun hand stuffed back into the pocket of her jacket and an expression of utter rage twisting her Mediterranean features.

Acid was right, there were too many people here for her to try anything. Despite his pounding heart, he couldn't help but throw the crazy nun a sly grin, doffing an imaginary cap for good measure as he joined Acid at an enormous set of revolving doors.

"Don't get cocky," she snapped.

Her face was hard, her eyes intense, but as they entered the first available section and leaned against the glass-panelled door, he noticed the shadow of a smile. She'd enjoyed his little display even if she wouldn't admit it. But the revolving door was slow-moving – thick brushes at the base of the heavy brass doorframe dragged against the carpet below. Turning, he saw Magpie – Sister Death, the killer of that sweet old couple both about his ma's age – stalking them through the foyer. She wasn't letting up.

"Acid," he huffed, swallowing his words, but she'd already seen her. Finally the door transported them through to the other side of the building and they stepped out into the early evening, blinking in the final rays of the day's sun as it made its descent behind the horizon. Before he could catch his breath, Acid was striding over to a large doorman who was standing by another set of revolving doors, arms rigid by his sides as though some sort of military guard. Danny followed her, his heart jumping into his mouth to see her gun sticking out the back of her shorts, clearly visible to anyone who might look her way. Quickening his pace, he grabbed at the back of her shirt and pulled the material over the gun as she reached the doorman.

"*Buenas noches, señor,*" she began, giving Danny a hard stare as he appeared next to her, her eyes saying, *Keep quiet. Don't fuck this up.*

The doorman peered down at her, substantial eyebrows morphing as one to take in this woman who was slight in stature, but more ferocious and intense (and yes, damn right sexier) than any woman Danny had ever met.

"I wonder if you can help?" she went on, dispensing quickly with the Spanish but replacing it with a breezy smile and – Danny couldn't help but notice – an accentuation of her chest. "I am a guest here at the hotel. I'm sure you recognise me."

The doorman's frown grew deeper, but his training kicked in before he answered. "Oh? Yes. Of course. Miss…? Erm…"

Acid giggled. "Oh you are silly. You know who I am. But I don't know if you're aware, I'm playing a concert here in your wonderful city as part of the festival, but I have a problem." Now her face dropped, an air of fear washing over the light-hearted countenance of whoever she was supposed to be. "I think I have a stalker following me. At first I thought she was a fan – and you know me, happy to sign an autograph or whatever." She smiled coquettishly. "But this weirdo got real nasty. Tried to attack me. And oh golly, here she comes. Please can you do something? My drummer here wants us to move hotels, but I told him this is the best in the city. With the best service. The best security."

Another smile coupled with her hand on his forearm and Danny had to bite his lip lest his own face give them away, captivated as he was by the whole act. Jesus, Mary and Joseph, this woman was affecting him in ways he didn't like. Dangerous. Very dangerous.

"Where is this person?" the doorman asked, following suit as Danny puffed his own chest out.

"Right there," Acid squealed, pointing to where Magpie was nearly through the revolving doors. "Please stop her so we can get away. I'm so very scared. Please help me."

Feck. Was that an eyelash flutter?

The lassie was pulling out all the stops, but Danny liked her style, and clearly this dirty old doorman did as well. With his head raised, he strode over to the doors and was in front of Magpie in a second, holding his arms out wide and blocking her path.

It was all they needed.

"Run," Acid told him, setting off at pace.

Danny couldn't help but give it a moment to see the

outcome, the mad nun shouting animatedly at the doorman as he tried to restrain her, not doing herself any favours. He smiled to himself and then took off, following Acid around the side of the hotel.

"Where are we going?" he wheezed as he caught up with her.

She kept moving, didn't look at him. "Not sure. As far away from the hotel as possible. Put some distance between us. Once we're clear, you're going to the airport. It's not safe."

The words hit Danny in his guts, sending a blistering sensation up into his neck. "What? No. We have to get the other egg. You said—"

"She'll kill you if you stay."

"Yeah, and so will Petre Kaminski if I don't bring him both eggs."

They got to the end of the street and took a right, moving down an alleyway that ran between two tall buildings, more hotels by the looks of it.

"Come off it, your uncle wouldn't let that happen."

"My uncle is an old man," he said, grimacing through the exertion. "Not as well-known or as well-feared as you think he is. Not in the circles I move in, at least. Plus, antiques are my whole world, if lose my credibility I lose everything – and I need that money. As much as I can get."

"Why? What's it for?"

"I just need it, all right? I'm not going anywhere."

Acid slowed her pace so he could catch up again. "But your uncle *could* help."

"He is helping, isn't he? That's why you're here." He tried a grin but it fell short. "Listen, I know a little place a few blocks from here. It's seedy and dark but no one knows about it. No tourists at all. Let me buy you a drink while we talk. Please, Acid. I need that money. Let me try and convince you. One drink, somewhere safe where we can lie low. Get our heads back in the game."

His feisty accomplice didn't answer.

So that was a no, then?

He quickened his pace to keep up as she leaned into the next corner and they found themselves on a long open street busy with people – hordes of locals and holidaymakers alike all heading for the festivities in the old town.

"Hey, you," he gasped, winding around families as he tried to keep up. "Wait. Can we just—"

"Fine." She stopped and turned so fast he almost crashed into her. Sweat dripped down her face and she was fighting to breathe. "One drink. But I'm not promising anything, you hear me?"

Despite his own discomfort – the lactic acid cutting into his side – he hit her with his trademark smirk, complementing it with a cheeky wink for good measure. "Grand," he said. "I reckon ya gonna love this bar, it's so you."

"One drink, Danny."

"Sure," he said. "One drink."

TWENTY-TWO

"*BÁJATE DE MÍ*," MAGPIE SNARLED AT THE HULKING DOORMAN. "*No me toques* – get your hands off me."

"*Perdon*," he growled, before slipping into English, an attempt at formality perhaps, or distance. "I cannot let you leave. There has been a complaint against you."

Magpie stepped back to take in the pathetic oaf. "By her? The woman you were talking with?"

He nodded solemnly. "I know you are a fan—"

"A fan? A fan?" She held her arms out. "You think she is some sort of famous person? *Imbécil*. So she smile at you and you believe all she says? That woman is no star. She stole from me. She is a thief. *Una ladrona*."

The man's face fell as he scrolled back through the last few minutes, perhaps realising his mistake. "*Estas seguro?*" he stammered. "You are telling the truth?"

"Yes. I am a guest here. She was in my room. Which way did she go? Quickly."

The doorman frowned, still coming to terms with how easily he'd been duped.

Well, make that twice. Estúpido.

"Which way?" she repeated, before he dumbly pointed down the side of the hotel.

Giving the fool one last sneer, she turned and gave chase, running alongside the Ramon Labaien Plaza, heading away from the river. At the crossroads of Camino and Okenda Kalea she paused, scanning each street in turn, both of them full of people even at this time of day.

The festival.

Mierda.

Her entire body seethed with an uncomfortable rage, but it was useless. She'd lost them. The crushing and debilitating fury continued to flow through her system as she stood on the corner glaring at passers-by, those casting concerned or curious looks her way, and stuffed her hand in her pocket, her fingers finding the handle of the 92, the gun an extension of her own body. A second went by, and another. She didn't move, fighting against an onslaught of powerful urges and almost blacking out with the pain of failure.

There'd be another time.

This wasn't over.

But working freelance, with no organisation backing her up (and without the technical wizardry of Raaz Terabyte to help locate the prey), it wouldn't be so easy. She'd struck it lucky today at the hotel, that brazen woman's desire for all things indulgent and expensive had been her undoing. But Acid Vanilla wasn't an idiot. She wouldn't make the same mistake twice.

Perhaps this is the way it should be, she told herself, as she set off walking. Hunting the old-fashioned way was purer, unencumbered by the entrapments of modern life. She tilted her head to the heavens. The sun was all but gone and the sky a palette of dusky yellows and lurid pinks.

"Ayudame Dios, dame fuerza," she whispered, so quiet her

plea to God to give her strength was lost to the buzz of traffic and revellers.

Down Okenda Kalea and she found herself back in the old town. It hadn't been a conscious decision to head this way, yet perhaps something had drawn her here. The Basilica de Santa María del Coro was a couple of streets away, and with no further thought she headed over there, walking up the stone steps and entering the ancient church's narthex entrance a few minutes later.

Mass had finished thirty minutes earlier and the cool, echoing nave was empty except for a tiny woman huddled under a black shawl on the front pew, lost in silent prayer. Straight away, Magpie's eyes fell on the confession booth on the left of the wide transept. The thick wooden doors were closed but the priest was in.

Was this why she was here?

With the church so silent, she could hear every gentle slap of her soft-soled espadrilles as she made her way down the aisle, pausing to take in the painting of Christ hanging above the altar. The artist had depicted him as a torn and broken figure, his face drawn and weary as he dragged the heavy wooden cross through the streets. She took a deep breath, letting the powerful image permeate her soul while Christ looked down at her through heavy-lidded eyes, informing her of what she must do. She raised her face to his, thanked him for his message. Then she turned and walked back out the way she came.

It took her fifty minutes to get back to the convent, and a further five to arrive at her own quarters in the annex building. Once there, she heaved the heavy door shut and stood with her back against it, chest rising and falling as she steadied herself. Her mind had been – mercifully – free from thought as she'd walked through the busy streets and followed the winding path up the hillside. Determination now her only motivation. To do what she must do.

She moved into the centre of the room and stood in front of the modest dresser unit that, except for the flimsy old bed, was the only piece of furniture in the room. A small round mirror hung from the wall above and from where she was standing she could see the reflection of her head and torso. She cricked her neck to one side, then the other, letting her lank hair fall across her face. With her head lowered, she unbuttoned the linen shirt she was wearing, peeling it from her sinewy frame where it was stuck with sweat from her earlier effort. The bra went next, that evil contraption of cloth and wire that she despised wearing even after all these years. She unhooked the clasps and let it fall to the floor, the cool air in the room biting at her nipples as she stared at herself in the mirror. Her face was hard, her eyes free from emotion as they drifted down to take in her breasts. They were modest in size and unremarkable in many ways, yet had been nothing but a burden from the moment they'd arrived – along with the tufts of hair and widening of her hips – when she was just twelve years old. A young girl, a child, yet without her agreement she suddenly had these symbols of adult depravity bursting out from her body.

Drifting lower her eyes settled on the crisscross of scars on her ribs and stomach. Some of them angry, purple stripes, others almost not there, like invisible ghosts of transgressions past. She turned around, peering over her shoulder to view her naked back where longer scars were visible, the shadows cast by the dim bulb above highlighting the raised welts and ragged hollows.

Reaching across the bed, with its threadbare blanket and anaemic single mattress, she hooked a long string of rosary beads from off the headboard and held them in both hands, moving the cold marble beads between her fingers, feeling the energy of their shared history. What redemption these beads had provided over the years. Hundreds of Hail Marys whispered into the darkness in an attempt to ease her suffering and assuage her shame.

But not today.

Not anymore.

Because prayer only got a person so far. And guilt was reserved for those with a soul. Turning back to the mirror she gripped the beads in her fist, making sure the heavy marble crucifix was hanging down in front. Then, with her jaw tight and her eyes blazing defiance into their own reflection, she began to whip the rosary beads violently over her shoulders and around her flank. Grimacing through the pain, defying herself to cry out, she kept going, each strike harder than the last and the edge of the crucifix tearing at her naked flesh.

Now at last she felt something.

And this was needed. Required of her.

"*Pecador repugnante*," she snarled at the woman in the mirror. "Disgusting, sinful creature. You deserve nothing. *No mereces nada.*"

Except she deserved this pain all right. She'd earned it. Like always. She'd let herself down.

It would not happen again.

TWENTY-THREE

A THOUSAND CHATTERING BATS PLAGUED ACID'S THOUGHTS AS she leaned against the raw brick of the wall, keeping one eye on the door while waiting for Danny to return with the drinks. The bar was tiny, with a small counter at one end of the windowless room and only three tables in the place. It was certainly dark. Seedy too. Danny hadn't been lying about that. But it was the rest of his story she had issues with. Why not simply sell the egg he did have and disappear? By the sound of it, that alone would bring him more money than he'd ever need. He could be in Antigua by next weekend, safely away from the Luis Delgados and Petre Kaminskis of the world. Why risk everything for the second egg?

"Ah, bollocks."

She looked at her hands, realising she'd been picking at the skin around her thumbnail. It was bleeding. She shoved it in her mouth, the sour taste of iron unpleasant on her tongue. There was something Danny wasn't telling her, but if she was honest with herself, her desire to find out what was only a smokescreen. The real question was why did she feel so crappy all of a sudden? Ever since she'd arrived in Spain (ever since she'd sobered up, if she was sticking with honesty) she'd been aware of a niggling presence on the cusp of her awareness. The bats had arrived in force, but that aspect of her mania she could handle, having long ago learned to hone the intense nervous energy into something powerful. The inspiration to try things others would never attempt, or to think fast, need little sleep – these were valuable attributes for the types of situation in which she often found herself. But this new presence was different. Darker. More sinister.

"Here we are, get that down ya."

The chirpy Irishman's booming voice cut into her train of thought. She sat upright as a bottle of beer appeared on the table in front of her.

"San Miguel? Seriously? I can get this in Dagenham."

Danny shrugged, already chugging back a mouthful of his own beer. "It's what he gave me."

"I thought you said this place wasn't for tourists."

He placed his bottle down and leered across the table. "It's not. So maybe the old St Michael is good Spanish lager after all."

"Maybe."

He grinned, baring his pearly whites. "Come on now. We just escaped certain death. You saved my life. You were awesome."

She picked up the beer and took a swig. Not as chilled as she'd have liked. "She's still out there, Danny. Still alive. That's no cause for celebration." She shifted on the hard stool to put herself on an angle away from that stupid look on his face, somewhere between lust and reverence.

"So it is true. Ya used to be… You were…"

This again.

She chewed on her bottom lip. Didn't look at him. "I was what?"

"Ya know. Same as the mad nun, same as my uncle."

"Oh, I thought he was always just *Uncle Jimmy* to you?"

"Yeah, but I heard the rumours. We all did. So it is true. Geez. I never kissed a hit woman before."

She turned to face him. "And you haven't now."

"But before… in your room. Sorry, but I'm taking that."

"Well, you shouldn't. Nothing happened." She swigged back a mouthful of lager. "It was a mistake."

"You're amazing, ya know that."

She glared at him. "Does this sort of shit usually work for you?"

The comment sent him fumbling with the label on his bottle, picking at the edges. But he couldn't hide his smile. It was a good smile. "Aye, usually it does. But then I've never met anyone like you before."

"Oh for heaven's sake." Even for her the eye-roll was dramatic. She sipped at her beer, her voice dropping to a sombre tone. "What were you talking about with the barman?"

"Carlos? He's a good lad, good craic." His face fell serious. "I didn't tell him anything of course. About you. Or the Sister Death, whatever she's called."

"Good to know." She leaned her head back against the wall. "I've got to say, Daniel, you do seem to be taking this whole situation in your stride. Getting shot at. A price put on your head."

A cheeky smirk lit up his face. "Maybe I'm too stupid to realise the enormity of my predicament."

She leaned over, eyes narrowed as she spoke. "I don't think so."

"Look, I've been dealing antiques for a long time, back in Dublin and in London. You meet a lot of dodgy people in that environment. I've been in plenty of scrapes over the years so that I've learnt to live on my wits. I've had guns pulled on me many times before. Although, granted, this is the first time I've had a price put on my head. That I know of, at least." He winked. "There's probably a few girls out there who thought about it."

"I bet."

Pushing his beer to one side, he folded his forearms on the table and leaned closer. If that wasn't disconcerting enough, the wry smile and spark in his eyes most definitely was.

"So come on then, tell me what it's like being a hit woman."

"Why, you thinking of becoming one?"

"How many people have ya killed?"

She shook her head, tutting. "Oh no. You never ask a person that. Anyway, I'm not… one of those. Not anymore."

"What happened?"

She stared at him as she took another swig from the bottle. He wasn't going to let it go. "Let's say I had the decision made for me."

"You were pushed?"

"Sort of." She tipped her head back, swallowed the last of the beer. "Though I had been feeling restless. Which I suppose was what led me to make a few mistakes, errors of judgement, that really pissed off my boss."

"I see. What did he do?"

She rolled the empty beer bottle in her palm. "He made his point," she said softly.

"Oh?"

"He took out an innocent. Someone close to me who had nothing to do with that world. The only person I had left."

"Shite, I'm sorry," he muttered, the cocksure smile replaced with one of sympathy. "Must be hard."

She shrugged it away. "It is what it is. I'm making my peace with it. Day by day."

"You don't want revenge?" he asked. And when she didn't answer, he added, "Does the crazy nun have something to do with all this, by any chance?"

Acid peered at him watching her all wide-eyed and eager. Maybe not as dumb as he looked. He was joining dots quicker than she expected. Or liked.

He finished his beer and brought the bottle back to the table. "So this is personal for you. And there was me thinking you were saving my arse cos ya liked me."

"Sorry to burst your bubble, Romeo." She leaned back. "But all right. Yes. It's personal. Maybe too personal, I don't know."

"How's that?"

"My friend Spook, she thinks I have unhealthy obsessions. A tendency to fixate." She sniffed, annoyed at herself. "Sorry, you don't need to know any of this."

Here she was, oversharing once again. A sure sign she was slipping into the red. The fact she'd been wondering what Danny looked like naked these last few minutes was another.

"You have a friend called Spook?"

She smiled. "Yes. And that is her real name."

"Acid and Spook? Jesus Christ. And what is it you call my uncle again, The Dullahan? Shite on a bike, am I in some bad superhero movie?"

"We're trying to save your arse, sunshine. Have some respect."

He scowled at her. "Oh I do. I *respect* you very much, Acid. I was only thinking just now how much *respect* I'd like to give ya."

"You never turn it off, do you?" she said, letting a sly smile escape across her lips.

Danny lifted his shoulders. "Man's got to try. Which reminds me." He reached around and removed something from his jeans pocket. "Here." He dangled a key in front of her.

"What's that?"

"A key."

"Yes, I can see it's a key, Danny. What does it open?"

He gestured at the bar. "Carlos has a little flat around the corner. Rents it out, but it's empty presently. He said we could stay there a few nights. Ya know, whilst we work out how to steal the other egg."

"Ah no. Not happening." She placed her hands palms down on the table. Resolute. "Today was too close. I need to get you to the airport and back home."

"The hell with that. I need that egg. Kaminski's going to kill me if I don't get it." He stared at her, his eyes full of concern and pleading. "C'mon, Acid. Help me. I'll make it worth your while, I promise ya. It's a lot of money."

Shit.

Her thoughts flashed to Spook and the debt she owed for her care. Then to that grimy terraced house she'd put up with for the last year. Surely she owed it to herself to find somewhere more comfortable, more conducive for her mental health.

The stool scraped across the stone floor as she got to her feet and snatched the key from his hand. "Come on then, Romeo," she said. "We've got work to do."

TWENTY-FOUR

THE SLIVER OF A NEW MOON HUNG ABOVE THE ROOFTOPS AS ACID followed Danny across the empty street towards the apartment building on the corner of the next block. Her mind was already scrambled with chaotic thoughts and severe doubts, that she'd just agreed to this ridiculous mission, and for a bloody golden egg of all things. But then again, what did she have to lose, and more importantly what did she have to go back home for? She was better off here, amongst the action. Risking your life on an hourly basis negates any desire for soul searching or self-reflection. So yes, it was better that way. Experience told her, swim too long in the ocean of your own psyche and you were likely to drown.

"It's the second floor," Danny told her as they entered through the doorless entrance and straight up an open-plan stairwell that wound around the side of the building. "I thought that was good. Safer, somehow."

"How do you figure that?"

"We'll see anyone coming, won't we? And they'll only have one route up to us."

"Yes and we only have one route down."

He stopped on the landing and placed his hand on her shoulder. "Not so, darling. I don't know if you remember jumping out of that window an hour or so ago, but there's always that same option."

She eyed him with mock contempt. "Remember when I told you not to call me *love*? Well, same goes for *darling*."

"Oh Christ, you're not one of those, are ya?"

She brushed past him and continued up the stairwell. "I'm not one of what?"

"You know," he said, scurrying after her. "A feminist."

Bloody hell.

What was she doing partnering up with this cretin? He was bad news. She knew it. Even if he did have the bluest eyes she'd ever seen. And that smirk…

Damnit.

"Here we are," he chimed, as they reached the top floor and a row of blue doors standing either side of a short landing. "Number twenty-six, there on the end."

"Been here before?" she asked.

"Once." He looked sheepish.

"I see. With a girl, was it? A little love nest?" She slipped the key from out of her pocket and unlocked the door.

"Something like that."

With one hand on the 9mm still stuffed in her waistband, she slipped through the door and swiftly scoped out the apartment. A bedroom (decent-sized, complete with bathroom) and a small utility closet led off from the hallway. Through to the main space and she found an open-plan lounge and kitchen area. A stale smell lingered in the air but it was clean enough, and empty of threats.

"We good?" Danny asked, closing the front door behind him.

She ran a finger across the kitchen worksurface. "Let's not get ahead of ourselves, shall we? It's adequate."

"I'll take that." He shuffled into the lounge where he collapsed onto the two-seater leather couch with a loud sigh. "God help me. I'm totally knackered."

Acid remained in the kitchen, opening and inspecting each unit. "Aww. Well, you rest up, sweetie. It's been a tough few days. Poor little Danny."

"Less of the little," he called back. "And how come you get to call me sweetie?"

She pouted through the question as she peered into the fridge, the pungent reek of half an onion doing nothing to diminish her relief on seeing three bottles of lager in the vegetable tray. Self-medication. It was still the best game in town.

"That's different," she replied. "*Sweetie* is a term of endearment. Calling a woman *love* is patronising."

"So ya are a feminist. I knew it."

She took two lagers from the fridge and shut the door. A quick inspection of the drawers told her there was no bottle opener, so she smashed the tops off on the corner and went through into the lounge.

"Is it comfy?" she asked, gesturing to the couch as she handed him one of the bottles.

"Not one bit," he said, the leather squeaking beneath him as he shifted to make room for her. She chose, instead, to sit in the small armchair (suspiciously Ikea-esque) standing against the wall.

"Well that's too bad," she told him.

"How's that?"

She swigged down some of the beer. It was ice cold. "Well, if we are staying here a night or two, that's where you're sleeping."

136

To further dissuade the lusty Irishman, she removed the nine from her shorts and placed it pointedly on the arm of the chair, facing him. But not before she'd released the magazine. Three rounds left in this one and she had two more mags in her bag. Not a lot of firepower, but then guns were never her first weapon of choice. Most of the operatives at Annihilation Pest Control specialised in the silent kill, the accidental death. From the late eighties until a few months ago, if you'd wanted rid of someone and the police not even consider it a homicide, then Caesar's crew were your best bet. But that was before Acid went rogue and began wiping them out one by one. She grabbed up her bag, sensing her chest tightening at the thought of her old mentor and wondering where he was right now. Whether he was still planning her demise, or if his lack of resources would keep him in the shadows for good.

"I'm going for a shower," she said, glaring defiantly at Danny, waiting for some pithy response.

His eyes sparkled. "Can I join ya?"

And there it was.

"Enough tomfoolery," she snapped. "We need to focus. If we're doing this, you need to start taking it seriously. Work out how we get this bloody egg of yours without us both getting killed in the process. Yes?"

"Okay, yes. Agreed."

Without another word, she went through into the bedroom and threw her bag onto the bed.

Jesus.

Did she just use the word tomfoolery? What the hell was happening to her? Chewing on the inside of her cheek she pulled out a change of clothes and got undressed, screwing the dirty items up into tight balls and stuffing them in the bag. The fact she'd left the bedroom door ajar troubled her, but she made no move to close it.

The bats were having fun at least. She wasn't sure she was.

In the bathroom she twisted on the shower dial and left it to warm up for a second or two whilst she turned her attention to the mirror above the sink. The woman glaring back at her looked worn out, yet her eyes were still fixed and glassy. The same look she always had when the bats were running wild in her psychology. She grinned at herself, checking her teeth, pulling at the skin on her cheeks and neck. Not bad for thirty-four, she told herself, and for someone who'd consumed little sustenance but a whole lot of toxins for the last few months.

But that stopped, today. The drink and casual sex had been a decent enough way to numb the pain and confusion circling the drain in her consciousness, but it was a delay tactic rather than a fix. To kill a demon you had to face a demon. It was the only way. She gave her reflection a nod before stepping inside the shower unit and closing the glass door behind her. The pressure of the water was lame but it was pleasingly hot. She placed her head underneath the jets and closed her eyes, trying to ignore the crushing cacophony of futile thoughts fluttering across her mind.

It was true, the bats were having real fun now, but even they couldn't drown out the dark presence which was getting closer by the hour. She turned around to search for shampoo, which was difficult when the glass shower unit was as cramped as a coffin. A larger person – Danny, for instance – would have trouble fitting, she thought, then kicked herself again for thinking about him in that way. Naked. Droplets of water dripping down his chest.

"Stop it, now," she hissed. "Not the time."

She turned the shower off and stood for a moment in the immediately silent and cold unit. Steam had filled the room but she could see there was no towels on the rail. Leaving a trail of water she padded barefoot into the bedroom, still not bothering to close the door, or even attempting to cover herself as she checked the dresser and small wardrobe for a towel.

"You okay in there?" Danny called through from the lounge.

"Yes. Thank you. You come up with a plan yet?"

She heard movement and shifted over to the door, hiding behind it as Danny approached. "I got the bones of one," he said. "Only thing is, there's a spanner in the works that we could do with sorting out first."

"Magpie?"

"Aye, the mad nun. With her still after me – us – it's all going to be so much harder. If we could just…"

"I know." She lowered her head. "You're right."

"So you reckon you can, ya know, take her out?"

She pressed her face against the door. The cool wood felt good against her skin.

"Acid?"

"I'm here," she said quietly. "I've been thinking the same thing. It's just…"

"What?"

"Nothing. Forget it." She straightened her back. Took a deep breath. "Yes, I can do that. I will do. I'll give my contact another call, see if I can get a location out of him, anything. But first I need rest."

"You sound different. Is everything all right?"

She glanced out of the window, now a square of inky blackness. "I'm fine," she told him. "Give me a few hours, I'll be sorted. I suggest you do the same. We've got a busy day or two ahead."

"Aye, I guess, but—"

"Good man."

She closed the door on him and, still wet, collapsed onto the soft bed. Sleep was a long way off, she knew that already. But she was glad to be alone at least, somewhere quiet and still. For once that was what she needed. And for now, all she could hope for.

TWENTY-FIVE

Sleep may have been a way off but had happened eventually it seemed. Not that she remembered drifting off. Or even much about last night. But she'd clearly slept all the way through, the day's scorching sun was already shining through the shadeless window.

Sliding off the bed, Acid padded to the dresser where she'd left her phone. After switching it on and waiting for the vibrating and flashing to cease, she checked her messages – one from The Dullahan, and from Spook too, both saying the same thing: the kid was on the mend.

It was a relief to hear, and the thought crossed her mind to phone but she quickly dismissed the idea. Speaking with Spook would either piss her off or have her questioning her decisions, and she couldn't afford for that to happen. Not now. She'd told Danny she'd help him steal the egg, and she never backed out of a mission once she'd thrown her hat in the ring. Plus, this was how she got Magpie Stiletto. Plus, now that she was this close to Magpie Stiletto, it would be a waste to leave without killing the sour-faced bitch. To avenge her mother's murder.

She typed out a brief text message to Sonny Botha's secure

line, asking him to ring her when he got a chance. Then she grabbed up the clothes she'd laid out the previous night (black leggings, plus her favourite *Cramps* t-shirt and Fox and Rose underwear). The fact her underwear matched gave her a moment's pause (she didn't want Danny thinking she'd worn them especially), but they were all she had left. She stepped into the lace pants and pulled them on, already annoyed with herself for even considering that he might see them. Because he wasn't going to. That would be stupid. Very stupid.

Once dressed, she brushed her teeth and attended to her hair in the mirror. It was knotted and stuck up in all directions from falling asleep with it wet. But it kind of worked, as well.

So screw it.

The sound of electronic music filled the main space as she opened the door. She placed her phone on the kitchen counter and went through into the lounge.

"Bloody hell, can we turn this crap off?" she croaked, through a dry throat.

Danny glanced up from his position on the couch, lying with his legs dangling over the arm. "What you talking about, this is a total banger," he said, nodding at the TV screen, some Spanish music channel. "You don't like dance music?"

He'd also taken his shirt off sometime in the night and Acid's gaze was drawn to his tanned torso, defined but not too muscular. "No, I do not," she said, averting her eyes. "It's dreadful. For idiots."

He scoffed. "What music do you like? Heavy Metal? Gothic shit?"

She slumped down in the chair facing him, taking in the faded shamrock and the words *Fighting Irish* tattooed on his upper chest. "I like real music, good music. Like these guys." She pulled at her shirt. "The Cramps."

Danny eyed her chest, emblazoned with the *Date With Elvis*

cover art. "Never heard of them." He nodded at the image. "But yer woman there looks terrifying."

Acid smiled. "That's Poison Ivy, the guitarist. She's amazing."

Danny laughed as he sat up. "Poison Ivy? I see. What else?"

"All sorts. Bowie, Black Sabbath. Johnny Thunders. Richard Hell and the Voidoids."

"Ha. Makes sense now."

"What do you mean?"

"Poison Ivy, Johnny Thunders, Richard fecking Hell. Sounds like *Acid Vanilla* should be in a band with those guys."

"It's not like that."

"Oh?" He sat forward. "What is it like?"

She considered him for a moment, breathing heavily down her nose. He seemed different this morning. More combative, sure, but more serious too. "Never mind." She sighed. "So do you have a plan worked out?"

He pulled his lips back over his teeth and waved his hand in a *maybe, not sure,* sort of way. "Still the bones of one."

Acid got to her feet, the need to move consuming her all at once, and walked to the large window opposite the kitchen. "Let's hear it then."

"Right, well, we need to get into the house somehow. Clearly I can't do that, so it'll have to be you."

She watched out the window as an old man shuffled along the street directly below her. It looked like every step pained him. He was also far too overdressed considering the heat. "Yes. I'd assumed the same. How do you see me getting in?"

"How d'ya feel about befriending Delgado?" She turned around to look at him and he held his palms up. "I'm not asking ya to do anything ya don't want to. I don't mean ya have to get fresh with him, but he has got an eye for the ladies.

I reckon with a little guidance from yours truly we can present ya as a believable art dealer."

"And you expect him to – what – simply invite me to his home, to see his paintings?"

"Aye. Something like that. Then it's a simple matter of getting to his office. Easy."

Acid scoffed. "*Easy?* I see. And what are you going to be doing while I'm alone in this dangerous man's house, surrounded by all his goons?"

"I'll be outside, ready to burst in if needed. We can hire a car as well, to make a quick getaway. But it shouldn't come to that. This isn't the hard part, as far as I'm concerned."

"What is?"

He got up and joined her by the window. He stank faintly of sweat and beer, but it wasn't unpleasant. "Killing that mad fecking nun. I'm afraid in that respect my plan comes up short."

Leaving him at the window, Acid moved to the sink, taking a glass from the draining board and filling it with water from the tap.

"You shouldn't drink that, ya know," he called over her shoulder.

With the glass half-way to her mouth she paused. "Bollocks," she muttered, tipping the water back in the basin and turning around. "Don't worry about Magpie. She's my problem. I just need to find her."

She was about to tell him she was waiting for a call back when, right on cue, her phone vibrated on the kitchen counter. Holding it up to show Danny, she side-stepped away, answering the call on her way to the bedroom.

"Sonny?" she asked. "You got my text, then?"

"I did. So what can I do for you?"

"It's Magpie. I need to know where she is." The line went

silent. She dropped down to the edge of the mattress and lowered her voice. "Please, Sonny. It's a lot to ask, I know. But I really need to find her."

Another pause, followed by a sigh. "All right," he grunted. "But you didn't hear this from me. You understand?"

"Absolutely. You know where she is?"

"Sort of." The line crackled as the wily gun-runner's stubble brushed against the speaker. "You sparked my curiosity before, so I'd already been putting the feelers out. I heard she's staying in an old convent up on the headland. Still in use, mind, so I don't know how true that is."

"No, that fits."

"I mean it, Acid, you did not hear this from me. The client I heard it from isn't the nicest or most reliable person you've ever met, so it could be bullshit. It could also be a trap."

"Right now it's all I've got." She glanced to the window. The sun was still low in the sky. "I need you to get something for me. Obviously I'll pay."

She gave him the details and agreed a price, more than she'd wanted to pay but he had her over a barrel now. They arranged to meet at noon, same spot as before, and she hung up.

"What was that all about?" Danny asked, as she returned to the kitchen.

"Do you have cash on you?"

"Erm, yeah, about half a monkey. Two hundred and fifty."

She held out her hand. "I need two hundred. Actually, give me the lot."

Watching her the entire time, he got to his feet and walked over to his holdall. "What's going on?" he asked, unzipping the inner compartment and taking out a roll of euros. "Who was that on the phone?"

"A contact, that's all you need to know." She took the

145

money, before grabbing up her gun and phone and taking them through to the bedroom. Once there, she packed them with a spare magazine into the canvas shoulder bag she'd had the good foresight to buy on her shopping venture yesterday. Because the one problem with leggings – no pockets. "I'm going out for a while," she called through, hooking the bag strap over her head and fixing it across her body. "I'm going to take the key. Lock you in."

"Lock me in? Kinky."

She went into the lounge and over to Danny, pointing her finger in his face. "Stop that. I mean it. The time for jokes is over."

"Aye. Fair enough." He ran his tongue across his bottom teeth. "What will I do with myself while ya gone?"

"You'll do nothing," she said, cold and prickly. "Do you understand? From this moment on, we're in dangerous territory. I need you to lie low until I get back. Can you manage that?"

He shrugged, smirked, looked about him at the sparse room and huffed. "I guess."

"Danny. I'm serious. If I'm helping you do this, you have to follow my lead. I know that might be hard for you to get your head around, taking instructions from a girl. But it's my way, or I walk, do you understand?" He nodded, reminiscent of a naughty school boy being scolded by his teacher. "Danny. Do. You. Understand?"

"Yes!"

"Good." She straightened up and rolled out her shoulders. "I'll be back sometime this evening. But if I'm not here by midnight, for whatever reason, you've got your new passport, you've got the one egg, get yourself out of Spain."

"Where the hell are you going?" he asked, all cheekiness gone. "What's happening?"

"I'm going to find Magpie Stiletto and I'm going to kill her. But I have to do this part alone."

"Fine." He sighed, begrudgingly. "But be careful. Please. I know ya can handle yourself, so don't start, but she's fecking crazy, ya know."

"Yes, well so am I."

She glanced around the room, at the sun's sharp rays shining across the counter tops and up the wall. Then she grabbed her sunglasses from the TV stand, gave Danny one last nod, and left the apartment.

TWENTY-SIX

THE MEETING WITH SONNY BOTHA WAS A MUCH BRIEFER AFFAIR than last time. Today he seemed in a hurry, troubled almost. Sweat dripped from his swarthy brow and his watery eyes darted about as he spoke. It might have been down to the fact there were other people milling around (sightseers, taking in the glorious views across the Bay of Biscay, cooing at the impressive angular sculpture), but it was more than that, she felt. It wasn't that she didn't trust Sonny, but something felt off. Invisible bat fangs nibbled at her nervous system as they made the exchange and Sonny promised to call if he heard anything else. She handed over the extra fifty euros as down payment – any further information he could get her on Luis Delgado.

"And I continue on this path?" she asked, as Sonny was climbing into the cab of his campervan.

"All the way along the headland. Keep the ocean to your left and you'll see the convent up on the hillside once you get around that patch of rocks."

Acid followed his gaze. "Got you. Thanks again, Sonny, I owe you."

"Doesn't everyone," he wheezed, a wide smile splitting his

craggy features. "You take care, miss. Like I said before, this is heavy shit."

"Heavy shit is all I know," she replied, before heading off the way he'd told her.

Over her shoulder she sensed him watching, could almost see him shaking his head in a combination of disbelief and admiration. Or more likely, perhaps, at her foolishness. But like she always said, one woman's foolishness was another's ingenuity. You had to think different to get one over on people like Magpie Stiletto.

As she made her way steadily around the headland, thankful of the sea breeze, her mind drifted to thoughts of her mother, and to a time when she was still the young, innocent Alice Vandella and life was so much easier than it was destined to become. Growing up, there had never been much money around, but somehow (Acid didn't like to think about exactly how, truth be told) her mum had gathered enough together for a week in Spain. It was the first holiday Acid had ever been on. The first and last with her poor mum, as it happened. But those seven days in Majorca, up in the north of the island, had been so wonderful, so full of laughter and fun. She remembered a feeling of lightness she never experienced again in her childhood. A year later her mum met Oscar Duke and Acid's fate was sealed. The memory of that cruel bastard, even after all these years, sent a shiver down her spine. But it wasn't fear, she now realised, but hate. Pure hate. She could still see him in her mind's eye, looming over her with that avaricious leer on his face and her mum's blood on his hands. Oscar Duke. Her first kill. She'd acted that night without a moment's consideration, driven by an intense rage and a pounding desire to avenge her mum's attack. That single moment changed everything for the young Alice. Yet given the situation again, she'd kill him in a second.

So why was she faltering now?

Where was her desire for revenge when she needed it the most?

Maybe Spook was right, the years spent as Caesar's most prized asset had taken their toll on her. And now, away from the organisation, she was struggling, unsure who she was in this new world. *Institutionalised*, was the word Spook had used. *PTSD* too. Was it time to admit the kid had a point?

Acid flicked her hair over her shoulders, as if the action might somehow shake the troubling thoughts into the sea. Up ahead she could now see the stone roof of the convent and the small chapel standing adjacent to it. She unzipped the canvas bag and removed the Viking and a fresh magazine. Once loaded she shoved it in the waistband of her leggings and lifted her t-shirt over the top. The other item in the bag was an oversized white dress shirt she'd borrowed from Danny which she put on, buttoning it all the way to the collar.

Time to get her game face on.

Like most people, Acid hadn't even stepped foot in a convent before, so was unsure what kind of conduct would be expected of her. Opting for a mixture of serenity and reverence (not so easy with her manic energy so rampant), she entered through an open doorway and walked across an enclosed courtyard to where a wooden door had been left ajar.

She removed her sunglasses and tucked them in her shirt pocket before easing the door fully open and stepping through into a small square room. A hint of incense hung in the air, and the bare stone walls meant the space was cool despite the intense summer heat outside. The only furniture in the room was a large oak table with a pile of dog-eared Bibles bound in maroon leather and a brass bell sitting on top. Opposite her was another wooden door and a stone stairwell that led to an upper level.

"*Hola,*" she called out. "Is anyone there?"

Nothing. She tried again.

"*Hola.* Hello. I need to speak to someone." She reached for the bell, unsure whether it was ceremonial or for situations such as this. Well, she'd get their attention or else mortally offend them. She could live with either.

The bell was heavier than it looked and let out a shrill chime as she rang it. A few seconds passed before she heard footsteps, leather souls flapping on stone. As they got nearer she straightened her back, relaxing her pout into the most agreeable and non-threatening expression she could muster. Finally the door creaked open and a thin-faced woman with nervous eyes peered around the side. She looked Acid up and down.

"*Le puedo ayudar?*"

Acid grinned sheepishly, again ruing the fact she'd not kept up with her languages. "Sorry," she said. "Do you speak English? Err... *Ingles?*"

The nun sniffed. "A little."

"Oh thank God. Shit... Sorry. I didn't mean... I was worried you might have taken a vow of silence or something. But you haven't. That's good." She shut up. The bats were at play. It happened. She composed herself. "I was wondering if you could help me. I'm looking for someone."

The nun's eyes widened. "*Quién eres?* Err... Who are you?"

"Oh shit... I mean shoot. Sorry. My name is Special Agent Angela Summers. I'm from Interpol." She reached into her bag and pulled out the wallet she'd purchased from Sonny earlier, flipping it open to reveal the card and badge and handing it to her.

The nun studied the ID for some time. "Interpol?"

"That's right, Sister."

She had wanted MI5 or CIA, but this was the best Sonny

could get last minute. She hoped it would offer her enough sway.

The nun's eyes met hers. "What is it you want?"

"As I said, I'm looking for someone and I believe she may be hiding out here. She's about my height but thinner, with two white streaks in her hair, here and here. Quite hard to miss." She smiled, encouraging the nun to respond, but her face didn't falter.

"I'm sorry, I can't help you."

"Oh? I was told—"

"I have not seen who you ask for."

Acid held her nerve. "Do you mind if I look around?" She took the ID from the nun and shoved it in her bag. "It won't take long, and I'll be quiet, don't worry."

With the nun muttering Spanish remonstrations in her wake, she marched over to the door and pulled it open. A long stone corridor lay in front of her, with tiny ornate windows carved into the stone on both sides.

"Please, some of us are at prayer," the nun whispered, flanking her as she got to the end of the dark corridor, where it led off in both directions.

"Don't worry," Acid whispered back. "I'll be respectful, but you have to realise this is important business. The woman I'm looking for is wanted for murder."

The nun swallowed audibly at this, but said nothing.

"What's down there?" Acid asked, gesturing to where the space opened up into a larger room. Squinting into the gloom she could make out an old table and chairs and two nuns sitting in silence.

Before the nun could answer, Acid was already striding down the corridor. As she entered the room both nuns jumped to their feet, visibly startled by her presence.

"*No se preocupe, hermanas,*" the nun behind her called out, shuffling past. "*Esta mujer es de Interpol.*"

Acid smiled, giving her new audience the same spiel as before – special agent, looking for a woman with white streaks in her hair. The nuns looked at each other, before shaking their heads.

The first nun smiled serenely, crepe skin stretched across skeletal bone structure. "As I have already told you, we have not seen this woman. She is not here."

Acid eyed her and sniffed. "Yes you did say that, didn't you? Okay, fine, have it your way. What's through there?" She pointed to another door hanging open, and through it to a brightly lit room that appeared more modern than this part of the convent.

"Our sleeping quarters. No one is there now. We are all at prayer or doing chores."

"I see." She chewed her lip, wondering if she could (should) lean on the woman some more. Yet she seemed resolute in her silence. A dead end. "I'd better leave you good people to it then." She smiled at the other nuns as they averted their eyes. "I can see myself out."

But the first nun had already scurried over to the door and was beckoning her along the corridor.

"I am sorry we could not be more help," she told Acid, as they walked to the main door.

"Makes two of us, but if you do see this woman – my height, little thinner, white streaks in her hair – will you call me? Do you have a pen?"

The nun shook her head. "We do not have a phone."

"Ah, I see. Well, never mind."

The nun heaved the door open. "*Dios te bendiga.*"

"Sure, Sister. Same to you.

As she stepped out into the hot afternoon sun and heard

the door close behind her, Acid couldn't help thinking that could have gone a lot better. She flinched, an attempt to shake the confusion away. Had that scrawny penguin played her just now? And if so, what was she hiding? And why? She stared out over the ocean and huffed.

What a bloody waste of time.

The clock on her phone told her it was a few minutes after two. She briefly toyed with the notion of heading into town and asking around, but she knew it'd be the same story. People like Magpie, well-trained, experienced, they didn't leave a trail. Better instead she head back to the apartment, see if Danny was any further forward with his plans. She set off walking, but as she reached the edge of the coastal path a voice called out behind her. She stopped and turned to see a nun running towards her, recognisable as one of the two younger ones who'd been sitting at the table.

"*Esperar. Por favor.* Please."

Acid raised her chin. "What is it?"

"You were asking about the… umm… actress?"

"Actress?" But as she said it, the nun mimed at her hair, moving her hands down either side of her face. Streaks. Both sides. "Oh? Yes? *The actress.* So she was here?"

The young nun (couldn't have been older than seventeen, she realised up close) glanced back at the convent. She looked terrified. Acid placed a reassuring hand on her shoulder. "It's okay. I'm from Interpol. You aren't going to get into trouble. This is the right thing to do. Just tell me the truth. The big man is watching, after all."

"*Sí. La verdad.* Truth." She smiled, her thin lips almost vanishing across her pale face. "She is staying here. I saw her leave a few minutes before you arrived."

"Staying here? But how? Why?"

The young nun snorted. "She made a contribution to the convent. Is a lot of money."

"I see." Acid tensed. "And it's definitely her, with two streaks in her hair?"

"Yes." The nun looked down into her hands. "She was allowed to wear our clothing. Is research for a movie, something like that. I did not agree. I still don't. It is not good."

"No," she said. "It is not good. Do you know where she went?"

The nun shook her head. "I am sorry. She seemed... angry as she left. No. Not angry. *Decidido.* Umm... determined. I heard her talking on her phone. Which is also not allowed here. But her voice – it sounded like El Diablo himself was inside of her. I heard her say she had all she needed, that she was ready to complete her mission. I do not know what this means."

The words hit Acid like a rifle butt to the guts. After stammering a brief thank you to the bemused nun, she turned and ran as fast as she could back into town. The bats screamed in her ears, telling her how stupid she'd been, how foolish.

Ready to complete her mission...

Somehow Magpie had found out where they were hiding and she was on her way to the apartment. Only, Acid was up here on the hillside and Danny was all alone. And sure, he was a big guy, and shrewd too. But he was also unarmed and unaware. If Magpie got to him first, he didn't stand a chance.

TWENTY-SEVEN

An intense pain stabbed into Acid's temples as she ran down the hillside towards the city. Like a stress headache, but one exacerbated by a million unseen bat wings beating against her nervous system.

How the hell could she have been so stupid?

Ever since she'd left Annihilation Pest Control she'd felt herself slipping, growing softer, losing focus. But to leave Danny alone, with one of the most vindictive and skilful assassins she'd ever met hunting him, she must be crazier than she realised. A screeching dissonance of silent chatter blistered across her synapses as she hurried down a flight of stone stairs leading to the roadside and jumped the final three. Her blood was on fire, pumping heavily through her veins as she pushed through the soreness in her thighs and calves, and fought the constricting pressure in her chest.

The old Acid Vanilla would have killed Magpie by now. Would have done it the first day. That version of her – tunnel-visioned, hyper alert, not resting until she had the mark in her sights – would be back in England by now. Or on the next job. But no. She'd messed around, searching for distractions, letting her focus drift to eggs and blue-eyed boys and money.

What was certain, she realised – as she zig-zagged though the labyrinth of alleyways and backstreets she hoped would take her to the far side of the apartment building – she didn't have the same bloodlust the old Acid had. Once, it was almost overpowering, and a driving force in her life. Even now, thinking about Magpie, about Caesar, about what they did to her mum, her desire for vengeance was ebbing. The ramifications of what that meant made her want to throw up.

"Fuck off. Get lost."

She barked the words viciously into the sky, an act of defiance towards more obtrusive thoughts. Up ahead she could see the apartment building and the corner unit on the second floor where Danny was. Despite the late afternoon sun the lounge light was on, visible through a gap in the blinds. She didn't see any movement. Another thirty seconds and she'd be there. She slipped the backpack off and pulled out the nine in readiness. She could still make this right. She would.

She had to.

With her breath held like a physical ball of energy in her throat, she entered through the back door of the building. Letting the Viking lead the way, she took the stairs two at a time, shifting around the first floor landing and up the final flight of stairs to room twenty-six. Nothing seemed out of order as she glided down the corridor, reaching into the bag for the room key as she went. Once at the door, she laid her ear silently against it. She could hear the faint rumble of synthesized bass, another of Danny's dance tracks coming from the TV, but nothing else. Slowly she slid the key in the lock, gritting her teeth at the *click* as it opened. Keeping her aim high, she opened the door and slipped through into the hallway. Scoping out the bedroom she saw her overnight bag laid out on top of the unmade bed, exactly as she'd left it. Nothing unusual there. The bathroom light was on but she couldn't remember whether she'd turned it off or not. Besides, Danny could have used it, it wasn't a sign of an intruder. Leaving the bedroom she moved to the end of the hallway and positioned herself flat against the wall. With her eyes closed, she cast her awareness into the room on the other side. Her heightened senses told her there was no movement, no presence of another soul. That meant one of two things. The room was empty, or she was too late. A quick scan of the floors and walls showed no sign of blood spatter. So with her breath tight in her chest, and gripping the pistol with all she had, she stepped around the corner. The couch still had a Danny-shaped indentation in the cushions and the TV was on (the same Spanish music channel, showing a crowd of bronzed millennials dancing moronically on a beach), but no Danny. And no Magpie.

"What the…"

She spun around to take in the far side of the room, as if perhaps she'd missed him in the kitchen. But no. The place was empty.

So where the bloody hell was he?

Her next thought wasn't a good one. Magpie had beaten her here, drugged him, and taken him somewhere to finish the job at her own sadistic pace. She had form for that sort of thing. She might have even taken him to Delgado, she mused, as dark chaotic images flashed in front of her face. It wasn't unheard of for clients to request pulling the trigger themselves. Although, she herself had never agreed to it in her sixteen years in the industry. For her that sort of murder tourism was gauche and undermined everything she'd worked so hard for. If someone hired her to do a job, then she did it her way.

She went into the kitchen. There was no sign anywhere of

a struggle. Would Danny have simply walked out with her? At gunpoint maybe, but knowing the brash Irishman even for a short time, she couldn't imagine it. He was a pain in the arse, and didn't seem to be able to take anything seriously, but he was tough and he was savvy.

With her head still spinning with possibilities, she pulled her phone out, wondering if she should call The Dullahan. He wouldn't be happy about the situation, but he also might have heard something. From Danny, even.

The idea was cut short however when a moment later she heard the sound of a key in a lock. Leaping over to the side of the room, she positioned herself next to the open doorway. It had to be Magpie. She'd disposed of Danny and was coming back for her.

She waited. Still and unblinking. That thousand-yard stare she'd perfected over the years. A face ready for battle.

Footsteps crept down the hallway. One, two, three... One more step and they'd be in the room. Acid adjusted her grip on the nine, holding it with both hands up at shoulder height as the intruder rounded the corner. Once in her peripheral vision she made her move, smashing a sharp elbow into their side before stepping around to take the shot.

"Shite. What the—"

"Danny?" She kept the gun raised, but already loosening her finger on the trigger as she stared at the bedraggled figure in front of her. "I almost shot you."

"Well please don't," he yelled back, holding a white carrier bag up to his face that clinked with the sound of glass bottles. "It's me. Calm down."

She lowered the gun. "What's going on? I told you to stay here."

"I woke up and I was thirsty. Went to get a few beverages

for us." He held out the bag for her. "See? Nice bottle of Jameson and a few beers."

"You fucking idiot," she shouted, in a rare and unrestrained show of emotion. "I thought you were dead, or... I don't know... But still, Magpie's on her way. She knows where we are."

"What? No she doesn't. How?"

The bluntness of his response shook her alert. She gulped back a mouthful of air. "She was coming down to the city... to finish her mission. Someone heard her... A nun..." She trailed off, doubting herself suddenly. Because without Raaz Terabyte's *eye in the sky*, it would indeed be hard for Magpie to know where they were. Unless she had some insider information. A mole. Carlos, perhaps? Sonny? Was that it? Or was this the bats and the baking sun (not to mention the dark presence, still there in the back of her psyche) leading her down a blind alley of paranoia?

She glared at Danny, her readiness to kill turning to confusion and now to rage. "I told you to stay here."

"Yes, but I wanted a drink. I was bored."

"Y-You were bored? Oh fucking hell, I do apologise, is being on the run from a trained killer too dull for you?" She shook her head, muttering more obscenities under her breath. "How did you get back in?"

Danny held up a key and grinned. "Got a spare from Carlos. No worries."

"*No worries?* You're a bloody idiot, you know that? I don't know what I was thinking going along with your stupid plan. But it's over. All of it. First thing tomorrow you're on a plane home."

"Ah come on, Acid. No. Please." He stepped towards her and lowered his chin, practically fluttering his eyelashes at her. "I'm real sorry, babe. Let me make it up to ya. I will so, I—"

Acid landed a heavy fist to the side of his mouth which shut him up and had him staggering backwards into the kitchen unit, the contents of the bag clattering as they hit the cupboard.

It was too much for her.

Far too much.

TWENTY-EIGHT

THE PUNCH SHOCKED DANNY. BUT LESS SO THAN THE INTENSE ferocity on Acid's face as she flew at him again. This time he managed to let go of the bag and grab her shoulders, holding her away from him as she swung her fists around.

"Hey, stop that." He leaned back, steadfast in his stance. "I'm sorry, all right? I wasn't thinking straight. It won't happen again."

She surged at him one more time before her body relaxed. Her face too. Although not entirely. Danny sensed a twinkle of murder still in her eyes, which was why he kept a firm hold on her, literally keeping her at arm's length.

"I thought you were dead," she spluttered. "I thought Magpie had come for you. And with me up on the hillside…"

"Ah, you were worried about me. That's sweet."

The angry assassin scowled at him through the hair covering her face. "I wasn't worried about you. I was just… mad at myself for being… I'm here for your uncle, remember? I owe him."

"Yeah, sure." He loosened his hold on her and stepped backwards, thankful when she remained still. "Look at me,

Acid, I'm fine. There's no way Sound of Music knows where we are."

"She was coming here. She said…"

Danny picked up the carrier bag and placed it on the kitchen counter with a clink of glass. "No one knows we're here except Carlos and he wouldn't have told anyone. I promise ya. How would she know?"

Acid frowned, shifting her gaze to the bottle of Jameson as he removed it from the bag. "She is working alone. Doing it old-school. That is, unless she's found someone else who can hack CCTV and the like."

"Do you think she has?" he asked, taking two tumblers from the cupboard and placing them on the counter.

"I don't, Danny," she spat. "That's why I was worried."

He screwed the top off the whisky and glugged out two large helpings. "Okay, I get it. But San Sebastian isn't that high-tech of a city. Even if she could, you see any cameras around here? I don't think she's coming, ba—" He stopped himself, the remembrance of the punch still smarting on his cheek. "Mate. Even if she was, we're two flights up with only one way in. And the front door's double locked."

He handed a tumbler to Acid and she took it, staring morosely into the amber liquid for a second before gulping down half of it in one go. She glanced at him, her expression softer now. "Maybe you're right. I'm being paranoid. It happens. Especially when…"

"When what?"

"Never mind." She raised the glass. "Cheers. I needed this."

"Cheers." They clinked glasses. "May the road rise up to meet ya."

It took them both just two swigs to finish the drinks. Danny

163

poured out some more as Acid went through into the lounge and flopped onto the couch.

"Getting comfy?" he asked, joining her as she unbuttoned her shirt. She rolled her eyes at him before taking it off and flinging it in a heap on the floor.

"Don't get any ideas."

"Oh believe me, I won't try nothing. Though ya can't stop me from having ideas. And by Jesus, some of the ideas I've been having about you." He turned, hitting her with his best, most effective grin. It got zero response.

Instead she let her head roll back and stared at the ceiling, seeing something only she could see. "You have no concept of how much danger you're in, do you?"

"I'm pretty sure I have. But what's the use in getting all het up and stressed about it? Besides. I've got you here looking out for me."

The comment elicited a loud snort down both nostrils. They drank in silence, Danny opening his mouth to speak a few times but thinking better of it. Because he wasn't the fool she thought he was. He knew when a situation demanded gravitas and solemnity. But at the same time, life was an adventure, wasn't it? If you didn't try to have fun, what was the fecking point of anything?

"Sorry for punching you."

The way she said it, whispered on an out breath, he wondered for a moment if he'd imagined it. But as he turned to her, she was gazing up at him. Her eyes were wide and a little watery, any hint of murderous rage supplanted by a wired nervousness that he at once found unsettling. And incredibly sexy.

"I deserved it. I usually do."

"Get punched by women a lot, do you?"

He sipped at his drink. "That's a loaded question, so it is.

But yes, there have been times. And I do always deserve it." He shifted, to better look at her. "I'm not the reckless rogue you think I am, Acid."

"Oh that is a shame," she replied, moving to face him. "I kind of have a soft spot for reckless rogues."

"Is that right?"

She shrugged theatrically. "I mean, they have to be good-looking. And they can't like that awful dance music."

He smiled. "Ah that is a shame."

"Isn't it?" She finished her drink and handed him the tumbler.

"Another?"

"No." She sat upright, the nervousness in her eyes suddenly shifting to a look of trepidation. "I have to get some rest. Got some thinking to do."

"Ah come on," he coaxed. "It's only, what, gone six? You can't go to bed now."

"I don't feel too good and I want to be up early."

"One more. We were getting on, at long last."

She looked at him with her mouth twisted to one side, clearly having an internal conversation with herself – her baser instincts fighting against what her head was saying. He'd seen the same look in many girls' eyes. In his experience, the baser instincts always won out.

But not this time. Steadying herself with a hand on his leg, she got to her feet. "I'll see you in the morning."

"Acid?"

She turned at the door. "What?"

"You will still help me? To get the egg, I mean. You weren't serious about going to the airport first thing?"

"I was," she said. "But yes, we'll get your damned egg. After I take care of Magpie though. Understood? I need her out of the picture as soon as possible. The venomous bitch is getting to me."

"Got ya."

And he did. At least he thought he did. Except this Acid Vanilla, she was certainly an enigma. Unlike any woman – any person – he'd ever met. Sure, she was sexy, funny, scary as hell, but there was so much more to her as well. In his younger days, the cocksure lad from Dublin might have labelled the fierce, feisty woman a challenge, but not now. Because now he saw something in her that he recognised.

Pain.

A deep sadness.

But that only made him like her more. Of course, he knew full well he was setting himself up for a fall. Even before you factored in the real present danger of Sister Death and the shitstorm raging around them.

Bollocks to it.

He finished his drink and closed his eyes, the alcohol making its presence known in his system. Surprising himself, he began to pray, asking the big man for forgiveness and to grant him the strength to do what he needed to do.

Danny talked a good talk, even to himself. But times like this – lying here alone with no outside stimulus, not even the television, to distract him – the twin demons of fear and worry soon rose up inside him. Despite what Acid said, he was taking this seriously. But he was also fecking terrified and if he thought too much about it he'd freeze. Go mad. Break down. So whenever possible he tried not to think too deeply. Like he had done all is life - . after his dad was killed, after his ma got sick. It was easier this way. And life *was* an adventure. People owed it to themselves to drink and laugh and screw and defy the Gods for as long as possible. Because Danny knew full well, it could all be over in an instant.

TWENTY-NINE

Despite his busy mind, Danny must have drifted off to sleep, because the next he knew he was blinking into the gloom as a figure approached him at speed. He sat upright as they leapt on him, clutching at his hair and planting soft lips firmly on his. He kissed back, breathing in the heady mix of expensive perfume and body odour.

"Acid," he gasped. "You sure you—"

"Shut up." She kissed him again, before grabbing at his t-shirt and pulling it off over his head.

He leaned back, taking her in as best he could in the dark room. She was wearing a black lace bra, which he removed promptly (a seasoned pro at the old one-handed-bra-clasp-unfastening) before letting out an involuntary *woah* at the sight of her naked form above him.

And it was happening.

It was really happening.

It couldn't have been a dream because she wouldn't have been pulling his hair quite so hard if it was. Her fingernails wouldn't have been scratching at his back quite so painfully. She lifted her hips, slipping off the couch, so he could remove his pants and then hers before (*oh shite*) she was back on top. She pulled harder at his hair, grinding on him as he groaned into her neck.

Oh fecking hell.

This *was* happening.

He was actually having sex with an assassin, a professional killer.

And boy did it feel good.

What didn't feel so good however was the leather couch, which was sticking to his bare arse and making him sweat more than he needed to. Making a swift decision he scooped Acid up, and with her legs wrapped around his waist they stumbled into the bedroom and fell onto the bed. Now things really took off. Danny had slept with a lot of women over the years, some of them more than experienced in the ways of passion, yet this felt different. It was more like a battle, a skirmish. And one he appeared to be losing.

Who would have thought it? Danny Flynn was being dominated, and he was even (mostly) enjoying it. But that didn't stop him giving as good as he got, grabbing hold of her in all the right places – with just the right amount of force, judging from the noises coming from her. Him too, both of them grunting like wild animals as they worked on each other, changing positions, flinging each other around the bed. There was more grunting, more hair pulling, before finally, with a mutual cry and a shudder that rocked them both, they collapsed onto the soft mattress.

"Fecking hell," Danny gasped, once he'd got his breath back and his vision had returned. "That was amazing. I can't feel my legs." He glanced at Acid, who had rolled onto her side, facing away. She didn't speak. "Hey, you okay?"

All he got was a nod. He reached over and stroked her shoulder in what he hoped was a reassuring manner, his finger resting on a small raised scar that looked like a bullet wound. So… it was probably a bullet wound. A closer inspection of her lithe, tanned back brought to light more scars. Some small, some large. But plenty of them. They didn't detract anything from her beauty, but the sight of them gave him butterflies. She was the real deal, all right. An actual trained killer.

"You get all these in your work?" he asked, running his finger down a long white scar beneath her ribs.

She sniffed, shrugged. "Yes. All part of who I am." Her voice was cold and clipped. Not the sort of pillow talk he was used to.

"Is everything all right?"

She rolled onto her back, making no attempt to cover her naked form like most girls might. And maybe that was why he was so smitten with her. He'd never experienced confidence like it. Yet even now, as she stared at the ceiling, he noticed again the sadness. Only a glimmer around her eyes, but it was there.

"I'm fine." She sighed. "I've got a lot on my mind, that's all."

"Good, because I didn't want you to think—"

"Listen, Danny, we both needed that." She turned her head to look at him. "It was a pleasant release, okay? But nothing more."

He smiled. "Fair enough. Ya know, I did wonder about you. Whether maybe ya batted for the other team. Liked girls."

"I do like girls."

"Oh, right. So you're like… bisexual?"

"Oh god." A pained expression twisted her features. "I don't like labels."

"So what do you like?"

She propped herself up on her arm, smiling now but with the devil behind it. "I like good sex. Plain and simple."

"I see. And was that… good sex?"

She sat up and slid off the bed before swaying over to the bathroom. In the doorway she paused. "It was above average, certainly," she told him. "But I think we can do better."

"Ya reckon?"

"Oh yes. Why don't you get us another drink and then we'll try again in a minute."

Danny baulked. "But I… I only just…"

"Come on now, Daniel. You're playing in the big leagues now. No time for rest. You've got work to do." She winked impishly. "Like I say, it's a release. After everything that's happened the last few days, I'd say we deserve it. So get the drinks and we'll go for round two."

"Round two. Wow. Okay." He swung his legs out of bed. "How many rounds are there?"

She disappeared into the bathroom and shut the door. "That's up to you, Danny boy," came the muffled response. "Let's see how much of me you can handle."

THIRTY

ACROSS THE STREET AND CONCEALED IN THE SHADOWS DOWN the side of a small supermarket, a lone figure watched the apartment building. This was it. The waiting was over. If anyone could see Magpie Stiletto at this present moment, they'd have been hard pushed to call what she was doing with her mouth a smile, but it was as close as she ever got. Despite the rage and bile always present in her demeanour (even more so these last few days, being in such close proximity with that *ramera*), she felt good, relieved even. The plan had worked exactly as she'd hoped, that foolish young nun having taken the bait perfectly.

After that it was a simple matter of concealing herself in the long grass near the convent and waiting. She'd been there when Acid arrived, then when that pious nun had chased after her. And once the seed had been sown, she'd followed her at a distance as she raced back into town, leading her straight to the mark.

Magpie Stiletto, stepping into her new role as Sister Death, the dark nun, curled her lip, disgusted but not surprised at what she'd seen. The front room blinds had been closed all afternoon but through the corner window there had been a clear view of the two of them. The mark and Acid Vanilla, both of them naked, and her wrapped around him like the whore she was.

They'd been drinking too. Confirmed just now when the mark returned to the kitchen and picked up a bottle before returning to the bedroom. His face was red and he had a big smile on his face. Pleased with himself.

Well enjoy it, muchacho. Because you have no idea of the pain and suffering coming your way.

But not just yet. The immoral and licentious cretins would be in situ for the next few hours at least, possibly the rest of the night – meaning she could carry out her plan to the letter. To do that, she needed something first from her supplier across town. Something potent but not lethal that administered correctly would make the next few hours a whole lot easier and much, much more satisfying.

She checked her bearings. The shore was in front of her, the mountains to her right, looming large over this part of the city. Peering around the side of the supermarket, she could see the corner of the Manteo Sports Centre up ahead. It had been many years since she'd ventured into this part of town, but if she headed down San Francisco Kalea she was sure to reach the Church of San Ignacio where the drop would take place. The whole journey there and back would take her less than an hour.

Less than an hour and the mark would be dead.

Less than an hour and she'd have Acid Vanilla where she wanted her. Drugged, bound, ineffectual. Unable to fight back.

Then the atonement would begin.

Sister Death would get her pound of flesh and that wretched *fulana* would experience the true embodiment of pain and agony. She'd already lived a lifetime of sin and now her flippant ways and loose morals would come back to bite her. The reckoning would be slow and methodical, engineered to cause the most amount of suffering for as long as possible. Her own *Via Crucis*. A pilgrimage of anguish and sorrow.

With the right tools she could draw out the experience for hours, days even. It would not be pleasant at all, but it would be just and it would be righteous.

A spluttering laugh emanated out from deep inside of Magpie, shocking her a little. She never laughed. Ever. The very fact her imagination was running riot and filling her with such emotion told her all she needed to know. This was the right path. The righteous path. Her work was His work. Like she'd always known it to be. With a final glance back at the apartment building, she moved out of the shadows and left to meet her supplier.

THIRTY-ONE

"What? Are you kidding me?" Acid stood in the bathroom doorway with her hands on her hips, taking in Danny's prone form.

So there was the answer to how much the roguish Irishman could handle her. Not very much at all. She'd only been in the bathroom a few minutes, splashing water on her face and pits, freshening up after their second go at something close to passion, and now here he was, snoring into his pillow with his bare arse in the air.

"Bloody lightweight," she sneered, tilting her head to one side and watching him as he slept.

But this was a good result. She had been gearing up for a third attempt, but mainly in the hope it would tire him out enough so he'd stay put for the night. She had to admit though (only to herself obviously), the boy had lived up to his own hype. She'd hit him with the 'only a release' line to keep him at arm's length (she'd seen how he looked at her and she wasn't having any of that nonsense), but as she went into the front room and gathered up her underwear she realised it was true. Even if literally screwing the sentience out of someone in your

174

care (what would she call him — her charge, her client?) was a reckless move, it had been a bloody good distraction. Exactly what she'd needed.

She slipped on her pants and bra and gathered up her phone from the kitchen counter. A brief glance at the screen told her it was a few minutes after ten — still early — and she was certain sleep was now far beyond the horizon. With this renewed but gnawing alertness came more obtrusive thoughts, chaotic missives darting haphazardly across her consciousness, too quick to even focus on but leaving their malevolent stench all the same.

She moved over to the small window next to the kitchen and leaned on the sill, gazing out into the inky abyss. There were a few stars in the sky and she wondered if that was Venus over to the east, but no answers. She rolled her head around her shoulders, sensing the dark presence waking in her psyche as her eyes fell on the bottle of Jameson. There was another release right there. A blessed release from the burden of being her.

No.

She had to stay sharp and work with not against the demons in her soul, weaponizing her dark energy like she always used to. With her head held high, she marched past the bottle — still calling her — and into the bedroom. Playtime was over.

Danny's snoring was more forceful now as she tiptoed around the bed and found her t-shirt and leggings balled up in the corner. She got dressed, picked up her shoulder bag and the Viking 9mm from the top of the chest of drawers and left, closing the door silently behind her.

She made her way out and down the two flights of stairs to ground level. The air was still warm with a slight breeze coming down from the hillside as she stepped out onto the empty street and headed towards the town centre. She had no destination in mind, just an awareness she needed to do something – change the scenery, clear her head. Although, easier said than done when you were Acid Vanilla and at any one time you had a veritable cocktail of over-zealous chemicals, past traumas and bad karma swirling around in your system.

As she walked she chewed on her bottom lip, aware of the road in front of her but seeing so much more. Shadowy memories rose up to meet her, as so often happened when she was alone and in deep contemplation. She thought of her mother, of Davros and Spitfire, and even Jacqueline, her therapist at the home for dangerous girls, the woman who'd introduced her to Caesar. As a professional killer, the fact that her past was littered with so many dead bodies came as no surprise, but now more than ever she felt the burden of karma breathing down her neck.

At the corner she took a right down Zurriola Avenue towards the seafront She'd always found the crashing waves and sound of the ocean spray as it splashed against the rocks to be a calming experience. But as she got closer she saw the tide was far out and the sea was restful for once. Maybe it was the universe balancing itself out somehow. Tonight it was she who carried with her the sea's violent, restless energy.

As she made her way along the length of the promenade, her thoughts turned once more to Magpie Stiletto, and her entire body shivered with intense hatred. She had to kill her. She had to. Yet she was aware now of another emotion, on the flip-side of her loathing, one she'd been struggling with ever since she arrived in Spain, unable or unwilling to face head on, to look it in the eyes, but perhaps it was time to admit it. She was scared. Except that wasn't even the main problem. She'd spent the last sixteen years pushing all her emotions down inside of herself. Staying cold, detached, focused – so she could do the job she was paid for. But now here she was on the outskirts of her own life, and she was floundering. Uncertainty gripped her like never before. Could she do this? Could she face Magpie? Could she avenge her mother's death like she'd promised?

Jesus, Acid.

She shook her head, gazing out across the horizon. If she couldn't bring herself to kill Magpie, then who the bloody hell was she?

THIRTY-TWO

IT TOOK HER ALL OF SIXTY SECONDS TO PICK THE LOCK. WHICH was longer than it would normally have taken, but she was taking it slow, working as silently as possible. As she felt the pleasing give of the final spring in the cylinder she straightened up and, with her face rigid with focus, opened the door and stepped through into the apartment. Moving stealthily down the short corridor, she took in the open-plan space.

Cerdos asquerosos.

Dirty pigs.

The air smelt of body odour, of sex and hormones. With disgust wrinkling her nose she passed through the kitchen area, eyeing the bottle of whisky on the kitchen counter, half empty. No surprises there, and it was what she'd counted on. The debased harlot had never been able to resist temptation. Whether it be carnal desire, or alcohol, or the many trappings of success she herself had stayed clear of, it was the same story – Acid Vanilla was a wanton and despicable *degenerada*. A debauched libertine of the worst kind.

Even Beowulf Caesar, once a man of such vision and drive (and someone she'd looked up to despite his decadent homosexual tendencies), had become flabbily obsessed with money and power at any cost. He'd let go of his purpose, allowed ego and his desire to be number one drive him into the ground. And look where they were now. The organisation was in tatters, Spitfire was dead, and Caesar was in the wind, a broken, frightened man.

Holding the pistol to her chest (a Sig Sauer P365, chosen for its compact size) she glided around the corner, finger ready on the trigger. In the front room she found signs of a struggle – the couch on an angle, cushions flung on the floor – but no mark, no Acid Vanilla. Stepping over a small pine table that had been knocked on its side, she cast her eyes around the room. Because despite her vendetta, she also had a job to do. And that meant she still had to locate Delgado's precious egg and USB drive.

With her countenance unflinching in its sneer, she slipped the Sig Sauer into her jacket pocket and unzipped the money belt she had strapped around her waist. Inside was a small leather pouch and foldaway blade. She shoved the blade between her teeth, retching at the taste of metal as she opened up the pouch and removed a vial of yellow solution along with an intravenous needle. Propofol. Used all over the world by top anaesthesiologists – as well as enterprising killers who needed to transport one or more victims to a second location with minimal fuss. She'd already spotted a moped parked up outside which she planned to use for the journey. It wouldn't be easy, but things that were important were never easy. It didn't mean you shouldn't try. Why couldn't more people on this dying cesspit of a planet understand that?

Once the syringe was assembled she swapped it with the knife between her teeth, leering at the shiny steel as it glinted in the harsh strip-light above. She crept back along the short hallway. To the bedroom where the two revolting miscreants were no doubt sprawled out in post-coital slumber. Carefully she removed the syringe from her teeth and held it in her fist with her thumb on the plunger. A swift jab and she'd empty the contents into Acid's neck, or failing that, a limb. If she hit a vein, the drugs would render her unconscious before she had a chance to know what was going on. After that she planned on opening up the mark's throat from ear to ear. She could picture it already, her delighting in his pain and confusion as he gasped for air, drowning in his own blood and sin. It would be a slow death and he'd know it was coming. Ample time for him to regret his recent choices. She even hoped for some kind of spluttering confession as he bled out.

With her breath held heavy in her chest, she leaned her forearm against the door and eased it open. The room was dark and a gentle breeze blew in from an open window. But as she peered into the gloom, a cry of deep repentant anguish escaped from her taut throat. The bed was empty.

"*Madre María! Esto no puede ser verdad.*"

This could not be happening.

But they'd been here. She'd seen them both. They were drunk, naked, intertwined. She moved around the room, picking up articles of clothing and bedsheets as though they were somehow hiding somewhere. They were not.

"*Estúpido tonto,*" she cursed herself.

This was what happened when you let desire get the better of you. The giddiness she'd felt had skewed her focus, made her complacent like everyone else. Because this wasn't her. This wasn't who she aspired to be. A loser. A fool.

She scoped out the rest of the room and the en suite bathroom, moving less furtive now, rooting angrily through drawers and the wardrobe, peering under the bed. If Sister Death couldn't deliver the penance she'd hoped to, then at least she might salvage something. Find the egg at least,

Delgado's USB drive. But no. Another circuit of the room, searching everywhere she'd already looked, then in the main space too, told her the egg wasn't in the apartment either.

With gnashing teeth, fighting a strong urge to burn the place to the ground, she stormed down the hallway and flung open the front door. Either they'd got lucky or somehow they'd known she was coming. But that didn't mean she couldn't still find them. They'd foiled her for now, but they were still out there. Donostia was a city small in size. She'd find them. With God's help, she'd find them.

THIRTY-THREE

Even after watching the crazy nun leave – her looking both ways down the street before scurrying off with a face like blackened thunder – Danny remained where he was for a good few minutes longer. Every muscle in his body was tense with fear and trepidation. He daren't move, more than aware it was only a sheer stroke of luck (luck o' the Irish, and all that) that he'd woken up needing a piss ten minutes earlier. If he hadn't, he'd be dead right now, or perhaps wishing he was.

Awake but confused as to where his bedroom sparring partner had gone, he'd wandered into the front room and happened to glance out the window at the same time as a lone woman – wiry-framed, with two shocks of white streaked through her straight black hair – was striding towards the apartment. He'd watched her for a moment, unable to comprehend what he was looking at through the fog of sleep and whisky, but as soon as he did he'd rushed to the couch and gathered up his clothes. After almost falling over stepping into his jeans on the way to the bedroom, he only had time to pull on a t-shirt and grab his holdall before a faint scratching at the door had him clambering out the window. It had been a decent drop to the street below and he'd jarred his leg on impact. But he'd escaped. For now, at least.

The sight of the assassin's callous and inhuman expression – illuminated briefly in the glare of a streetlight – had been enough to shock him into alertness. It was the cruelty in her eyes as she scowled down the street that got to him, more so even than the suggestion of a blade, gripped tightly in her paw and shimmering in the moonlight. The woman was evil. Pure evil. And she meant business. As he waited in the shadows he suddenly felt dumb, like a young child who'd been playing at being an adult. Acid was right. It was really time to take things more seriously.

Acid. Shite.

Where the hell was she?

Gripping the holdall to his chest, he moved around the side of the building, walking swiftly but cautiously up to the end of the street and peeking around the corner. His calf and shins throbbed like hell after jumping two storeys, but he could walk okay, most of the pain overridden by the sheer amount of adrenaline shooting through his system.

He checked both ways, double-checked to make sure, but the nun was nowhere in sight. But then neither was Acid. Danny had a vague memory of her getting out of bed, but in his dreamy state he'd assumed she was going to the bathroom and must have fallen back asleep.

Had he done something to piss her off?

Upset her?

From what he could tell she'd enjoyed herself, having made all the right noises, but what did he know? She was a complete and utter mystery to him. Unlike any woman he'd ever met. And still his mind was drawn to that hint of sadness he'd noticed. Only slight, almost undetectable, but it was there. Something was tearing her up inside. Despite the fact she could definitely handle herself – and would no doubt be pissed off with him – he set off towards the centre to find her. She was alone in the city, unaware that the crazy nun was nearby. She might be a tough lassie and dangerous with it, but that meant diddly-squat if she was caught off guard.

As he pressed on, Danny told himself to stay on track, not let his imagination run riot. Only, the sight of Sister Death had freaked him the hell out, even more so than on their first encounter. Now the determination coming off her was profound, like a zealous fury that radiated into the night sky. She wasn't messing around. And he couldn't afford to either. He had to find Acid before she did.

THIRTY-FOUR

THE BARMAN SMILED WEARILY AS ACID CAUGHT HIS EYE. "*Otra cerveza, por favor,*" she purred, giving the lispy pronunciation both barrels. *Thervetha.*

He scooped up the empty glass, carrying it to the tap at the far end of the bar and pouring one out for her. This was her second already of the evening, but the glasses were small and the beer weak, nowhere near strong enough to derail her, or to take the edge off the chattering symphony going on in her brain. But that was okay, she told herself. Important, even. It meant she'd stay vigilant. Although why that mattered was fast becoming a moot point.

She shoved a folded ten euro bill at the barman as he placed her drink down, and held her hand up for him to keep the change.

"*Gracias, señorita.*"

Hunched as she was over her glass, she was able to watch him through her hair as he took her in. He wasn't a bad-looking guy. Typically Spanish, with shiny black hair and a good nose. His mouth twitched as though he wanted to say more, but he must have thought better of it because a second

185

later he turned and busied himself with a trayful of clean glasses, removing each one in turn and placing them on a shelf above the bar. It was a wise choice, Acid felt. Whatever he was about to say, it wouldn't have worked out well for him.

She slurped the froth off the top of the malty beer and sat upright, flicking her hair over her shoulders and catching a whiff of it as she did. Geez. It stank. She stank. Of sex and whisky. Of sweat and misery. A good wash and some sleep would have helped, but right now those things were pretty far down on the list of things Acid needed. The top items being: Magpie Stiletto dead, Beowulf Caesar too, and for this draining revenge mission of hers to be over. After that she'd appreciate some peace and bloody quiet, perhaps a deeper knowledge of what she might do with the rest of her life. As it was, she had none of those things. All she had was a rapidly diminishing Spanish beer and a heap of infuriating and unfathomable questions.

She looked up to see the barman was staring at her again. He smiled, but any further suggestion of kindness was parried by her deep sigh that sent him scurrying to the far end of the bar. As is most people's go-to distraction in these sorts of situations, she pulled out her phone and began to scroll through the menu. Before she'd even acknowledged to herself what she was doing, or why, she'd found The Dullahan's number in her contacts list and hit call.

He answered after one ring. "Acid? Everything all right?"

She sniffed. "Define all right."

"Is Danny safe?"

Define safe.

She stopped herself before she said it. It wasn't fair.

"Yes. He's… asleep," she replied instead. "And he's also a fucking liability. Are you aware of that?"

"Is he?"

She sat up from the bar. "He's given me the runaround, let's say that." She stopped short of telling him about the egg, about their planned heist. All of a sudden she felt stupid for calling. She should be handling this.

"What's going on, Acid? I thought you'd be back in London by now. Danny, at least. Where are you, a bar? I can hear laughter."

"I'm doing a little recon work," she lied. "Danny wanted to stay with me, got a few things he wants to sort out before we fly home. But he's safe."

"What about Magpie? She taken care of?"

"She's a slippery sod, but I'm on her trail," she told him, glancing down at the near-empty beer glass. "Don't worry, I've got it under control."

"Righto." He didn't sound convinced. "You want to speak to Spook?"

The question landed heavily on her shoulders. "Is she there?"

"Aye, I'm at the surgery now. Came to check on her. She's on the mend, so she is. Here y'are…"

"No, Dullahan, it's fine. I—" She stopped as the line crackled and another voice came on.

"Hey, Acid."

Spook. Little Spook. Her voice was croaky but she sounded well.

"You gave me a fright, you know that?" Acid told her. "Don't you dare do anything stupid like that again."

"What, save your ass? It's not the first time, if I remember rightly."

Acid stifled a smile, lest it be conveyed down the line in her voice. She gulped back the last dregs of the beer. "Whatever. It's good to hear you're on the mend."

"How's it going over there? How are you?"

"I've been better, I'll be honest. But I'm doing better than the last time you saw me, so... all relative, isn't it?"

Spook was quiet when she spoke. "Be careful. Please. The Dullahan has filled me in. That Magpie – man, she sounds terrifying."

Acid sucked in her cheeks, catching sight of herself in the mirrored wall behind the bar. She looked dreadful. Her hair was stuck up like she was in an 80s metal band, and her eyeliner smudged to panda-bear proportions. "She's not so scary," she replied. "Just thinks she is. It's a fine line."

"I'm sorry I can't help you with anything," Spook said. "I asked the doctor if I could have my laptop but he said no. Got to stay rested a few more days."

"It's fine. I've got this." She paused, swallowing back a ball of emotion. "It's good to speak to you, kid. I think we need to talk when I get home. You were right about a few things. Quite a few things."

"Oh? Wow. I wish I was recording this."

"Don't push it. Sarcasm doesn't suit you."

"Well, I have learnt from the best. But I understand. I'm sorry." Her tone had risen, a smile there in her voice. "And I'm glad. If you're ready to open up, I'm ready to listen."

Acid nodded at her reflection, an uncomfortable feeling in her stomach. Something like shame. "Thanks." She cricked her neck to one side and jutted out her chin. "Okay. Good talk. I need to get back to it now."

"Please be careful. I mean it."

"You just focus on getting yourself better. I'll see you soon."

She hung up and slipped the phone back in her bag before raising her finger to attract the barman. One more beer wouldn't hurt. One more and then she'd head back. Get some rest. Then tomorrow it would be a completely different story. No more of this bullshit. No more getting bogged down in a pathetic quagmire of thoughts and *what-ifs*. She was still Acid Vanilla, for Christ's sake, a highly trained and deadly assassin. She'd been the best. And so what if she'd had a slight wobble? It happened. The trick was to keep moving. You stand still too long in this life and the darkness envelops you.

"Oh, shit."

The barman was on his way to her when she saw something through the window behind him. Or rather, some*one*. It was dark outside, and the window was awash with reflections from the brightly lit taberna, but she'd know that profile anywhere. The sharp nose, the cat's arse mouth. The white streaks in her hair.

"You want another?" the barman asked, but Acid was already off the stool and flinging the bag over her shoulder.

"No, change of plan," she called back, as she rushed for the door and yanked it open. "I'm meeting up with an old friend. Must dash."

THIRTY-FIVE

ACID BURST OUT THE DOOR OF THE SMALL TABERNA AND YELLED out to Magpie Stiletto, who spun around and locked eyes with her. Despite the late hour, the narrow winding streets in the old town were busy and a stream of people, merry with drink and sunshine, wound around the two stationary women as they faced each other.

A moment passed.

Neither of them moved.

The assassin's code, adhered to around the globe, stated plainly that all jobs should be carried out with the utmost stealth and secrecy. Not always possible, of course, but unnecessarily drawing attention to oneself was a definite infringement of the code. Especially so as Caesar's operatives, who all prided themselves on delivering a certain artistry in their work. Shooting up a crowded street was vulgar and it was uncalled for.

Even so, that didn't stop Acid from dropping the bag off her shoulder and slipping her hand inside, feeling for the reassuring weight of the MP-446 Viking. In front of her Magpie raised her head, looking down her nose at her the way she always did. In turn Acid hit back with a broad, ironic grin, more than aware of how manic and feral she appeared. Sometimes being a little crazy was a bonus.

"So what now?" she mouthed at her old colleague.

But Magpie remained stoic, a slight curl of the lip but hardly noticeable.

Another moment passed.

It felt to Acid like they were the only two people in the world. She took a step forward. Magpie took a step back. Keeping the distance between them, like always. Neither of them blinked. This was it, Acid told herself, as the bats woke up and began beating their leathery wings. No going back. One of them was going to die. Not here, perhaps. Not in this crowded street. But somewhere. And soon.

She flinched as Magpie slipped a bony hand inside her black silk jacket. Still unblinking she gave a curt nod, informing her she too was carrying. Not a surprise. But now they both knew. If one pulled, they both pulled. With this many civilians around it would be a total bloodbath.

Acid gripped the handle of the nine, her finger poised on the trigger. If this was how it was going to be, she was ready. People would die. Innocents. But right now everyone but Magpie Stiletto was static on the radio. She drew back a deep breath, focusing on slowing her heart rate whilst relaxing her muscles at the same time. High-pressure situations like this – where the victor was decided in a split-second – required fluidity of movement. If you were stiff, too on edge, you made mistakes. And right now, one mistake would be all it took. She exhaled. A light tremor shook her breath. Her lip quivered and she caught it between her teeth, burying it beneath a smile.

"Your move," she called over, enunciating each word before giving her hair a gentle flick. She followed this up with a wink, only brief, a mere suggestion of flirtation, but enough to rile the rancid prude.

Magpie shook her head in repulsion. "No more games," she shouted over. "You and me, we finish this."

Acid nodded, her hand still holding the gun in her bag. "I'm ready," she said, making to step forward, but before she had a chance a cluster of drunken men (early twenties, English unfortunately but weren't they always) stumbled into her and broke her focus.

"Hey," she yelled, raising her foot and shoving one of them away with it. "Watch where you're going."

The man grunted as his friends laughed and jeered – "Calm down, love" – but holding their arms up in a gesture of apology all the same.

She gave them a curt nod, *forget it*. But as she regained her focus, she saw Magpie turn and disappear down a side street.

Pulling out the 9mm she gave chase, pushing past people, zig-zagging around others and following after Magpie. Away from the main thoroughfare, the narrow street, more of a back alley really, was dark and almost deserted. Just one other person, a man, taking a piss against the back door of a taberna. Up ahead she saw Magpie leaning into a turn, ready to vanish around the next corner. Acid raised the pistol momentarily, but from this distance it would be a wasted shot and would only draw attention. Cursing herself, along with those drunken fools back there, she set off after her, pounding the dry pavement as she thundered past the pissing man and around the corner.

This next street was busier, a pedestrian walkway with a steady flow of people all heading in the same direction – towards the park, where she could hear fireworks going off. Without losing her stride, she crossed over the street to where a set of stone steps led to a raised shop-front. Leaping up the four stairs in one bound, she turned back to see over the heads of the human traffic, catching a glimpse of Magpie's black and white hair up in front as she spun around to lock eyes with her. The slow-moving crowds had lessened her lead and now the bats were screaming across Acid's consciousness, telling her, *Take the shot. End this.*

With gritted teeth she fought against the urge, instead jumping down the steps and hitting the ground at pace. All the way to the end of the street she ran, following Magpie around a bend where she found herself on a neon-lit strip populated almost exclusively by late bars and nightclubs. The atmosphere here was electric as crowds of clubbers and drinkers alike laughed and joked with one another in raised voices, straining to be heard over the twenty different genres of music drifting out from underground caverns and merging into a heavy wall of sound.

Acid hung back a moment, throwing her gaze over the revellers and spotting Magpie up ahead. She was standing outside a nightclub, talking to a man dressed in typical bouncer attire, black jeans, white shirt, huge black bomber-jacket even in this heat. She saw Acid and shot her a strange look before raising her arms to the sides to let the bouncer frisk her. Down each arm he went, down her ribcage, nothing. Somewhere along the way she'd ditched her weapon and now she was... Really? Going inside a nightclub?

What the bloody hell was she playing at?

Magpie glanced back at her again before descending a steep flight of steps where she dissolved into the darkness of the underground space. With her mouth still hanging open, Acid squinted at the sign in bright yellow neon tubing. Club Tropical. The 'T' was done out to resemble a palm tree. The last place she'd ever expect to see the tightly wound Magpie Stiletto.

So what was this? A futile attempt to escape, or a trap?

She didn't have time to work it out. With manic energy burning up her spine like a fuse wire, she side-stepped over to the closest garbage bin and shoved the Viking, along with the spare magazine, on top of a mound of food wrappers. Then, with her chest out and a huge smile ironing out her furrowed brow, she skipped over to the entrance.

"Can I come in?" she asked, breezily.

The bouncer looked her up and down with no hint of friendliness. "B*razos*," he growled, raising his own arms to show her.

"Oh, sure," she trilled, assuming the position. "But you don't have to worry, I'm no danger."

"*Bolso*." He nodded at the bag and she handed it over.

While he scowled at the contents for a moment, she cast her attention down the stairwell leading into the club. The steps and walls were painted bright red with three mirrored panels bolted together on the roof. It was these little touches, along with the neon palm tree and the sticky handrail, that told her it was a real classy joint.

"Is fine," the bouncer growled. He shoved the bag at her and stepped aside, already more interested in a group of boisterous young men standing behind her.

"Good luck, boys," Acid muttered to herself, as she hurried down the steps. At the door of the club she paused to get her head back in the game. Whether she was walking into a trap or Magpie really was running scared, the same guidance was true – she had to be focused and she had to be ready. There was no room for mistakes. Magpie was a dangerous woman, and they were playing for keeps. Acid rolled her shoulders back, leaned into the heavy door and entered the club.

THIRTY-SIX

THE HOT STUFFY AIR HIT HER FULL IN THE FACE AS SHE LET THE door swing shut behind her. In front of her was a corridor, with a coat attendant to her left and an illuminated hatch in the wall to her right. Another bouncer, friendlier than the one outside but only relatively, gestured for her to move towards the hatch where she was confronted with a blue-haired girl wearing a skin-tight silver top and a fake smile.

"Hello," she sang. "Is thirty euros."

"Woah, thirty, okay." Acid reached into the bag and found the roll of notes, peeling off a ten and a twenty and handing them over.

"You want to put bag in locker?" the girl asked, taking the money.

She shook her head. "No, I'll keep it with me. Is that okay?"

The girl replied with a brief shrug as she bopped her head to the music coming from the main room. Electronic dance music. The sort Danny liked. The sort Acid hated.

She offered up the back of her fist for the girl to stamp and nodded thanks before sashaying along the corridor. It opened out into a circular dancefloor which took up most of the room. High tables had been placed at intervals with chairs around their circumference, whilst a long and curved bar took up a quarter of the back wall. Next to this was what some might call a 'chill-out area' comprising of six booths underneath a mezzanine level that jutted out over the edge of the dancefloor.

It being early for this sort of thing, the club was only a fraction full, but Magpie was nowhere in sight. Acid prowled around the edge of the dancefloor, scanning her gaze around the faces. Her heightened senses were on overdrive, but in the dinginess of the basement club her vision was skewed. A growing fog of dry ice pumping out from hidden units in the walls didn't help. Half a circuit of the club and she found herself at the bar eyeing the extensive array of liquor on the back wall.

No. Not a good idea.

Except over by the entrance she clocked the bouncer, watching her with a curious expression on his face. That settled it then. Whether you were the hunter or the one being hunted, it was important to blend into your environment. The only problem was, right now Acid had no idea which of those two positions she inhabited. *Hunter or hunted.* If she knew she could act accordingly rather than feeling out of step, unbalanced. But perhaps that was exactly what Magpie was hoping for.

Shit.

She was overthinking it again. Second-guessing herself. It wasn't like her, and it certainly was not a good head space to be in currently. Magpie Stiletto was getting to her.

And maybe *that* was exactly what she was hoping for.

She rested one arm on the bar top, keeping side-on to the room. Next to her a group of giggling girls wearing skimpy dresses were necking back a row of bright blue shots. Ignoring them she leaned over the bar as a swarthy young barman spotted her and walked over.

"Please?" He had big expressive eyes and his thick shiny hair was pulled back into a ponytail.

"If I order a spirit, will it come in an actual glass?" she asked.

The man – a boy, really – tilted his head to one side, demonstrating with an over-the-top expression he was confused.

She sighed. "What glasses do you use for the whisky?"

Still frowning, the man picked up a bright pink beaker made of plastic. "You want whisky and coke?"

Acid baulked at the sight. "God no. I'll have a beer. Please. *Cerveza, gracias.*"

With a big smile (bright blue teeth under the UV lights), he spun around and returned almost instantly with a bottle of Mahou. He placed it down in front of her and made a show of opening it with a bottle opener attached to his belt by a piece of elastic. "Ten euro," he told her.

Biting her tongue, she pulled out another ten note. "Here you go," she told him, before scrabbling around in the bottom of the bag and retrieving a handful of coins. "And here. For you."

The man smiled again, scooping up the change and taking it to the till. Acid took a long swig of the beer. It was ice cold and incredibly welcome. But she wasn't here to have fun.

Holding the drink down by her side but keeping her arm tense, ready to employ the glass bottle as a weapon if needed, she moved away from the bar. By the entrance she clocked the three men who'd arrived just behind her. They were standing by the door and taking in the club with greedy eyes. Yet as Acid watched, she also noticed a certain stiffness in the way they held themselves that belied the cocksure attitude on show. They were young bucks. Harmless enough. And wasn't everyone wearing a mask of some kind? Some were just easier to spot than others.

She carried on around the club, drifting past the chill-out area, seeing most of the booths were already inhabited by young loved-up couples, some already engaged in high-energy kissing sessions. Others laughed and joked together, their eyes fixed only on each other. Then as she circled around one of the large round pillars that supported the upper level, she saw her. Only a glimpse at first, her head just visible over the top of the booth's high-backed, red leather seat. But it was her all right. Magpie Stiletto. Sister Death.

Acid froze as a million possibilities flew through her mind. To underestimate Magpie now would be dangerous, but fate had brought them here and she was curious. Sometimes the only way out was through. Besides, neither of them were armed, and even if they were, killing someone in a crowded club, having to pass by two huge bouncers to use the only available exit, it was reckless at best.

"Is this seat free?" she asked, appearing at the side of the booth. The club's acoustics had been cleverly designed so the music was muted here in the seated area, but she still had to raise her voice.

Magpie didn't flinch. Only turning her head slightly to take in Acid, with that same old wicked sneer tainting her lips. "Be my guest."

After a brief glance at the exit, mentally rehearsing her escape route, Acid slid into the booth to face her old colleague.

They stared at each other without speaking, like they had done earlier in the street. As though winning a staring contest would be all it took.

"You look well," Acid started, giving it as much sarcasm as she could muster, nodding at Magpie's gaunt appearance and dry straggly hair.

Magpie let out a throaty, humourless laugh. "Looks were always so important to you, weren't they?"

"Costs nothing to take pride in your appearance, sweetie."

Magpie raised her head a touch. "It costs everything. This desire for attention from anyone who'll give it, it is detrimental to the soul."

Acid took a swig of beer. This was new. Magpie had always been spiteful and nasty with her words, especially those directed at Acid, but she never sounded so pious and... well, creepy.

"I think we both gave up our souls a long time ago," she replied. "But, hey, thanks for the tip."

"Always joking. So tragic." Magpie sat back in her seat, placing both hands flat on the table in front of her. With her stiff, slender neck and sinister but deadpan expression, she had a look of the Sphynx about her. She glared at Acid. "You want me dead, I take it. That's why you are still in Spain. Why you were at the convent."

Acid took another gulp of beer. The bottle was almost empty. "You always were rather astute."

"I'm paid to be. But tell me, what are you paid for these days, Acid? What is your role here?" She sat forward, slapping her hands against the table. "I knew you were trouble the moment we met. So full of ego and confidence you were. Then, as time went on, and your skillset grew I thought maybe I'd been wrong about you. But no. Here you are, a pathetic, broken wretch, unsure of who she is, of what she is. You think you scare me? At all? You do not."

"I see." Acid ran her tongue along the inside of her cheek. Couldn't let her see she was getting to her. "And what about the game of dress up you've been engaging in recently? Is that who you are? A new calling?"

"Not a new one. Sister Death is simply another part of me. Always there. But risen to the surface recently. She is a stronger, better person." Her tone changed, from deep and threatening to sounding almost affable. "I almost became a nun once. Did you know this?"

"Is that so? Wow." She held her nerve, keeping one hand on the bottle, one eye on the door. "A life with God, hey? Isn't that a little at odds with... you know, all the killing you've been doing the last twenty years?"

"Not so," Magpie spat. "When we rid the world of filth and sinners, are we not doing His work? Tell me, do you believe those you have killed deserved to die?"

The question almost floored Acid. Because it was true. She'd always told herself as much. It had been a way of justifying what she did so she could sleep at nights, but it was still true, the large majority of her kills had indeed been total shits of the highest order. Corrupt, despicable people who the world was much better off without.

"I take it from your lack of response that you agree," Magpie went on. "But this idea of *Sister Death*, it goes much deeper."

Acid leaned forward as the music grew louder. The club was filling up fast and it would be easy now to disappear into the throng. Could she do this? Finish it here and now. Another name off her kill list. The penultimate one. She ran her fingers down the slender neck of the beer bottle. The bats were united, wings smashing against her frayed nerves.

Take the bottle. Smash it off the table.
Into the bitch's throat.

"You have heard of St Francis of Assisi?" Magpie asked.

"I recognise the name. Friend of yours?"

"You jest, but you are not far wrong, Acid. St Francis was a clever and spiritual man who in his later life decided to make a friend of Death. Sister Death became a part of his life, not something to fear but to simply accept. By doing so he freed himself from his human frailties. This is what I do now. Who I am." She spat the words out, her manner growing in intensity and rage as she went. "Death is not my enemy but a part of me. I do not fear it. Every day I am ready for it. So let me ask you this, Acid, are you ready? I remember a time when you feared nothing and had an almost nihilistic view of life. Is that still true? Do you still not care? Have you made Death part of your family?"

Acid listened without reaction, but a sense of unease prickled up her spine. This despite the bats screeching for blood. "I don't have any family left," she rasped. "You killed my mother, remember?"

"You and this pathetic vendetta. Don't you see, no one is to blame for this but you? You brought death to your mother's door, Acid. It was your actions that killed her." She sat back, sliding her hands off the table and letting them fall onto her lap.

Acid swallowed and nodded sagely as a dull pain bore into her temples – the tension of remaining outwardly calm whilst inside a heavyweight cocktail of rage and desolation threatened to envelop her. Problem was, most of this anger was aimed at herself. Magpie was right. Her mum was dead because she'd fucked up. And here she was still doing it.

"I'm going to kill you," Acid snarled through gritted teeth.

"So do it."

Out of the corner of her eye she noticed the three men from earlier. On the prowl now and heading their way, with plastic pint glasses held proudly in front of their puffed-out chests.

"*Hola, señoritas,*" the smallest of the three growled, but with a clear London accent. "You okay?" He stopped next to their table, smiling, and nodding at them to respond.

Acid kept her eyes on Magpie as she addressed him. "Get lost."

"*Excusez-moi?*" he exclaimed, slipping into pidgin French. "You hear this lads? Got a feisty one here."

Magpie's eyes narrowed. "You see," she hissed. "These are the kind of people you attract. Immoral oafs. No better than rats."

"Woah, she knows you well, mate." The men laughed with each other, but there was an uneasiness to them now. She'd rattled them.

"Run along, boys," Acid followed up. "I mean it. You've picked the wrong table here." The men hesitated, unsure if she was joking. She looked up at them, proving with her wide, manic eyes that she was deadly serious. "Go away."

She glared at them, not blinking, until they turned and shuffled off towards an empty booth a few feet away. She shook her head, about to say something when she felt a burning pain in the front of her thigh.

"What the hell?"

Her hand went to the source, itchy now, but as she touched her leg she realised it was numb. Completely numb. And the numbness was spreading. Fast. The other leg now. Her arms too. She felt nauseous. Dizzy. The room was spinning.

"No," she gasped. "You didn't…" Her tongue felt loose, like it didn't belong to her. She looked around, trying to get someone's – anyone's – attention. But no one was even looking in their direction.

"Don't fight it," Magpie told her, rising from her seat and moving around next to her.

Acid strained at her throat. "Bi… fu… nnng…"

She fell back against the seat, unable to keep her head upright. The last sight she saw before she blacked out was the harsh face of Sister Death leering down at her and cackling the shrill laugh of nightmares.

THIRTY-SEVEN

AN INTENSE FORCE SHOT THROUGH HER BODY, ROUSING HER awareness, but not so much she knew where she was. Or what was happening. She fluttered her eyelids, tried to keep them open, but all she could make out was a swirling fog of nothingness. The shaking went again, rattling her teeth and bones as her muscles contracted and her consciousness spread.

She'd been in that club.

And she'd passed out.

Was this one of the bouncers, shaking her awake?

Another jolt rocked her body, but now with her growing cognizance came a deeper pain that took her breath away. The pain originated in her legs and travelled up to her heart before bursting out through every pore. She groaned, hearing her voice as though coming from another room. As the next jarring shake arrived she instinctively went to cross her arms over her chest. To protect herself.

Only she couldn't.

What the…?

She forced her right eye open, seeing her arm splayed out to the side of her. A heavy leather cuff was fastened around her wrist and this in turn was fastened to a thick chain connected to the ceiling. She tried to make a fist but her hand hardly moved. She rolled her head to the other arm. Same story.

Another jolt forced her fully awake and the agonising pain that followed close behind had her screaming into the room.

"She lives," a voice bellowed from behind her. It was deep and throaty, with the hint of an accent. "I thought I may have made an error with the dosage. That would have been a real shame."

Panting, exhausted already, Acid raised her head and scanned her eyes around her. She was in a featureless room about fifteen feet square with yellowing walls. An open doorway stood in the corner with only darkness beyond it. On the wall directly opposite her hung a huge mirror in an embossed gold frame and to her left was a small metal table with raised sides, the kind you might find in an operating theatre. Above her a solitary, shadeless bulb hung from the ceiling, casting deep shadows down her face as she lolled her head back to take in her reflection.

Well, she'd certainly looked better. Her leggings and shoes had been removed and strands of lank hair stuck to her swollen, bleeding face. And there was the source of the pain. Magpie had attached jump leads to her ankles, their sharp metal teeth pulling and tearing at her skin. She traced the thick red and black cables along the floor to a small black box with meters and dials on its side. One hell of an alarm clock.

"Do you know why you are here?" Magpie Stiletto asked, moving into view.

Acid took her in, lost for words for once. The crazy bitch had ditched the silk jacket in favour of full nun's habit, including coif, wimple and veil. It would have been funny if she didn't feel like she was going to throw up.

"Do you know why you are here, Acid Vanilla?" she asked again, with an intense shrillness.

"In this room?"

"In Spain."

She swallowed. Her throat was dry and it hurt to speak. "I'm here for The Dullahan," she croaked. "For Danny."

"No!" Magpie yelled into her face. "You're here because I brought you here."

Huh?

"Did you really think I didn't know who the mark was, who his uncle was? I knew the old fool would send you to the rescue. It's the only reason I took the job. Why I spared the mark's life until you arrived in Donastia." She sat back. "He was nothing to me but bait."

Acid nodded weakly. It was all she could do. "So, what? You're going to kill me?"

Magpie wheeled the metal table closer so she could see the assortment of torture devices laid out on top – knives, bone saws, gauging devices, plus an electric drill and what looked like a hand-held jigsaw. Acid closed her eyes.

"Where is the USB drive?" Magpie asked. "The egg?"

She opened her eyes a fraction. "I thought it was me you were interested in."

"I'm interested in the money Delgado is paying me to retrieve his possessions." She picked up a surgical scalpel and held it up in the light, eyeing it greedily. "Money is important now more than ever since you ruined everything." With a swish of her habit she lunged at Acid, thumping a sharp fist into her stomach which left her winded. Before she had a chance to catch her breath Magpie had her hand around her jaw and was pressing the cold steel of the scalpel against her cheekbone. "Being taken on as an operative at Annihilation Pest Control changed my life. For the first time I had real purpose. Significance. I'd found people who truly understood me. It was a place I could work on my craft whilst learning from the best."

"You should have said," Acid rasped, both eyes on the scalpel. "I'd have shown you the ropes."

"*Imbécil!* You were never the best." Sour spittle hit Acid in the face, accompanied by a sharp burning pain as Magpie slashed her cheek open. "I was the best. I am the best." She stepped back. "And you took it from me. Because of you the organisation is in ruins. Caesar has fled. Maybe never to return. You have taken everything from me."

Acid raised her head. She was starting to feel her body again, the numbness leaving her system. Whether that was a good thing or not, she wasn't sure. She pulled at the chains but they were fastened tight.

"Did you think I was going to let you get away with what you did?"

"Not this again."

Magpie placed the scalpel down and picked up a wooden-handled gauging spike about half an inch long. "Our message was clear, was it not?"

"I guess not."

"You betrayed your work, helping a mark to escape like you did. It almost took down the organisation. Everything we'd all worked so hard for. Surely even you can see you had to pay for your mistake?"

"Yes, me. Not my mother. Not her."

"She was, how they say, collateral damage."

Acid gnashed her teeth, rattling the chains overhead. "Bitch. I'll kill you. I swear it. I'm going to fucking kill you... Argg—"

A sharp pain in her side splintered through her abdomen as Magpie pierced her flesh with the gauging spike. Not deep enough to hit any major organs but enough to tear through layers of skin and muscle. Enough to leave her riling and weakened.

"Where is the egg?"

"I don't have it."

She struck again, another spear to the side, ripping the spike away as Acid stiffened, fighting the pain. "Tell me."

"You'll kill me if I do."

Magpie stood facing her, eyes wild with energy. "I'm going to kill you either way. So choose. One path is quick, relatively painless, but the other... well..." She lifted the gauging spike up to her face. "It will take time. A long time."

Acid lifted her head, moving away from the weapon as much as her constraints allowed. "Lingchi."

Magpie nodded. "Death by a thousand cuts."

The technique, originating in ninth-century China, had always been one of Magpie's specialities. It was a brutal and protracted way of killing someone, but it sent a clear message, and the more notorious and sadistic of Annihilation's clients liked that sort of thing. Acid remembered Caesar explaining to her – with some degree of veneration – how his new recruit had picked up the practice working for the cartels. At the time she'd thought the stories were bullshit, told by Magpie to make her sound more deadly than she actually was. But maybe not.

"What happens then?" she asked. "If you kill me. What then?"

Magpie frowned. "Then I find the mark and retrieve the items for my client, what else? So please, don't tell me where they are. Choose the path of penance. Perfect for a sinner such as you."

"You still want Danny? I thought you only used him as bait."

"It was, how you say, two birds with one stone. I got you where I want you, yes. But I took the job so I will complete it."

"For money? Isn't that a sin?" Acid yanked some more at the chains, testing the strength of them, lifting her feet a little off the ground.

Magpie watched, laughing derisively. "The love of money is a sin. For me it is simply a tool. And I care a great deal about my reputation." She sneered. "But I understand now. You see, I saw you together. Writhing naked, like disgusting animals. I always knew you were a loose-moralled *puta* who couldn't keep her legs together, but you actually have feelings for the mark."

Acid shot her a look, the numbed helplessness she'd experienced since waking switching to an intense rage. "This is about Spitfire, isn't it? I saw the way you used to look at him."

Magpie sneered again, but under the folds of the wimple headdress Acid noticed her eyebrow twitch.

"What can I say, Mags. He wanted me, what could I do? And shit, was it good. *Reeeally* fucking good."

"Stop." Another swift lunge with the spike, getting her in almost the same wound as before.

"Nnnggg." The pain was extreme and she had to fight to stop herself from blacking out. She snarled at her attacker like a wild animal. "Fuck you."

"You should calm down, Acid. Conserve your energy. It's going to be a long night for you." She moved around the side of her, stabbing deftly and fluidly with the spike, puncturing her flank and upper thigh as she went.

All Acid could do was squirm away, screaming with each tear of her flesh, the sound coming from a space deep inside of her.

Satisfied with her work, Magpie stepped around the front to take her in. Acid's bare legs were almost crimson with blood as it dripped down her body and pooled at her feet.

"I'm going to kill you," she whispered, her eyelids heavy. "I'm going to— ARGG!" A sharp pain shot through her as Magpie tore the spike through the thin skin of her underarm. "You rotten bitch. I'll— Shit!"

More pain.

The spike stabbing into her back. Her shoulders. The tops of her arms.

"I swear… I'll kill…"

"Shut your foul hole," Magpie spat. "You're embarrassing yourself. I hate to see it."

Fighting through the pain and dizziness, Acid murmured, "For my mother. For me. You will die. You will fucking die…"

"Stop!" Magpie screeched into her face. "You pathetic iniquitous dog. You don't talk to me anymore." She marched back to the metal table and threw down the gouging spike. A quick perusal of the implements and she selected the scalpel once more. "Maybe I'll cut out your tongue. Shut your wicked mouth once and for all."

"Try it," Acid muttered, as the fluttering onslaught of a million invisible wings beat against her mindset.

The bats were arriving in force.

Now alongside the pain and panic she felt a resourceful, shimmering energy that was at once overwhelming but also empowering. Like a full body orgasm only more potent and driven only by hate. Her limbs and chest tingled with a manic vigour.

She lifted her head as Magpie stepped forward, scalpel gripped in her bony fist. But before she had chance to strike, Acid took her weight onto her arms and lifted herself off the ground. Summoning all her strength (and with memories of her gymnastic training flooding back to her), she kicked out violently with both feet, catching Magpie in the face and sending her toppling backwards into the mirror.

"Go to hell, you crazy fucking bitch." Her voice was back, strong in her throat and with a rancorous fury sharpening each consonant.

"*Perro estúpido,*" Magpie squawked, getting to her feet and launching herself at her.

Acid leaned back on the chains ready for another go, but as she raised herself up a dark presence swooped across her eyeline, launching at Magpie, grabbing her around the waist and sending them both crashing into the wall. Before the screeching nun knew what was happening, the figure dressed in a black hoodie had smashed her head into the concrete, knocking her out cold.

Acid stared open-mouthed as her shadowy saviour got to their feet and turned around.

"You all right, love?" Danny gasped, lowering the hood and wiping a hand across his mouth. "I wondered if you might need a little help."

THIRTY-EIGHT

DESPITE WHAT SOME PEOPLE MIGHT THINK, DANNY FLYNN wasn't stupid. And he wasn't blind or deaf either. He knew how most people viewed him. The cheeky chappie, the carefree charmer, the loveable Irish rogue – he'd heard them all, but usually did little to dissuade any cliched assumptions. Why would he? He knew from experience, whenever people underestimated you it gave you an advantage over them.

Because whilst all these traits were genuine (charming, loveable – absolutely), they were only a small aspect of his persona. And when it came down to it, Danny Flynn could be as mean and crafty as the best of them. Hell, he wouldn't have lasted two minutes amongst the villains and charlatans with whom he often associated otherwise. And whilst he preferred the role of the charmer, he was still his father's son, still his uncle's nephew. Fierce Irish blood pumped through his veins.

It was this fiery spirit that had compelled him to follow the mad nun as she'd headed towards town an hour earlier. He'd taken it steady, staying a safe distance away but keeping her in his sights as she cut down backstreets and weaved her way across crowded squares. He'd been witness to her silent showdown with Acid, seen the two women going into the nightclub. He'd even tried to follow them until a gruff bouncer grabbed him and told him in no uncertain terms that he wasn't welcome. As it transpired, a recent conquest of Danny's was a good friend of the bouncer's and he'd seen her with Danny a week or so earlier. It wasn't clear whether the bouncer was sweet on this girl himself or just pissed off with Danny for ghosting her after promising the world, but his position was clear – he was not letting him in the club.

Knowing better than to argue, he'd moved to the taberna opposite to wait with one eye on the exit. It was there where he'd seen Magpie emerge from the basement club dragging an almost paralytic Acid alongside her before scrambling into the back of a waiting taxi.

That same fecking bouncer had even helped her.

After grabbing up his holdall he'd jumped in the next available cab, yelling for the driver to step on it (*"Rápido, por favor"*) as they pursued Magpie and Acid across the city until they pulled up outside a derelict butcher's shop, *la carnicería*, on the outskirts. He'd paid for the ride and asked the driver to wait for him, telling him there was another hundred euros in it if he did. Then with the sound of muffled screams drifting up into the warm Spanish night, he'd made his way down to the basement of the old butcher's shop, unsure what he was going to find and not daring to even breathe.

"Danny," Acid murmured now, watching him through heavy-lidded eyes as he got to his feet. "You were here... this whole time?"

"Sort of," he replied, rooting through the array of sharp instruments on the table, hoping to find a key for her restraints. "I've been waiting outside in the corridor there, biding my time, so to speak." He located a small silver key and hurried over to release her.

"Danny…" she gasped.

"It's all right, I'm here." He unfastened the cuff around her right wrist and lowered her arm limply to her side. She was a real mess. Blood poured from the open wounds. "I'm sorry I didn't jump in sooner. I had to wait until I saw an opening, then I went for it."

Acid's head rolled back as he unlocked the other cuff. She was fighting to stay conscious. "But… she's…"

Danny had the key in the lock ready to turn it when he heard the sound of scraping metal behind. He spun around just in time to grab the mad nun's wrist as she brought a scalpel down inches from his face.

"*Imbécil*," she screeched, her rancid breath hot on his cheek. "*Te mataré.*"

She lunged forward and smashed the heel of her hand into his nose.

"Feck!"

The punch blurred his vision but the angle meant she hadn't put much force behind it. He was still in the game. Twisting her wrist to the side, he made her drop the scalpel before he stepped forward and a driving headbutt found its mark on the bridge of her nose.

"Mother of…." he yelled out, the impact sending them both staggering backwards.

He shook the pain away as Magpie grabbed a large serrated knife from the metal table and swung it towards him. He managed to jump to the side, parrying and dodging the blade as it whistled close to his face.

"*Te mataré*," she screamed. "*Te mataré, te mataré.* I will kill you like I killed that tight-lipped old fool."

She sprang forward and Danny leapt back, his heart in his throat. "What ya talking about?"

Knife poised in her hand, a wry smirk pulled the crazy

woman's lips to one side, sending a shiver down his spine. It was the same look he'd seen on her earlier outside the apartment. Pure evil.

"She died because of you, Danny." She lunged forward with the blade, slicing it down his forearm, enough to break the skin.

"Who? Who died?" he said louder. And when she laughed, he shouted, "Who, ya fecking bitch?"

Her eyes shone. She jabbed with the knife, taunting him. "Such a shame that she put so much faith in you. That she couldn't see you for what you really are." Her lip curled in disgust. "She protected you to the end, la estúpida mujer."

Danny's legs weakened, he dropped back against the wall. "Camila…"

"What a waste of a life, protecting someone like you. In her naivety, she would say nothing that might harm you. You, un bastardo sin valor." She spat at his feet. But he did nothing. Only tried to comprehend what she was saying and if he could believe her. If he could believe anyone would be that cruel. "She said even less when I cut out her tongue. And slit her throat—"

Danny barged into her, slamming a sharp elbow into her neck. Not giving her a second to recover, he administered a heavy right hook, connecting with her nose and sending blood and snot splattering up the wall. Magpie staggered against the wall and dropped to one knee, like a fallen boxer defying the count. A glance over at Acid. She was still drifting in and out of consciousness but he could tell she was fighting it. He moved over to her and began working desperately on the last wrist cuff as the crazed nun reeled onto her feet.

"Kill her," Acid wheezed. "Leave me. Just… do it."

But he couldn't leave her.

He wouldn't.

Still struggling with the cuff he dragged Acid to one side, away from the large knife flying their way. It was no good, his fingers were sticky with blood and his hands too shaky to even get the key in the lock. Acid opened her eyes and snarled his name. A second later he felt a heavy pain across his shoulders, like someone had hit him with a brick.

"Shite."

Reaching back he felt something hard and metallic lodged into his trapezium muscle. Without a second thought he yanked out the weapon (a blade about six inches long, like an evil serrated machete) and flung it defiantly at the mad nun. The knife clattered to the floor a few feet from her as she made for the door.

No. Not a chance. This ends now.

With legs like jelly, but full of more piss and vinegar than he'd ever experienced, Danny pounced on the vile assassin. He got his arms around her waist, throwing his full weight against her as they sprawled into the metal table sending the contents spilling noisily over the concrete floor. They landed with Danny on his back, Magpie on top of him. He tightened his hold on her but a swift elbow to the face followed by sharp nails in the open wound on his arm released his grip. As she scrambled to her feet his fingers found the wooden handle of a small blade and he grabbed it up, slashing wildly but only managing to slice through the material folds of her nun's costume. With a guttural war cry she stamped backwards, landing a heavy foot on the side of his jaw that left him dazed and reeling.

"Danny," a voice cried through the red haze. "Look out."

Punch-drunk and bleary-eyed, he couldn't even get to his knees before another stamping kick sent him tumbling over himself.

"She's getting away. Danny!"

He opened his eyes as wide as they'd go in an attempt to stop the room from spinning, seeing Acid grabbing the nun's robes with her one good hand but unable to hold on. He staggered to his feet, using the wall to steady himself. But by the time he'd regained his bearings she was gone.

"Go after her!" Acid yelled, fully conscious now. "We can't let her get away."

But Danny shook his head. "I can't," he gasped. "Can't leave you… Can't catch her."

He slumped against the wall, defeated. His legs were shaking and it felt like his heart might explode. Acid glared at him, blood seeping from the tiny wounds all over her body.

She was in a bad way.

So was he.

This was the right move, he told himself, as he slid to the floor and retched up a mouthful of stomach acid and beer.

"Sorry," he gasped.

Because he knew, even if he conjured the energy to chase after her, and by some amazing feat caught up with her, what then? He was a big guy, sure, and he could handle himself. But she'd caught him on his damned glass jaw, and right now he was a mess of quivering legs and a fuzzy mindset. If she hadn't have legged it just now, she'd have killed him. And the thought of that only made him want to throw up again.

THIRTY-NINE

A<small>CID'S FACE WAS NUMB AND HER LIPS FAT AND SWOLLEN, BUT IT</small> didn't stop her chastising the pathetic Irishman as he made a big show of getting to his feet and staggering zombie-like towards her.

"Are you bloody well joking?" she snapped. "You had her. Why didn't you jump on her, hold her down, anything?"

All Danny could do was shake his head forlornly. "I don't know what happened," he muttered, as he clocked her fierce expression through glassy eyes. "She blindsided me. Knocked all the focus out of me. I'm sorry, I'm a fecking idiot. What she said about Camila…"

"Camila?" she asked, watching him as he shoved the tiny key into the remaining cuff lock, closing one eye and grabbing her arm to steady himself. His hand shook, fingers slipped off the key and he swore.

"My landlady. Of the room I was renting up until a couple of days ago." He looked up at her. "She wouldn't really have… Would she?"

Acid didn't answer. But he took what he saw in her face,

swallowed hard, nodded once and reaffirmed his grip on the key.

"Well I couldn't leave ya, could I?" he said, unlocking the cuff and releasing her. "What if I'd have... If she'd... Ya know. You'd be tied up here for who knows how long. Bleeding out—"

"I'd have been okay."

"Would ya?" he snapped, then dropped his gaze away.

She hobbled over to the mirror to better examine her injuries. As well as her bust nose and cut cheek there were around twenty puncture wounds in total. Some of them had already clotted but not all and they would require attention. As the adrenaline and sedatives left her system, they were also starting to hurt like hell. She wanted to shout. To smash something. To scream the scream of a million bats.

How the hell had this happened?

She'd had Magpie in her sights and she'd screwed it up.

Again.

She'd hesitated.

Again.

Maybe her old adversary was correct. She'd lost it. Nothing but a pathetic joke. An insult not only to her years of training and discipline but to herself, and her mother most of all. Poor, innocent Louisa Vandella. She'd had the chance to avenge her death. To do what she'd been longing to do. And she'd failed.

Again.

She got up close to the mirror, her breath steaming the glass as she stared into her own eyes, her mind drifting to that famous Nietzsche quote. *If thou gaze long into an abyss, the abyss will also gaze into thee.*

She sneered at her reflection.

She who fights with monsters... and all that jazz.

"What now?" Danny asked, joining her at the mirror and speaking to her by way of his reflection.

"Not entirely sure. Do you think the apartment has been compromised?"

"I know it has," he replied. "She was there. Luckily I saw her before she arrived and jumped out the window. Hurt my leg actually, which was another reason why I couldn't—"

"Wait." She held her hand up. "She was there? So has the egg, the USB?"

"Ah no," he replied. "I did have the foresight to bring my bag when I left. I… Oh no… Oh shite on a bike, no."

Before she could quiz him further he was out the door and had disappeared into the gloom of the corridor beyond. She was about to follow him when she heard a noise. It sounded like the last pitiful wails of a dying animal.

"Danny," she said sternly. "Don't tell me she…"

He put his head around the doorway and his expression said it all. "I'd left it outside the door here. She's taken it."

"And what was inside?"

He looked down. "Everything. The egg, the USB, money. My passport."

"Oh for heaven's sake." She made for the door but stumbled as her legs gave way beneath her. The trauma caused by Magpie's sordid torture session, coupled with the tranquilisers, had drained all the lifeforce out of her. She hadn't felt this damaged in a long time.

"Here, let me help." Danny shoved his head under her arm, supporting her as they shuffled along the corridor and out of the building. She didn't even have the strength to resist. And as the bats screeched across her soul, a heavy existential weakness overcame her. She hadn't felt this vulnerable in a long time, either.

They got to the steps, where Danny reached down and

gathered up a piece of black cloth, part of Magpie's habit tossed away whilst fleeing the scene. "Here, wrap this around yourself."

"I don't need it," she mumbled. "I'm not cold."

"Yeah, well it's not for your benefit," he said, brushing her hair forward, covering the cut on her cheek. "We both look enough of a state without all the blood."

She gazed up at him, her head spinning some more as she did. "What do you mean?"

───

TEN MINUTES LATER AND SHE UNDERSTOOD, SAT IN THE BACK OF the taxi as the driver, pleased with the extra hundred euros coming his way, sped through the night streets. She rolled her head to one side to take in the plucky Irishman who was sitting forward in his seat, pensive for the first time since they'd met. At least he appeared to be taking the situation seriously for once.

"Where are we going?" she whispered.

Danny glanced at her, then back at the road. "The apartment." He held his hand up. "I know, I know, it's been compromised, but we don't have any other options. My guess – my hope – is she'll stay dark, for a day at least. Lick her wounds, so to speak. Besides, I just gave yer man here my last hundred euros."

"You have more at the apartment?"

"I'm hoping so, if she didn't find my stash. Plus we need to get you patched up. We've got work to do."

She let out a bitter huff. "Come on. It's over. We both know it. You don't know Magpie, don't know what she's like. She's not the type to lick her wounds, for Christ's sake."

He moved his head from side to side. "Mmm, reckon I've got a pretty good idea what she's like."

She was about to respond when a deep cough erupted from out of nowhere, hacking at her insides and leaving her feeling weaker still. Danny was right about one thing, she needed patching up. Even if all she was doing in the next forty-eight hours was catching a plane home (something she was adamant would be the case), she needed her wounds attending to. And then some rest.

She closed her eyes, leaning into Danny as the taxi took a sharp corner. "Hope, hope, hope," she muttered into the darkness. "You shouldn't live on hope, Danny. That's what gets you killed. *Prolongs the torments of man.*"

He sniffed. "Quoting Nietzsche now? Shite. Things must be bad." One eye flickered open to see him peering down at her. "Oh, you're surprised I knew?"

"A little. Impressed, mainly."

"I am Irish, remember. We do know a thing or two about bleak existentialism. I've read Nietzsche. Beckett too, and Ulysses – well, most of it. I'm not just a pretty face and a wily art dealer, ya know."

Acid patted him on the thigh, smiling to herself despite the pain. "Who said you had a pretty face?"

FORTY

BACK AT THE FLAT ACID STRIPPED OUT OF HER REMAINING clothes and headed straight for the bathroom. Not pausing to look at herself in the mirror, she leaned into the shower unit and twisted it into the red.

"Can I help?" Danny called through from the bedroom as she peered around the bathroom door.

"I'm going to clean myself up. Then once you've done the same, we can dress these wounds." She nodded at his arm. It had stopped bleeding. "How are you feeling?"

He looked glum, his usual cheekiness gone. "It looks worse than it is. I think. I'm just angry at myself, so I am. This stupid glass jaw of mine. Ya know, I could have been a great cruiserweight if only—"

"Danny," she snapped. "Enough. It's fine. But we need some supplies. If you're feeling up to it, can you go to the shop while I'm in the shower?"

"Aye, I think there's an all-night store a few blocks away." He looked up, eyes wide and fearful. "But what if she comes back?"

"What if? We need things. Surgical tape. Bandages.

Anything you can get. Plus get some bananas, peanut butter and chocolate milk, if you can."

"Sure thing, Elvis. Want some ice cream as well?"

She sighed. Her glycogen levels had depleted so much she didn't even have the energy to pretend-laugh. "Just go," she told him, before moving back into the bathroom and closing the door.

Stepping under the shower she huffed with the pain. The water was almost too hot and as it ran down her body, rinsing out the puncture wound and slashes, her entire being chimed with an intense agony. But it also felt good. She relished the feeling – upset when a few minutes later the pain began to subside – because at least she felt something. Her heart, her head, they were just numb. A crushing sense that something should be there, but it was missing.

"Sorry, Mum," she whispered as she put her head under the shower, watching the red foamy water swirl around her feet.

She stayed there with her forehead pressed against the tiled wall until she heard the front door being unlocked and someone entering the apartment. Danny, most likely, back with the supplies. But if it was Magpie here to finish the job, then so be it. She wouldn't resist. How could she?

She turned off the shower as she heard his brusque Irish brogue filtering through from the kitchen. "Couldn't get chocolate milk," he called. "But I got some normal stuff. And some protein bars. For energy."

Ignoring him, she remained in the shower cubicle a few minutes longer as the water dripped from her, then she stepped out and stood in front of the mirror, wiping the steam away with the palm of her hand. Her wounds looked even worse now than they had done before she cleaned up – the heat puffing up the surrounding skin. But at least the blood had stemmed in most places, even the deep slashes on her underarms, although they still stung like hell.

She padded into the bedroom, still without a damn towel, and yanked a sheet from the bed, wrapping it around her as she joined Danny in the kitchen. He held up a banana for her.

"How you feeling?" he asked, as she accepted the offering.

"How do you think?"

"Bit sore, but raring to go? Ready to make a new plan? To get the eggs back?" He grinned, but it was half-baked to say the least.

Acid peeled the banana and walked through into the lounge area where she sank onto the couch. "It's over, Danny," she told him. "You know that. We lost. Our best plan – our only plan now – is get you a new passport. It'll take a day or so, but then you need to get gone. Go to Ireland or London or wherever. Keep your head down and your nose clean. Forget this sorry state of affairs ever happened."

He shook his head, and she noticed there was an annoyance to him now she'd not seen before. "No. Sorry. Can't do that, Acid. I need those eggs. I need that money. We have to get them."

"Are you fucking serious?" She was shouting now, so unlike her, pointing the banana at him like it was a weapon. "I'm done, Danny. I can't help you. I thought I could. And it's not like I don't need that money myself, because I do. But I don't have the… energy. Or the means. Or the capability any longer."

"What are ya talking about?" He sat on the edge of the couch, a frown planted across his brow.

"Back when I was working for Caesar I could do anything – would do anything – to achieve my mission. To get my mark. The reason Magpie hates me so much is everyone said I was the best. And I was, once. But not anymore. I've lost it. Lost whatever it was that used to drive me, that made me who I was."

She sat back.

Well, shit.

That was it, right there.

The realisation hit her like a claw hammer to the chest. Because Spook was right. Acid had been an assassin all her adult life and now she couldn't cope with being a civilian. It wasn't working out. She was bored, not to mention confused and unsure of how to be in this new life she was creating for herself.

And if that was the case, what did it say about her?

Spook had said she had to step out from the shadow of her past, but she saw now that was impossible. Because she was the shadow all along. And if she stepped out from that, what else did she have. Who was she?

"Acid?"

She looked up to see Danny staring at her, in a way that implied he'd been speaking to her.

"Sorry... what?"

"My plan. What d'ya think?"

She got to her feet and walked past him to the bedroom, grabbing up the bag of surgical tape and bandages from the kitchen unit as she went.

"I was saying, I've got an idea – for getting the eggs back. A good one. It could work."

Once in the bedroom she threw the bag onto the bed and placed her luggage, thankfully untouched, alongside it. "I've told you, it's over. We need to get out of Spain as soon as possible—" She stopped herself, the rest of the sentence echoing in her head... *like we should have done in the first place.* If she hadn't have been so damned stupid.

"Yeah, well I've told you. I'm not leaving without those eggs."

She turned to face him as a brittle clarity hardened her. "How the hell would we even get them back to England?"

"Ah, that's easy." He hit her with that cheeky grin of his. "I'm a professional, remember. This is what I do. I've got papers for them already printed out. Fakes, obviously, but the customs guys won't know. I've done this sort of thing many times. Like I keep telling ya, I'm not just a pretty face."

She snorted but didn't respond, turning her attention back to her luggage and rummaging about in the side pocket. "Here." She pulled out a packet of Quikclot combat gauze and a small vial of antibiotics. She popped off the top and shook two in her hand before swallowing them dry and offering the tube to Danny.

"No thanks, I'm good."

She scanned his body. "Come on, that wound on your back could get infected. Sit. I'll put some on."

He did as he was told for once, wincing as she cleaned the gash and applied the gauze. "Does it hurt?"

"A little."

"You hurt anywhere else."

"Only my heart and my pride."

"Jesus." She finished off and pushed him away. "Pass me the tape, will you?"

He crossed the room to get it and she dropped the sheet to examine her own injuries.

"Danny, what's the h…" She looked up to see him staring at her naked form. He shook his head out and offered her the tape.

"Sorry, here ya go."

"Tear me some off," she said, removing a piece of Quikclot

227

gauze from the packaging and placing it over the laceration under her arm. "Put it here and here."

OVER THE NEXT FIFTEEN MINUTES THE TWO OF THEM WORKED on dressing Acid's multiple wounds. Her instructing Danny in a curt, clinical manner, and him (thankfully for once) doing as instructed without further comment. Once finished, she grabbed a pair of clean knickers from out of her luggage and slipped them on.

"So what now?" Danny asked, looking at her in that almost coquettish way he had. Like Princess Diana with stubble. It made her want to punch him in the dick.

"I've told you already," she muttered, finding her jeans and pulling them on, grimacing as the tight denim scraped at the wounds on her thighs. "We lie low and wait for my contact to get you a new passport. Then we go home."

"But what about the eggs? What about Magpie? Don't ya want to kill her?"

She busied herself locating a fresh bra as well as the crumpled top she'd bought on her first day. "I can't. I'm sorry."

"Ya can't? Feck me. I didn't realise it was that bad. And what's this *I'm sorry* shite? Sounds weird coming from you."

"What do you mean?" she asked, as she finished dressing.

"I mean you're the most amazing woman I've ever met. Not like all the crazy chicks I usually... ya know... hang out with. You're smart, funny, fecking tough as nails. Ya don't strike me as the sort of person who apologises for anything. Ya certainly don't strike me as someone who feels sorry for themselves."

"Yeah, well, maybe you don't know me as well as you think."

"Ah, that's just a get-out."

She spun around and was in his face in a second. "No, Danny. It isn't. My head's in bits. I feel broken, confused, and full of so much pent-up rage that all I can do is turn it inwards. Because I've failed, all right? I've failed you, I've failed The Dullahan, I've failed myself and I've failed my mum. Once I was the best and now look at me. A fucked-up mess of a person who doesn't even know if they've got it in them to kill Magpie. Or Caesar. An assassin who can't kill – what a fucking joke."

Danny swallowed, a frown narrowing his baby-blue eyes. "But you're you, aren't ya? You're Acid Vanilla."

"And who the hell is she? Because if you know, please tell me. I'm serious. All I know is Acid Vanilla is the ghost of a concept that doesn't make sense in normal society. She doesn't fit in anywhere. Don't you see? I'm nothing." She stopped, gasped for air. "You know, my real name, my birth name, is Alice Vandella. Little innocent Alice. What would she think of all this?"

"Alice. She sounds nice."

"Oh yeah, real nice. Up until she wasn't." She glared into his eyes, defying him to look away. "I grew up with a single mother who did everything and anything she could to support us. And yes, I mean anything. After all she went through for me. After all she did. To be murdered because of me… I made her a promise that day that I wouldn't let these bastards get away with it. But, oh look, I let Magpie get away and now she's in the wind. Maybe for good. Once again I've failed my mum, and you have no idea how incredibly shitty that feels. So take your positive thinking and motivational bullshit and stick it up your arse. I'm done. I can't help you. I can't help anyone."

She sank back onto the bed, exhausted, sitting with her back to him and facing the window. A moment went by. And another. She could sense Danny's eyes boring into her. The tension in the room showed no sign of abating.

"I do know how that feels," he said. So softly she hardly heard him.

"You know how what feels?"

"Letting your mum down, thinking you've failed her."

"Oh?" It wasn't the response she'd expected. She shifted along as he sat next to her on the bed, both looking out into the inky nothingness of the midnight sky.

"I haven't told ya the full story," he said with a sigh. "About the eggs, and the money, and why I need it."

He looked at her but she didn't flinch. No doubt there was more bullshit on its way, and from someone she'd almost trusted.

"Go on then," she told him. "Spill."

FORTY-ONE

DANNY PICKED AT A CALLUS ON HIS PALM WITH HIS THUMBNAIL, knowing he had to tell her the full story. No more games. They were at zero hour, the last resort, and if he didn't convince her to help him, it was all over. Literally. All of it.

"The thing is," he started. "I actually owe Petre Kaminski quite a large sum of money. Selling him the eggs was a way of covering those debts."

"How much?"

He sucked back a sharp breath. "Over six hundred thousand. I know, I know... See, we were supposed to go in together on a deal with this guy I'd met in Switzerland. Vases, made from Nazi gold. I vouched for the guy and he ended up screwing us over. Kaminski was not happy. That's why I've been in Spain the last half year. On the run." He sat upright, puffing his chest out as he did. "When I saw the Fabergé eggs it was like a moment, ya know, I saw a solution. Kaminski loves the old antiquities. I rang him and told him I'd steal them if we could come to some mutual arrangement. And now he wants those eggs. *Really* wants them. To the point if I don't get them... Well, I'm sure you can imagine."

231

"Hang on," Acid said. "You said you were sharing the profits of these eggs with me."

His hand hovered above hers. "Sure, and I will. Only, it might not be as much as I first mentioned after Kaminski has collected his debt. Plus interest. There'll still be plenty of green left over though. More than a million each for the two of us. I swear."

Acid got to her feet. "So let me get this straight. If he doesn't get the eggs, you can't pay your debt and he kills you. But by stealing the eggs, Delgado puts a price on your head. Am I missing something? Why not stay hidden, change your identity?"

"I can't stay in Spain. I need that money."

"For Antigua?"

"For my mum." She stopped pacing to look at him, but he couldn't meet her eye. "That's what I meant when I said I know how you feel. She's sick, ya see. Early onset dementia, the docs call it. It's totally shite, she's only in her fifties. I mean she's all right at present, sort of, she gets confused but she knows who I am. But it's only going to get worse."

Acid snorted and he looked up.

"My mum had the same thing," she said. "It does get worse. A lot worse."

"I see. Right." He went back to picking at the callus on his palm. "I want the best care available for her. And am happy to throw as much money at it as I can. And yes, I'd love to take her to Antigua. Let her live out her remaining time somewhere hot. Somewhere peaceful. Away from all the bullshit and strife – most of which I've caused, admittedly, over the years."

Acid snorted a second time. "This could be me talking."

"Please, Acid, help me get Kaminski off my back so I can go home. To be with her. I need those eggs."

"What about your uncle, can't he help? With money? Or getting this Kaminski guy to back off?"

"Like I said before, he's not a part of that world. Plus he's retired. His name doesn't have the same sway it did even ten years ago. Maybe he could help out with ma's care, but he's been through the mill himself with my aunt Sheila. And she's *my* ma. *I* want to help her." He risked a glance her way. "I promised her."

The room fell silent for a moment, broken only by the sound of Acid softly huffing. Danny watched her as she stared unblinking out the window.

"I know you're doubting yourself," he said. "But we can still do this. I know we can. So what if you don't have the same bloodlust ya used to have? Maybe that's not a bad thing. The way I see this going, we don't need to kill anyone. We can get the eggs and be out of here soon as possible, no drama. No killing." When she didn't answer him, he asked, "Did yer ma know what ya did?"

She didn't move from the window. "No."

"So the person she knew, who was that?"

Another long silence, before, "It was me, obviously."

"And is that person alive?"

She frowned. "Yes."

"Right. So a part of you existed before - independent from all the training and the killing." He paused, waiting for a reaction, but none came. "Look. I get you've had a tough old life and maybe you're a little messed up, got a few more demons than most to deal with. But don't give up just because you don't know how to be in normal society. Cos I've got news for you, darling, no one does. And anyway, there's no such thing as *normal society*, if ya ask me."

He kept his eyes on her, searching for a tell. A moment passed and then Acid raised her chin, her ruby red uber-pout slipping. And there it was. A softness in her face he hadn't seen before.

"What did I tell you about calling me *darling*?" she purred.

"Ah, get away with ya," he replied. "Deflect all ya want, Acid. Tell yourself you have to be a certain way if it helps. But sounds to me like maybe you aren't letting your ma down at all. Because maybe she'd never have wanted this life for you in the first place."

He shut up and sat back, realising his heart was beating heavy in his chest. In front of him Acid chewed on her bottom lip.

Jesus, she was attractive. Even with a face like thunder.

She turned to him. "You think you've bloody well cracked me open, don't you? Sat there with that smug grin on your face."

He held up his hands, dropped his expression. "Not smug. Optimistic. Expectant. Go on, we can do this. Steal the eggs and run. In and out. No fuss."

She huffed loudly before joining him on the bed, smiling in a way that made his heart beat even faster. "Fine," she said, indignantly. "We'll get your damned eggs. But I'm not promising anything, Danny, okay?"

He shot her a grin. "Of course."

She shook her head in that *I must be mad* sort of way that Danny recognised all too well.

"Go on then," she said, looking him dead in the eyes. "Tell me this plan of yours."

FORTY-TWO

THE SUN WAS HIGH IN THE SKY, SHINING DOWN ON LUIS Delgado as he strolled confidently along the busy Mirakruz Kalea. It had been a good morning so far, having already brokered a sweet deal with the Albanian trafficking gang led by Murat Sula for a flat three million euros. A decent day's wage, considering, to be paid in three parts – one million to be handed over this evening on inspection of the product, another to pay off Delgado's many contacts in the police and the customs service, and a third million when the shipment (seven young girls, most of them from Eastern Europe) had successfully passed through Spain and was on its way to the UK.

It was a dirty business – and not one that married well with Delgado's alter ego as one of the most celebrated and renowned citizens of Donastia (with whispers he could even be the next mayor), not to mention as a generous provider for his two ex-wives and six children – but the girls were peasant stock from countries ravaged by the effects of civil war. So really, he was doing them a favour. And then of course there was the money. Oh, the money. That sure did make him feel a whole lot cleaner.

Besides, Delgado had always been skilled at compartmentalising the different aspects of his life and business. Like today, shifting effortlessly from the murky deal to indulging in another great passion of his alongside money – art. Although admittedly, dealing art had also brought in a decent chunk of wealth.

His destination this afternoon was the El Destello Gallery in the south of the city. A modest enough establishment founded by Delgado in early 2010, it had fast become the go-to place to experience new and exciting Spanish artworks. Today was no exception. Hanging in the gallery right now were sixteen brand new paintings by the young Murcian artist, Pablo San Miguel – commissioned by Delgado and expected to earn him more than eight hundred thousand euros. Enough to clean most of the first payment from the Albanians.

As he entered the calm, white space of the gallery, Alfredo, the curator and an old friend, welcomed him with open arms at the exact moment Delgado's phone began to vibrate in his trouser pocket. Holding one finger in the air, an instruction to Alfredo to wait, he retrieved the phone and swiped at the screen.

"Yes?"

It was Hugo, his right-hand man. "I have confirmation," he said. "The egg has been retrieved. The files also."

Delgado turned to face the street, lowering his voice as he spoke. "And the Irishman?"

"I am told there were complications. But I have her word he will not be a problem for much longer."

Delgado gritted his teeth, affecting a smile as two handsome middle-aged women walked past and nodded in acknowledgement. "We can be certain? What do you think?"

Hugo laughed. "I think the Irishman is a chancer and an idiot. But he's not stupid. Within the next twenty-four hours he'll either be dead or on a one-way ticket out of Spain. He's nothing but a petty thief who made a big mistake. Not someone we need worry about anymore."

"But it is the principle. He must pay for taking from me."

"I understand your concern," Hugo replied. "And we'll see to it that Danny Flynn pays for his mistakes, but for now we have bigger issues at hand."

Delgado turned around, seeing Alfredo still waiting patiently in the centre of the gallery for him. "Fine. I trust your judgement. Have our friend deliver the egg and the files to my house this evening."

"What about the Albanians? They are coming also."

"Hey, the more the merrier," Delgado boomed, smiling at Alfredo as he spoke. "No reason I can't get all my affairs in order at once."

It was a statement full of bravado, but he meant it. As a man of many means and as untouchable as it got, nothing was too much of an issue for Luis Alejandro Delgado. He hung up as Alfredo unfroze and stepped tentatively his way.

"You've done a good job, my friend," he told him, spinning around and eyeing the gallery space – the sixteen huge and colourful canvases suspended from the ceiling with fine wire and hanging a few feet from the walls to create the effect they were floating in space. "Looks good. Looks really good." He glanced around. "Has there been any interest?"

Alfredo, sweating even in the cool air provided by the state-of-the-art temperature control units, waved one hand from side to side. "Not as yet. But we have only been open a few hours. They will come. Although this one has been here some time." He gestured to a woman standing on the far side of the gallery with her back to them. She was taking in San Miguel's *Sin*

Título 3, a square canvas painted a light grey and flecked with violent streaks of petrol blue and bright crimson.

"Is she a buyer?" Delgado asked.

Another non-committal gesture followed from Alfredo, this time his head moving from side to side. "Perhaps. She has spent many minutes in front of each canvas, looking in great detail." He moved closer. "She is very beautiful. A very sexy girl."

Delgado eyed his old friend suspiciously. It was unusual for him to talk this way. "Thank you, Alfredo. That is all for now. Leave me to appreciate my art, will you?"

"Of course."

He waited for the bumbling oaf to scurry back behind his desk on the far side of the room before sauntering over to join the woman in front of the painting. He approached slowly, taking her in as he did. She was wearing a red dress that was frilled at the bottom, like a modern take on a flamenco dancer's *traje de gitana*, and which hugged her feminine form in all the right places.

It was no secret (perhaps why he already had two ex-wives) that Luis Delgado liked the ladies. And all kinds of ladies, at that. White, black, brown, yellow, red. If they had a pretty face, a good set of titties and a nice round ass, why discriminate?

Drawing closer he felt a familiar swell of excitement as she tossed her dark wavy hair to one side and he caught a glimpse of her profile. What cheekbones she had. And that pout, resplendent in blood red lipstick. However, despite the dress and her colouring, he assumed her to be foreign. American perhaps, or even English. It was something about her stance, the way she held herself.

"Hello there," he chimed, slipping into what he'd always felt was a perfect English accent. "You are enjoying the exhibit?"

The woman turned to face him. "Oh, hello. Umm... Yes, wonderful. Really something." She smiled politely, but he noticed a glimmer of something else as her eyes quickly ran down his body. Attraction, perhaps. Nothing unusual there. Delgado knew he was a good-looking man and had never had any issues attracting female company, not even as a young man, poor and wayward – the money and the expensive clothes only increased his pull.

"Are you an artist yourself?" he asked, knowing this sort of question always worked well with beautiful women. Have them believe you consider them more than just a piece of ass.

"Gosh, no," came the reply, holding her hand to her chest in mock disbelief. "But I am an art lover. A collector actually of modern art, but also antiquities. It's how I got this bloody injury here." She turned her head to show him the cut on her right cheek, covered by foundation but visible all the same.

"Oh my. What happened to you?"

"Wasn't looking what I was doing whilst packing up a five million dollar samurai sword."

Delgado was impressed. "Five million dollars? Extraordinary."

"Yes. A Kamakura, actually. Thirteenth century but still as sharp as a razor. What ho." She let her hair fall back over that side of her face. "Sorry, I do apologise, I haven't introduced myself. Gabriella Goldstein."

She held out her hand and he took it in his. "Gabriella? *Perdona. Eres Español?*"

"Oh no," she said, looking bashful. "But my grandma, on my mother's side, she was Spanish. Her name was Gabriella too."

"Ah wonderful." He sighed. "Well it is good to meet you, Gabriella. My name is Luis Delgado and I am the owner of this gallery. I actually commissioned all these pieces you see today. From a young Spanish artist, Pablo San Miguel. He is good, no?"

"Absolutely. And I know who he is. I've been following San Miguel's career ever since his Murcia exhibition seven years ago."

He stepped back to take her in some more. "I am impressed," he said. "It is not often I meet someone with such impeccable taste."

"Oh I don't know about that," she said, fixing him with the sort of look designed to send a man wild. "But I certainly know what I like."

"*Por Dios*," he exclaimed. "Your eyes, I notice they are different colours. Amazing. Like a work of art in themselves."

She glanced at the floor, but smiling. "You are a charmer, Mr Delgado."

"Please. Call me Luis. So tell me, Gabriella, do any of the pieces tempt you to buy?"

She sighed and turned back to the canvas in front of them. "I do like this piece. But to be honest with you, I was sort of hoping some of his earlier works might be on display. There's one painting in particular that I've been searching for. Just to see it would be wonderful. To stand in front of it, absorb its power and presence. Do you know the piece I'm talking about – his *Campo Complementarios Número Tres*?"

"Of course I know it." A shiver of eager anticipation ran down his arms. "Because I own it."

She looked at him and her full lips made a perfect circle. "Is that so?" she gasped. "I knew it was with a private collection but, wow, that's unreal. I don't suppose I could…"

"Of course," he boomed, already one step ahead of her. "In fact, I am having people to my house this evening. A little business, but a little pleasure too, you know how it is. There will be drinks, good food. Why don't you come along?"

"I'm not sure I should," she said. "I don't want to get in the way if you're busy."

He touched her softly on the arm. "My house is grand. Room for everyone. You will not be in the way. After I've finished doing business we can... talk some more, get better acquainted."

She glanced at the floor before gazing up at him with those big exotic eyes. "Well if you insist," she purred. "Thank you. I'd love to."

"Wonderful. Give me your address and I will send a car to pick you up this evening. How does seven-thirty sound?"

Gabriella smiled at him, a glimmer of something else in her eyes now. Lust, he hoped. "It sounds absolutely perfect," she replied.

FORTY-THREE

ACID YANKED THE BLACK DINNER DRESS UP OVER HER CHEST and jiggled it into place, trying to ignore the way Danny was looking at her, his expression a mixture of admiration and concern sprinkled with more than a hint of frustration. It reminded her of the way Spook often looked at her, and it was pissing her off.

"Ya will be careful though, right?"

"Jesus, Danny, this was your idea, remember? Your plan." She straightened up and checked her profile in the bathroom mirror, sucking her stomach in as she did. "Like you said, it's a simple job, in and out. From what he was saying it sounds as if he's got a lot on this evening, so he won't miss me if I nip to the bathroom and accidently find myself in his office. It's all good."

She turned from the mirror and stepped into the bedroom where Danny was sitting pensively on the end of the bed.

"How do I look?"

"Amazing," he said, shaking his head. "As always."

She sucked back a deep breath. "Aren't you sweet. But I need you to get your head in the game. If things do go awry you have to be ready to move in a second. Do you understand? Have you got everything?"

He nodded to the unit opposite where a black Harrington jacket was laid out with a set of night vision binoculars, a Bersa 380 and two spare mags of ammo (all procured from Sonny an hour earlier). "Aye, all set. So you know where you're going?"

"Yes. For the tenth time. Don't worry." She picked up the black Gucci handbag off the bed and checked the contents – mobile phone, a lipstick and a roll of euros. They'd discussed the possibility of her carrying a weapon (the handbag was big enough, having being chosen to easily conceal two Fabergé eggs without making it obvious), but the view was she'd probably get searched going in and it wasn't worth the risk.

"Are you nervous?" he asked her.

"I don't get nervous."

He shook his head. "How the hell do ya not get nervous?"

"Easy. You focus your attention only on what you have to do next, regulate your breathing, listen to your guts." She caught his eye, him staring at her with a worrying intensity. "Worst thing you can ever do in situations like this is overthink it. In fact navigating cerebrally at all is a bad move. Best to go by feeling. Instinct. I trust that I'll know what to do, when I need to do it."

"And that works, does it?"

"Hasn't let me down yet."

Danny got to his feet. "First sign of trouble and you're out of there, agreed?"

"Agreed."

Because it was the right move, deep down she knew that. Get the eggs and get out of there with minimal impact. But hell, what she wouldn't give to show that sick fuck Delgado and his cronies what she could do. Give her a Glock and a handful of ammo and their trafficking days would be over.

Shit.

She shook her head, a bitter laugh dying in her throat. Who the hell was she trying to kid? They were right. They all were. She'd lost it.

"Acid?" She looked up, the fog clearing as she saw Danny's concerned expression. "You with me?"

"Yes. Sorry." She tapped her temple. "Going over the plan, that's all."

"Good, cos for a moment there it looked a lot like you were overthinking it."

"I'm fine." She stuck her shoulders back, chin up.

"Listen, I know he comes across all sophisticated but don't underestimate him, or his fella Hugo. They're bad men." He walked over and put his hands on her shoulders. "Are you sure you're up to this? I know I'm the one that's leaned on you, but after everything ya said, I'm having second thoughts myself and—"

"Hey," she hissed. "I'm not one of your little twinks, Daniel. I've been carrying out covert missions like this for sixteen years. It's what I do."

Danny raised his eyebrows, gave her a thin-lipped smile. "It's what you *did*. That's not who you are anymore. You're better than that."

She sniffed, shook his hands away. "Tonight it's who I am. If you want this to work."

"Fair enough. What time is it?"

She opened her bag, checked her phone. "Ten to seven. I'd better get going."

She'd told Delgado she was staying at the Hotel Maria Cristina, which was where his driver was picking her up. She went to the bathroom and checked her hair and make-up one last time.

"I'll leave now as well," Danny called through. "Get in position, ready."

He was waiting outside the bathroom door as she entered the bedroom. "You look great," he said, leaning in for a kiss.

"Woah, none of that." She swerved around the side of him to get past.

"Oh right, sure. Game face on."

"Something like that."

"Please don't do anything stupid," he said. "I know I sound like an old woman, but I mean it. I'll be thirty seconds away, ready, armed and waiting. You've got your phone set to call me if ya need to send the alert?"

"Yes," she snapped, opening her eyes wide and wiping at some wayward mascara. "Stop worrying. I can handle myself."

"I know… but…" He trailed off as she shot him an impish smile. "Just be careful, all right?"

She tapped him gently on the shoulder on her way to the door. "You know me well enough by now, Danny boy," she purred. "I'm always careful."

FORTY-FOUR

Luis Delgado had sent a limo for her. An actual shiny black stretch limo, with champagne in an ice bucket in the back and a surly driver out front (who looked like he might be more than a driver if and when it was required of him).

"This is a bit fancy," Acid cooed, still channelling Gabriella Goldstein, as she took a seat at the rear of the spacious car.

The driver grunted in response before pulling the car away. Either he didn't speak English or didn't want to speak it. But as they drove along Acid tried engaging him in further small talk, a way for her to better get in character.

"How long have you been driving for Mr Delgado?" was her next tact, but got the same grunted response.

Fine. Have it your way.

Despite his muteness it didn't stop the driver from peering at her via the rear-view mirror every minute or so, watching her as they drove along the quiet coastal road towards Delgado's mansion.

Whilst the silence and stares were a little disconcerting, it was nothing she couldn't handle, and the bats helped – not as dominant as she'd have liked, but screeching their support all the same. She closed her eyes, connecting with the restless feeling of invulnerability and only opening them when the car ascended a steep hill and she could see her destination up ahead. At least, she guessed it was Delgado's place – a single storey sprawling complex standing in its own grounds away from any other buildings and lit up like a football pitch. The limo slowed to a stop at the main gates and the driver's window whirred open so he could bark something gruffly into the intercom. He glanced back at Acid and a second later the huge double doors shuddered on their hinges and began to open.

"Whoa, what a place." She gazed out the window as the limo circled around the front of the property and pulled up before a brightly lit entrance hall. The doorway was at least eight foot high, beautifully ornate and done out in royal blue to complement the white exterior of the rest of the house – but she also noticed it was reinforced with bulletproof panelling.

"Thank you for the ride," she told the driver, as a tall man approached the limo and opened the door for her.

"Ms Goldstein?" He held out his hand and smiled an incredibly white smile, highlighted all the more by his swarthy complexion and jet black hair.

"That is correct. Thank you." She took his hand and he helped her out the car.

"My name is Hugo Torres," he told her, steadying her elbow with his other hand as she wobbled on her heels. "I am Mr Delgado's assistant."

"Assistant?" she purred, casting her eye over his muscular frame, bulging at the seams of his beige suit.

Hugo laughed. "Assistant. PA. Right-hand man. I do what is asked of me. It is a good job." Once she was out of the limo, he shut the door and slapped the roof and it drove away.

She watched it for a moment as it waited for the gates to

reopen, telling herself, *Stay focused.* Telling herself, *You're Acid bloody Vanilla.*

She could do this.

Hugo's deep voice in her ear startled her. "Might I say how beautiful you look this evening, madam?"

"Oh. Yes. Of course. Thank you very much," she replied, composing herself and hoping she'd passed the moment off as embarrassment. "You are too kind."

"Not at all."

"Is Mr Delgado here?" she asked as Hugo, a hand resting gently on her lower back, guided her into the house.

"Of course. But at present he is in an important meeting in the north wing of the property. I hope you can appreciate, he is a busy man, a lot of people have demands on his time."

"He did tell me he had business to attend to this evening. And I understand. I'm the same, to be honest. No rest for the wicked."

She laughed. A shrill, neighing laugh that she hoped was ridiculous enough to chill the sudden frosty atmosphere her comment had caused. Hugo's face remained hard, but a second later he relaxed, beaming another big white one her way.

"Mr Delgado has asked me to settle you in and to tell you he will join you shortly. Oh, one thing," he said, gesturing to her handbag. "Because of the many rare and priceless artworks we have on display in the house, we ask that visitors surrender all phones and photographic equipment whilst in the property. I do hope you understand. May I?" He held out a large, manicured hand.

Another laugh covered the tension in her jaw and shoulders. "Of course, here you go." She pulled the phone from out of her handbag and handed it to him. "Can't be too careful. Don't want every cat burglar in the country knowing how much money is hanging on your walls."

"Indeed," Hugo replied, frowning at the flip-top burner phone in his palm.

"A temporary phone. While I'm in Spain on business." She fixed him dead in the eyes. Serious face. "I'm an art lover, Mr Torres. Here to appreciate the wonder it brings and perhaps buy some pieces also. I like to keep distractions to the minimum so my sensibilities are not eroded by social media and silly gaming apps."

He nodded, satisfied with her response. "Please. After you." He stepped aside to allow her to enter, before closing the heavy door behind them. She waited in the cool white corridor, featureless but for an enormous canvas along the wall to her right. A Picasso, if she wasn't mistaken.

"You like?" Hugo asked, joining her in front of the painting, a swirling outlandish composition but still discernible as a bowl of oranges and a gold jug.

"Who doesn't?" she whispered. "Always was a keen lover of Cubist art."

"Oh?" Hugo half-turned her way. "But this piece is from Picasso's Surrealism period, painted some years after he moved away from Cubism."

A breath froze in Acid's chest. She swallowed back, painful on her dry throat, the action making an audible squelching sound that didn't help the situation.

"Of course it is," she trilled, leaning into Hugo and resting her hand on his forearm. "Just testing you. Although to be fair, the old masters aren't my cup of tea. I always say I like sculpture and artefacts as ancient as possible, and hanging art as modern as possible. I feel the juxtaposition created by, say one of Hirst's Spin Paintings, hanging alongside an ancient spear from the Hadza tribe is incredibly powerful. The old and the new. The brutal and the bold. Fantastic." She bowed her head, watching Hugo out of the corner of one eye as he nodded in agreement. The words had spilled out of her fast and loose, a lifetime of thinking on her feet preparing her well for moments such as this. But, shit. She had to be more careful.

"Would you like a drink while you wait for Mr Delgado?"

She was about to respond (hell yes, she needed a drink), when a noisy commotion at the far end of the hallway stopped her. A woman appeared from around the corner and staggered towards them. But as she got closer Acid could see she was younger than she first appeared, no more than eighteen, if that. She was dressed in a short red dress that clung tight to her slight frame and which showed off an array of round purple bruises mottling her thighs which looked suspiciously like fingerprints. Her dark hair was scraped back into a high ponytail and it was clear she was under the influence of something, either drink or drugs. Probably both.

"*Ajuta-ma*," she slurred, leaning against the wall to keep upright and holding a spindly arm out to Acid. "*Help me.*"

She'd only travelled a few steps down the corridor when a man appeared behind her and grabbed her by the tops of her arms, guiding her forcefully back the way she'd come. He looked up and saw Acid and Hugo before holding up a hand in silent apology.

"Oh dear," Hugo chimed, through a tight smile, the anger in his voice apparent despite his attempts at flippancy. "One of our other guests seems to have overindulged a little."

Acid watched as the man dragged the poor girl around the corner and out of sight. "Is she okay?" she asked, feigning shock. "She didn't look well."

Hugo placed a hand on her arm. "She is fine. As I say, she is I believe the girlfriend of one of Mr Delgado's business partners and has had too much to drink. That is all. Not your concern."

She raised her head, smiling sweetly at him. "Of course. These young girls, hey? They shouldn't drink if they can't handle it."

"Indeed. Please, follow me. Mr Delgado will join you as soon as he is able."

Once more she felt his hand on her back, but guiding her more firmly now as he directed her down to the end of the corridor where they took a right, going in the opposite direction from where the girl had come from. They walked in silence to the end of this corridor, where it opened out into a vast room with one wall made entirely of glass and the remaining three displaying five huge canvases. Pride of place, on the wall adjacent to where she was standing, hung San Miguel's *Campo Complementarios Número Tres*. She'd spent most of the afternoon doing her research on the piece (or rather, Danny had taken her through it, what she'd need to know) and was confident now she wouldn't be caught out.

"There it is," she purred with delight. "My god. What an impressive piece."

She turned, noticing Hugo had left her side and was standing by the wall in front of a large antique chest, on top of which stood an impressive selection of spirits and wines. Beside the chest on a silver stand, a silver bucket was filled with crushed ice and three bottles of Champagne. As she watched on, Hugo slid a bottle from its icy bath and held it up for her to see.

"Would you like some?"

She squinted at the label. "A drop of Moët? Absolutely, darling. *Perfecto*." Relaxing into her role as Gabriella, she accepted the glass of fizz with a flirtatious wink and gulped down a mouthful. "What an amazing space."

Leaving Hugo by the door, she sashayed into the centre of the room where three enormous couches in tan leather had been set up in a U shape facing the walls.

"Please, sit. Enjoy the art," Hugo said, backing out of the room. "Mr Delgado won't be much longer."

She mouthed *thanks* and gave him another wink before perching ladylike on the edge of the grand couch. The corridors in the sprawling complex carried the sound well, so she could follow his footsteps as he continued down the hall and took a left back towards the front entrance.

She gave it another beat before getting up and moving quickly to the window. With the bright lights in the room and the outdoor floodlights trained on the property, it was difficult to properly determine which direction she was facing. Her best guess was this part of the house faced north, towards the sea. If that was the case, Danny was positioned behind a small copse of trees up to her left. She hoped he could see her as she gestured out into the blackness of the night, opening her purse and turning it upside down before miming the time-honoured sign of a phone, shaking her head and drawing a finger across her throat.

No phone. They took it.

It wasn't the best start to the mission, but one they had considered. In this scenario, Danny would move with her around the property as best he could. He knew the layout of Delgado's place well enough. Knew the spots they were likely to go – this room, the reception area, maybe the dining room, and hopefully Delgado's office where the eggs were on display. Acid squinted out into the darkness and gave a last curt nod before moving back to the couch as footsteps reverberated down the corridor towards her. They were wide strides, slow and measured, but purposeful. A moment later Luis Delgado entered the room, throwing his arms wide before gliding over to her and grabbing her offered hand in both of his.

"Gabriella Goldstein," he boomed, over-egging the pronunciation. "Welcome to my home." He held strong eye contact as he spoke, before reaching down and kissing her hand with wet lips.

"Thank you for having me. It's wonderful to be here," she told him, retrieving her hand and wiping it surreptitiously on the hip of her dress. "I was, of course, admiring your wonderful collection."

"The San Miguel. What do you think, seeing it now in front of you?"

They both turned to take in the painting. "It's breathtaking," she gasped. "Absolutely beautiful."

"Not the only presence in the room that takes one's breath away." He leaned against her. "This dress you are wearing, the way your hair falls down over your shoulders – *bella*."

"Why, thank you." She turned to take him in, smiling as she raised her champagne flute to her lips. "I need to keep an eye on you, you charmer."

He tilted his head to one side. "Maybe I need to keep an eye on you also, Ms Goldstein. And what a name you have." He went at it again, giving each syllable a real flourish. "Gabriella Goldstein. I have never heard such a wonderful name. A wonderful name for a wonderful woman."

He laughed, and so did Acid, despite the chill rushing down her spine. Because she'd noticed something just now that had sent her instincts spiralling. It was a blink and you'd miss it moment, a slight twitch at the corner of one of Delgado's eyebrows. But with her senses heightened, on full alert, she'd clocked it. Tension. Anger, even.

"As I say, it was my Spanish grandmother's name. I've always liked it. She was a good woman. Strong. Like me." At that moment she didn't know who she was most trying to convince.

Delgado stared at her for a few moments more. The look on his face, she recognised – him trying to get a read on her. "Would you like a tour of the rest of the property?" he asked.

"Oh yes. That would be super," she purred, glancing out the window. "I bet you have many fine pieces in your private collection. I'd love to see them."

He smiled, his dark eyes crinkling up at the corners. "And I would love to show you them. Come, my office is the closest. We shall start there."

FORTY-FIVE

ACID'S EYES LANDED ON THE ORNATE GOLDEN EGG THE MOMENT she entered Luis Delgado's impressive office through two huge double doors. Although calling it an office was really a misnomer. The space was bigger than most people's apartments and more like a bijou art gallery than a place of work. In fact, the only concession to it being an office was a large leather-topped desk opposite the doors, decked out with a ubiquitous Apple Mac and an antique banker's lamp.

"Oh my," she exclaimed, gliding over to the huge walnut display cabinet standing to her left. "Is that… a real Fabergé?"

Delgado joined her at the cabinet. "You have a good eye, Ms Goldstein." He picked up the egg with no hesitation and held it to the light. "*The Hen with Sapphire Pendant.* An incredibly rare piece. Lost for generations."

"I'm aware. How did you come to own it?"

Smiling, Delgado placed it back on its round metal plinth. "I'm afraid I can't reveal my sources, Ms Goldstein. Not to other dealers, even ones as beautiful as you."

"I understand," she replied, then moving along the cabinet

and pointing to an empty plinth a few feet away, "Oh, what happened to this one?"

"Another Fabergé. Another rare piece. But it is currently… elsewhere."

She turned to him, noticing the tension in his jaw was even more pronounced. "Oh dear. I would have liked to have seen it. Is it far?" Despite the way Delgado was staring at her, she kept her face open, her eyes inquisitive.

"Not far," he said. "In fact, I have someone bringing it back to me this evening." He moved to the couch and sat, shaking his head as he did so. "You see, it was stolen from me."

Acid remained where she was, not taking her eyes off him. "Stolen? From your house?"

He nodded, a grave expression on his face. How a hammy actor might signal disappointment. "It was someone who worked for me. Who I thought I could trust. Can you believe this?" He sighed. "You cannot trust anyone in this world, it seems."

"How terrible."

He shot her a look. "Indeed. But come." He patted the couch next to him. "Sit with me a moment."

She hesitated. "I'm okay standing."

"Please, Ms Goldstein – Gabriella – I do not bite. Not unless you want me to, at least!" He leaned forward, emitting a loud laugh before cutting it short, adding brusquely, "There is something I want to ask you. Please, sit."

Acid held her ground as her amygdala fizzed and bubbled, sending a heady cocktail of stress response chemicals soaring through her nervous system. The bats screamed in her head. *Step careful.*

"Something to ask me," she said, walking over and sitting as far away from him as the seat allowed. "Whatever is it?"

Delgado grinned, sliding an arm across the back of the

couch. His eyes were like slits as he considered her. A second went by. And another. Acid glanced up at the large window behind the desk. Heavy wooden shutters hung open either side but the external pane had steel bars criss-crossing the glass. Not a surprise for someone in Delgado's position. She wondered if Danny could see her right now, and how quickly he'd be ready to move if things turned sour. Because something in the air had shifted and she didn't like it. Not one bit.

"You know, I have lots of contacts in the art world," Delgado told her. His voice was soft, but more monotonous suddenly. "Dealers, artists, collectors. Many in Spain, but all across Europe, America too, the UK."

She took a deep breath in through her nose, keeping the smile fixed in place. "I'm sure you do, a man of your stature. I know in my own life I—"

"No one has ever heard of Gabriella Goldstein the art collector," he spat, lurching forward and grabbing her by the wrist. "Not one person. Anywhere. So who are you? Who do you work for?"

"Hey," she cried, trying to remove her arm from his grip but failing. He was stronger than he looked, the palpable fury coming off him helping his case. "What the bloody hell are you talking about?"

"I'm talking about you not being who you say you are. Lying to me. So talk. Fast."

"Okay, fine," she gasped, thinking on her feet. "My name is Louisa Horowitz. But I am an art dealer, I swear. Or at least, I'm trying to be. I thought... maybe if I put on more of a show, you'd be more interested in what I had to say. And like me more." She looked down, before gazing up at him through her eyelashes, a forlorn expression wilting her smile, doing the whole bit. "I am so sorry, sir. I am such an idiot."

Delgado frowned, not convinced, but visibly softening,

releasing his hold on her. "You knew who I was?" he asked. "Before we met?"

"Of course. You're Luis Delgado, art dealer, entrepreneur, most eligible bachelor in northern Spain." He smiled at this, couldn't help himself, but it faded fast.

"You are a gold-digger then, huh?"

"Not at all. I'm attracted to you. I wanted to meet you, that's all. Wanted to find a way to get you to notice me." She leaned in and put her hand on his thigh. "That's all. I swear."

Sixteen years of experience in high-pressure situations such as this meant muscle memory had taken over, even if her mind and heart were both racing to a finish line she didn't like the look of. She remained calm, her body loose but ready to act. She smiled her best smile (sweet and innocent but with a hint of thirsty yearning) and slid her hand further around the curve of his thigh. "Please, Mr Delgado," she purred breathlessly. "I only wanted a chance to meet you."

"Well, here we are."

"Yes."

With eyes half closed and her lips parting, she leaned in closer, him doing the same. Short panted breaths met somewhere in the space between them and she braced for impact, waiting to feel his lips on hers. She'd expected firmness, a little aggressiveness. What she wasn't ready for was him grabbing her face and holding her at arm's length.

"You think I can't tell when people are lying to me?" he snarled, sharp fingernails digging into the flesh of her cheeks as he squeezed them together. "You're still doing it."

With her face squashed together this way all she could do was convey with her eyes and a shuddering shake of her head that he was wrong. That she was sorry. That she was also afraid. Because right now she didn't need to pretend. The air was tense as hell and despite her subconscious frantically searching for a way out of this situation, it appeared she was out of options.

Delgado pushed her back and got to his feet. "I have business to attend to. You will wait here until I have decided what to do with you."

"But I—"

He held his hand up to her. "I won't be gone long but while I am I suggest you consider carefully what you're going to tell me when I get back. Because believe me, Ms Goldstein – Ms Horowitz, whoever the fuck you are – I want answers. And if I don't think they're the right ones, then this will be trouble for you. A lot of trouble." He got over to the double doors and grabbed a handle in each hand, ready to back out of the room. "Mark my words, if you know as much about me as you say you do, you'll know I'm serious. You'll know I'm not someone you want to piss off."

Acid watched in silence as he left the room and shut the doors with a heavy thud. A second later she heard the grinding sound of metal against metal. Him locking her in the room.

"Bollocks," she whispered to herself. "Looks like we're going to Plan B."

She hurried over to the window and peered out into the blackness. She had maybe ten minutes to get out of here before Delgado returned. It was up to Danny now. She waved impotently at the window, hoping he could see her. Hoping he was on his way.

Hope.

Shit.

There was old Nietzsche again, echoing across the ages. What had she told Danny before – hope was what got you killed. She chewed on her lip. She still believed that. But right now it was all she had.

FORTY-SIX

But Danny had indeed seen the goings-on in Delgado's office. After tracing their path through the building he'd found a vantage point behind a patch of thick wild grass to observe, his heart racing and his fists clenching as he watched that son of a bitch grabbing at his girl. Now, with the pistol gripped tight in his fist, he came out from his hiding spot and made his way down the uneven hillside towards the house.

As he already knew, Delgado was a cruel and arrogant man but had few enemies in the region, meaning the place wasn't guarded up to its eyeballs. Still, there were men patrolling the property – one front and one back – both armed with what looked to Danny like submachine guns. UZIs, if he had to guess, but only because they were the only submachine guns he'd heard of (a misspent youth watching Arnie movies to thank for that). Though he did understand enough about guns to know if they began trading bullets he wasn't going to last two seconds with the measly handgun in his possession.

But they'd calculated for this eventuality. Sort of, at least. And the idea was to keep it a stealth mission. Get Acid and the eggs out without drawing attention to themselves.

Fecking hell.

It had sounded so simple back in Carlo's kitchen, but he was fast starting to realise that plans such as this were easier made than done.

Keeping to the shadows, he reached the bottom of the hill and concealed himself behind a large olive tree that overlooked the western side of the house. Delgado's office was at the far corner, and from this position he could see Acid at the window. She was looking straight at him but he was unsure whether she could actually see him.

He raised his hand regardless, mouthed, *I'm coming, don't worry* – wondering even as he did, who's benefit he was saying it for.

There were no guards on this side of the building but the heavy metal bars meant there was no way he could get her out through the window. Going in through the front door was his only option. Without taking a breath he moved quickly over to the perimeter wall and peered through one of the hexagonal holes cut into the stonework. The guard was standing with his back to Danny a few feet away. He thought he recognised him as a guy called Pietro that he'd met on previous visits, but it was difficult to tell from the angle and the way the severe spotlights made his black hair shine a reddish brown.

Before he could talk himself out of it, Danny shoved the pistol into his waistband and grabbed onto the top of the wall. It stood a little more than five feet high but he was able to pull himself up easily enough, swinging one leg over, and then the next, and sitting there a moment. Pietro was still facing the other way. His shoulders were flat and the UZI, held in two hands, rested limply at waist height as though he was weary – a long shift in hot weather would do that to you. Holding his breath and with gritted teeth, Danny lowered himself down off the wall, landing on the dry earth of an unused flower bed without making a sound. Seemed he wasn't too shabby at this whole covert mission thing, after all. But he quickly shook that thought away.

Stay focused, laddo. Not the time.

He stayed low, shifting his weight onto his haunches and ready to leap forward if needed. In front of him Pietro didn't flinch. Now, without daring to breathe, Danny moved his hand slowly and deliberately towards the pistol stuffed in his jeans and gripped the handle. In the distance he could hear the chirping symphony of thousands of cicadas, like background static suddenly rising up and filling his awareness.

Was it a warning? A sign?

Danny remained still, not taking his eyes off Pietro as he weighed up his choices, of which really there were only two. Shoot the guy and risk alerting the other guard (as well as those in the house), or take him out silently the way Acid had instructed. Undoubtedly there was a clear winner, but that way was also the hardest option and was giving Danny real cause for concern as he made the split-second decision and slipped the pistol from his waistband. In two strides he was behind Pietro, and in the same movement he flipped the barrel of the gun into his palm and swung the heavy metal handle at the side of the guard's head. The impact made a dull thump and sent Pietro stumbling to one side. But didn't knock him unconscious.

Shiting hell.

Danny followed up with another heavy blow, this time to the nape of the neck which knocked the man to his knees. A final hooked swing to the temple finished the job. It had all happened in a moment, but he felt worn out as he knelt over Pietro's prone form to see blood pouring from a deep gash in the back of his head.

The sight had him a little dizzy, and he felt a strange

sensation in the top of his groin. Not delight, per se, certainly not arousal, but it wasn't entirely unpleasant either. Whether he'd just killed a man, he wasn't certain, but the way Pietro was laid out, with his head twisted to one side (not to mention all the blood), he wasn't going to cause them any trouble for the foreseeable future.

Danny was over to the front entrance of the house in two more strides, pressing himself against the wall and stretching his arm out to try the handle. It was open. Holding the pistol the correct way around now, he slid across the front of the door and leaned against it, easing it open and leading the way with the muzzle of his gun.

The long hallway was empty as he stepped through into the house, but he could hear voices floating down from Delgado's luxurious lounge in the south-facing wing of the property. He paused, mentally travelling through the layout of the building. The office, where Acid was being held, where the eggs were, was all the way to the end of this corridor and through a door leading off to the right. With muscles tense, and creeping as softly as his frame allowed, he moved down to the end of the hallway. The voices were louder now and he could pick out Delgado's booming baritone amongst gruff Eastern-European accents. They were speaking English, but it was difficult to pick out precise words. He glanced around the corner, seeing the door to the lounge open a few inches. In front of the immense, Bond-villain-esque fish tank that ran the length of one wall, sat Luis Delgado with his henchman Hugo and two other men. They talked and laughed whilst a line of young, skimpily dressed girls paraded about in front of them.

Dirty bastards.

Danny's finger twitched on the trigger of his gun. The only time he'd ever come close to firing a gun was at a funfair, or on his Xbox, but despite his lack of experience the firearm felt comfortable in his hand. How wonderful it would be right now, he thought, to walk in there all guns blazing and put a bullet in all four of their sick skulls.

Save the girls. Kill the baddies.

But no.

That wasn't the plan.

Focus, Danny. Focus!

The mantra Acid had drummed into him all morning, all afternoon too whilst they planned the heist, echoed around his head. She was correct, of course. If he lost focus now, he could get them both killed. They were here to get the eggs and get out without making a scene. That was it. The start and end of the plan. So whilst it was shitty for those poor girls – like Acid told him – you can't save everyone. If he started shooting up the place, Delgado's men would be on him in seconds. He'd be no use to anyone dead. Then what would happen to his poor ma?

Wrenching himself away from the scenes in the lounge, he glanced both ways before moving silently along the next corridor towards Delgado's office. Once there, he tried the doors but they were locked. He stepped back to better examine the set-up. The two heavy iron bolts top and bottom were easy enough to get open, but a large mortis lock front and centre, not so much. No key.

Where was the damn key?

"Acid," he whispered through the narrow gap between the doors. "It's me. You there?"

He heard movement behind the door, then, "Yes, I'm here."

"Did he hurt you?"

"No, but I need to get out of here. Where is he?"

"Entertaining some guys down the way. He must have the key on him... or wait..."

"What is it?"

He pushed against the doors and they gave way a little with the pressure. "Ya reckon I can bust it open?"

"Reckon you can do it without drawing attention?"

He glanced down the corridor as Delgado and his cronies guffawed vociferously at something unseen around the other side of the door.

"All right, here goes nothing."

As more laughter emanated from the lounge he took a step back and launched himself at the double doors, barging his shoulder against the lock. He heard a satisfying crack of splintering wood, but the lock remained.

"Come on, ya bugger."

He raised the pistol, half expecting to see Hugo running down the corridor. But the occupants of the lounge seemed oblivious to any commotion. No doubt they were too engrossed in their sordid little fashion show to notice. With his heart in his throat, he went again, pushing off from the opposite wall, smashing into the doors with all he had. The impact sent a judder of electric pain shooting through his body, but with a loud crack the lock gave way and he burst into the room with a flourish of energy.

Feck yeah.

He'd done it.

He grabbed Acid's hand as she ran over to him, feeling suddenly like he could take on the world, feeling like Arnie, Indiana Jones and James Bond all rolled into one.

"Come on," he growled. "Let's get those eggs and get the hell out of here."

FORTY-SEVEN

Acid stared open-mouthed as Danny yanked at her hand. "We need to move. Now."

She swallowed back a ball of emotion. To say she was impressed by how expertly he'd negotiated her rescue would be an understatement, but there was more going on than just that. The dark presence that had been lurking on the edge of her awareness was finally rising to the surface, threatening to consume her.

She swallowed again and found her voice. "Wait, there's a problem. Only one of the eggs is here."

Danny scowled at the display cabinet, then back to her as she opened her purse to reveal the single Fabergé egg. "Righto. That's the Hen with Pendant egg," he said. "Not the one I stole originally. D'ya think…"

"…Magpie's still got that one? Yes. I know she has it."

She watched his expression, the excitement on display as he'd burst into the room now fading as the realisation hit home.

"Can't be helped," he said. "Let's worry about that once we're safe."

They hurried over to the door and peered around the frame. No one in sight. "You got a location on Delgado?" she asked him.

"He's entertaining some associates at the far end of this corridor. The lounge. It's big. Open plan. Looks to be doing some sort of deal. It's not good."

She turned to look at him. "How do you mean?"

"Girls." He grimaced. "Young girls."

The dark presence inside of her let out a silent sonic cry. The pressure in her head made her ears ring and her skin tingled with an unbearable rush of heat energy.

They left Delgado's office and padded along the white shag-pile carpet, taking a side each and sliding along with their backs to the wall. Danny had his gun raised, but Acid was unarmed and she didn't like that. She felt naked. Vulnerable.

Once at the T-junction of the two corridors, they paused. From this position Acid had sightline into the lounge and could see the four men sitting on the couch, grinning lustfully as three young girls swayed nervously in front of them. They were each wearing a short babydoll nightdress but in different colours, a red one, a yellow one and a pastel blue one. She clocked Red as the girl from earlier, but they all had a similar appearance – blonde, Eastern-European, young. Very young. They all looked to be fogged up in the same sort of stupor. Half-asleep. Half-drugged. Pliable. Unlikely to cause their captors any problems. The sight of them, drop-shouldered and unsteady on too-high heels like small children playing dress-up, it sent deep shockwaves firing up from her belly. The bats were now insatiable in their response as the darkness overtook her.

"Acid?" She glanced up to see Danny beckoning wildly at her, pointing to the exit with the muzzle of his gun. "This way."

Grabbing her arm as he passed, he led her down the long

white hallway towards the front door, shifting around so he was walking backwards and keeping his aim up the way they'd come. Before she knew it they'd reached the entrance hall.

Safety.

Almost.

A warm gentle sea breeze hit her in the face as Danny opened the door and guided her outside onto the driveway. She saw the body on the floor, saw the blood pooling around the man's head like a crimson halo.

"I think he's dead," Danny whispered, needlessly. "Let's go."

Acid watched as he hurried over to the perimeter wall. He had one hand on top, ready to pull himself over, when he stopped and turned back. "What's going on? We need to get out of here. Come on."

She didn't move.

The bat wings beat against her soul, screeching wanton encouragement as a familiar prickle of strength shot through her system. She was at once filled up with a strong sense of imperviousness. No thoughts entered her head. Just feelings, instincts, impulses she trusted. Like in the old days. The world had suddenly switched from fuzzy grey to bright technicolour and everything had a sharper edge – including her senses, bristling as they were with a keen new awareness.

"Acid, please." Danny was back by her side, gently taking her by the arm and pulling her forward. "We wait here any longer they'll realise you've gone."

She shook him off. Remained where she was.

Danny was a good man, deep down, but he didn't understand. No one did. It was so clear to her now what had been going on in all those months of confusion and darkness, where she'd tried to drown out her feelings with booze and distraction. The dark presence that had weighed her down, it was guilt. Guilt that she was letting her mum down. Guilt that she'd become flabby and flaccid in her desire for revenge. For blood.

But not anymore.

Seeing those girls just now, they were her mother, they were Paula Silva, and they were young Alice Vandella as well. Every young girl who'd ever been snatched up and used by the system, their innocence lost to the whims of evil.

And she wasn't going to let it happen.

Not today.

Without a word she reached out and took the Bersa 380 from out of Danny's grip. "Acid, no," he whispered. "You're not thinking straight. We're so close here."

But she'd already spun around and was heading back the way they'd come.

The next few minutes went by in a blur. She was aware of walking down the long corridor towards the lounge. Straight into the room, where she put a bullet through Hugo's smarmy skull the second he got to his feet. But after that it was all a bit sketchy.

She had vague knowledge of picking up a wine bottle as she marched over to where Delgado and the two other men were sitting on the couch. There were more gunshots. From her. Wiping out both of Delgado's cohorts with well-placed shots to the heart and neck. And from a guard too, who burst through a side door with an UZI but who was taken out instantly with a flurry of shots from the Bersa. Moving over to Delgado she put a bullet in his knee, sending him to the floor where he belonged, before bringing the wine bottle down on the side of his head. Expensive vintage glass splintered and shattered across her vision, shards slicing into the skin on her arms and face. The noise swelling in her ears was overwhelming. A red mist descended from the sides of her vision. She saw Oscar Duke in front of her. Saw the faces of all the girls men like him and Luis Delgado had devastated. She saw Beowulf Caesar, Spitfire Creosote too, before all these images were obscured by a haze of blood and rage. Blinded by the red mist, she straddled the dark form in front of her, bringing the wine bottle down over and over again with a dull thump. Glass on flesh. On bone. Her muscles burned with an intense rage she could no longer control. Somewhere off in the distance she heard the muffled sound of her own screams. Heard her mother's name. Her own name too.

Louisa. Alice.

Louisa...

Alice...

Then, as soon as it began, it was over. The cacophony in her head stopped, as though she'd switched off a droning TV set or a vacuum cleaner, leaving nothing but a white noise hum ringing in her ears. An absence of sound rather than a sound itself. In that same way you don't realise any background noise was present until it stops.

"Hey. Acid."

She looked up to see Danny looming.

"He's done. It's over." His eyes were wide and unblinking, his face white, flecked with tiny droplets of blood. Behind him, the three girls cowered together, stiff with fear.

"Woah... I..." She peered down at herself. She was completely covered in blood, her dress, her arms and legs. A glance in the large mirror hanging above the stone fireplace to her right showed her face was the same. Covered in it. Thick claret, sticky and warm, but not a drop of it hers. Lying between her legs was Luis Delgado. At least, she assumed it was him. His face was so swollen and mashed up it was difficult to tell. A real mess and no mistake. As she got to her feet, aware now of the violent rise and fall of her chest, he let out a low, pathetic groan. Still alive. Just. Still panting she pointed the gun at his face, and as he raised one shaking hand in defiance, she pulled the trigger. To say it felt good did not do the euphoria flooding her soul justice.

And like that, she was back.

Whoever she was, whoever she'd needed to be, to do what she had to do. That person was back.

It felt good.

"Okay," she said, taking in Danny and the girls. "Now it really is time to get out of here."

FORTY-EIGHT

ACID'S SKIN WAS STILL PRICKLING WITH WHITE HEAT ENERGY AS she and Danny herded the three girls away from the bloody carnage in the lounge and down the corridor. At the first corner she paused, holding her hand up for the rest of them to stay back while she moved around the side of the wall, leading with the Bersa.

"Clear," she rasped. "Let's go."

She stayed back, letting the girls stagger past her and covering the rear in case any more guards should appear. Although, by her reckoning no one was coming. With the commotion and gunfire that had taken place over the last five minutes, they would have shown themselves by now. So either they were all dead or they'd legged it.

Regardless, she kept her senses in check and the gun raised as she side-stepped along the corridor, covering both directions. They'd almost reached the exit when she stopped in her tracks. Her aim snapped to attention as a familiar figure, dressed in black and holding an UZI (no doubt procured from the dead guard outside), stepped through the door. Magpie saw Acid at the same time and raised the submachine.

"Wait," Acid yelled, her finger tense on the trigger of the Bersa and not taking her eyes off Magpie. "Not here. Let the girls go."

The three young girls, still drugged and oblivious to proceedings, stumbled against each other like crane flies trying to negotiate a locked window.

Magpie raised her chin a fraction at the sight of Acid (covered as she was in so much blood), but kept a tight grip on the UZI, holding it at waist height and ready to cut the lot of them down. "Why should I?"

"The code," Acid spat. "Our code. There's no contract on them. They're innocents. Not part of this."

Magpie glanced over Acid's head, before nodding at her appearance. "You killed Delgado?"

"I killed everyone, sweetie." She threw up an eyebrow. "It's what I do."

Neither of them moved, each watching the other with stern expressions and rigid jaws.

"What you did," Magpie growled. "You talk of the code, but what code? I have no code. You took that from me. I had it good. We all did."

"You had it good? Wow. Because I don't remember you cracking a smile once. And you know what they say, Mags, if you can't be happy killing corrupt government officials and drug barons, when can you be?" She nodded at the silk satchel slung over Magpie's shoulder. "Is that the other egg? The one you took from Danny?"

"The one he stole. The one I was hired to retrieve. You want it? Come get it."

Acid didn't flinch. "Let the girls go. Danny too. We'll sort this like adults. Me and you. With honour."

"Honour? Don't talk like you know what that means. There is only right and wrong in this world. There are sinners and there are the righteous."

"And which are you?" Acid asked, her grip slick with blood and sweat on the gun handle.

"I am the righteous," Magpie screeched. "I am judgement."

Acid ground her teeth, her finger heavy on the trigger. A tiny bit more pressure and she'd shoot the mad bitch through her eyeball. She remained still. Couldn't risk it. "Let the girls go," she said again.

Magpie narrowed her eyes. "Fine. Go. Quickly." She beckoned the girls forward with a flick of her chin. They glanced about them for a moment before Danny shoved them forward and they tottered away arm in arm, heading for the open door.

Time slowed. Acid stayed poised and ready. She had one shot at this. Literally. Her arm was numb with tension as she raised the small handgun in front of her, trained in between Magpie's eyes. The Bersa (small, inexpensive, what they called a *Suicide Special*, not her first choice of weapon) used a ten-round single-stack magazine, and in her blind fury she'd not counted how many she'd fired. Although, to be fair, she never did. If it was a Glock, or a Beretta even – a gun she knew like the back of her own hand – she might tell from the weight how many rounds she had left. But not today. She took a deep breath, slowing her heart rate as the girls shuffled past the grim figure of Sister Death. One shot. One go at this. She glanced at Danny who'd been staring at her the entire time.

He gestured with his eyes to a door on the right, a few feet in front of him. "Ya get me?"

Acid sniffed and shot her attention back to the door. As the last girl wobbled out past Magpie she faltered on her ridiculous heels and stumbled into her. Not enough to break her concentration, or her aim, but it was a break, and it was all they needed.

"Now," she yelled, rushing at Danny and bundling them both through the door. A burst of machine gun fire traced their trajectory, peppering the walls with a line of smouldering shots as they ran across the room and dived behind a large walnut-topped dining table.

Acid stood her ground, squeezing off her final shot to hold her back as Danny upended the table and they took cover behind it.

It wasn't a moment too soon, as a flurry of bullets pounded into the thick wooden tabletop, splintering the edges and sides. Magpie didn't let up, screaming like an insane banshee as she sprayed the room with bullets.

"Here," Danny gasped, handing Acid one of the spare mags.

Spurred on by a chaotic but impenetrable resilience, she shoved in the new cartridge and threw her arm around the side of the table, firing off a few more shots in retaliation but not expecting to find her mark. She needed a better view and was considering how she might distract Magpie enough to take a real shot when the onslaught of automatic fire suddenly ceased, leaving only a desperate clicking sound that was all too familiar. But for once the impotent sound of a gun without bullets was not her problem. In fact it was her redeemer.

She sprang to her feet to see her old nemesis frantically shaking the UZI. She let out a terrible scream before snapping her head up to see Acid.

This was it. Acid raised her arm, relishing the moment, ready to shoot the acerbic harpy a new blow-hole. But before she had a chance to pull the trigger Magpie flung the spent UZI at her, forcing her to dodge to one side. As she fired, the shot went high, taking out a glass lampshade which exploded into fine dust. Before she could right herself, a dark flapping object was hurtling towards her. This time the makeshift missile found its mark and the Fabergé egg bounced off her forehead, sending her staggering backwards.

"Hey, I got ya."

Amidst a spinning spiral of confusion and colour she felt Danny's strong arms catch her. He pushed her upright as she gasped for air, fighting to stay conscious.

"You all right?"

She blinked. Shook the dizziness away. There was a crushing pain in her head but she didn't have time to worry about that.

"Let go of me," she wheezed. "She's getting away."

As the room rushed back into focus, she caught a fleeting glimpse of white-streaked hair in the doorway. Magpie turning on her heels. Escaping into the night.

No. Not happening.

She shoved Danny away and leapt over the table.

"Acid, wait." She turned as she reached the doorway to see Danny holding up the eggs. "We've got them. Both of them. Let her go. It's over."

She eyed him penetratingly as her focus clicked back online and a squawking chiropteran battle cry reverberated across her nervous system.

"It's not over yet," she snarled. "Get the girls out of here and get back to the apartment. I'll see you there." She held her hand up as he opened his mouth to speak. "If I'm not back by morning, get on the next plane out of here. Okay?"

With Danny shouting protestations of caution and carefulness in her wake, she grabbed onto the doorframe, swung herself around the corner and ran out of the house.

The three girls were standing in the driveway, glancing nervously about and hugging at themselves with spindly arms.

"Wait here," Acid told them. "Help is coming. You're safe. Yes? *Safe.*"

They looked through her with hooded eyes, still pretty far gone. But she didn't have time to explain further. To the right of the house she saw the outline of Magpie Stiletto as she leapt the wall and disappeared down the side of a grassy ridge.

She was getting away.

With the gun still clutched tight in her fist, Acid sprinted after her, scrambling over the wall and practically falling down the steep embankment in her haste. Righting herself she continued down the narrow winding path leading to the seafront. The way the hillside curved around the bay, she only got brief glimpses of her old rival as they both weaved their way down, and in turn Magpie was sticking to the nearside of the path, knowing Acid couldn't get a clear shot if she did. That didn't stop her firing off a few rounds out of anger and frustration, but hoping it might unsettle Magpie too so she could claw back the upper hand. The bullets pounded impotently into the grass hillside, sending tiny eruptions of sand and earth into the night sky.

"Magpie," she roared. "I'll fucking destroy you."

The words burst out from deep inside of her, like an echo of her past – the demon she'd always carried with her rising to the surface and finding its voice once more.

Another shot pinged off the metal railing that ran alongside the steps to road level. Magpie was taking them three at a time, leaning on the railing to steady herself as she went. Raising the pistol as she turned the final corner, Acid fired off a succession of shots, not easy whilst running, but one of the bullets found a home in Magpie's shoulder. She recoiled clumsily against the stone wall of the steps, almost stumbling to the ground, but managing to right herself at the last moment.

A quick look of her shoulder and she disappeared around the hillside.

"Shitting hell," Acid screamed into the night.

The rage had her squeezing the trigger once more, firing off two more futile rounds before she felt the slide catch lock and the bolt open.

"Mother shitting bitch," she yelled, flinging the handgun angrily into the long grass as she reached the top of the steps. She scuttled down the first couple before jumping the remaining few, and hit the ground running. Up ahead Magpie had now crossed the wide coastal road and was making her way down another steep path that led to the beach.

There were no cars on the road at this time of night, no other soul, but even if there had been Acid wouldn't have noticed. Every cell in her body was homed in on the woman in front of her. Magpie Stiletto. Sister Death. The penultimate name on her kill list. The moon was high in the sky, painting the scene with an eerie glow as she hurried down the path towards the rocks and sand. Someone was going to die tonight.

Once on the beach Acid halted, casting her eyes across the dusky terrain. Jagged rocks ten foot high in places stuck out from the sand whilst, in between, large pools of tepid seawater had formed. Kelp and seaweed plants stretched their slippery limbs out of the rock pools and across the sand. But no sign of Magpie.

"Come out," Acid yelled, at a tall group of rocks that had formed together like the bastard cousins of Stonehenge. "I know you're here. It's over."

There was no reply, but she wasn't expecting one and it didn't matter. Her senses were all screaming in unison. Magpie was here. Moving slow and shifting into her peripheral vision in case of any surprise attack, Acid reached down and selected one of the rocks at her feet – small enough to hold with some purchase, but weighty enough to do some real damage with the right swing behind it.

Her stomach tight and her muscles burning with exertion and bile, she circled around the side of the large rock formation.

Step careful, the bats told her. *Be ready.*

Be ready…

Shit!

Something struck her upper chest, knocking her clean off her feet. A thick clump of seaweed on the flat rock beneath her broke some of the fall, but she was winded and worried for a second that she'd cracked a rib or even punctured a lung.

"*Ramera repugnante.*"

Acid scrambled to her feet as Magpie swung the heavy piece of driftwood at her again, this time catching her on the side of the head with a heavy blow. The momentum sent her stumbling forward but she remained upright, turning around and launching herself at her ex-colleague with a guttural roar.

"You piece of shit."

She caught her with a sharp shoulder to the sternum and pushed her back against the rocks, following up with a right hook that split Magpie's lip and sent tiny electric shocks shooting up her forearm. The two of them staggered apart, gasping for breath but not taking their eyes off each other.

"He never loved you," Magpie hissed. "It was all an act. To keep you compliant."

"Seriously?" Acid wiped the blood from her eyes, hers or Delgado's she wasn't sure. "This is about Spitfire?"

"It's about you. Ruining everything. Like always." In the moonlight Acid noticed her usual cold, dead eyes were alight with rage. "You thought you were invincible. But look at you. Without the organisation behind you, you're a mess. Worse than a mess. Caesar made the right call."

Acid's fists were so tight her knuckles ached. "Not worked out too well for him though, has it?"

"You thought he cared about you too, didn't you?" Magpie went on, spittle flying from her bust mouth. "But you were nothing to him but a pay check. You brought him power, money, esteem. That's all it was. You thought you had a family at Annihilation. You didn't. They all hated you. Like I hate you."

"Yeah, well, feeling's mutual, toots."

Fizzing with manic energy, Acid threw another heavy fist her way. But this time Magpie anticipated the blow and parried it well before countering it with a searing chisel punch to the throat.

The two women glared at each other, both fighting for air, waiting for the other to make a move, to make a mistake. In the distance the waves crashed against the shore.

"I'm going to kill you," Acid spat. "You hear me?"

"So you keep saying," Magpie sneered, exposing two rows of bloody pink teeth. "But I think not. You're washed up. Nothing but a pathetic, wanton nobody."

Magpie leapt for her, the moonlight glinting off the steel of a stubby push dagger as she slashed wildly at Acid's neck.

But she was ready.

More than ready.

Stepping to one side, she let Magpie lurch past her before grabbing her around the back of the neck and using her own momentum to propel them both forward. With a loud splash they tumbled into an enormous rock pool filled with sinewy black seaweed. Acid held on tight, grabbing the wrist that held the push dagger and trying to work it free as they squirmed in the seawater. They thrashed around, both fighting desperately for the upper hand, dunking each other under and gulping down mouthfuls of salty water before gasping for air as they surfaced. As Magpie rolled under, Acid reached out blindly and grabbed hold of her hair. She yanked her old rival's head back whilst simultaneously forcing her arm still holding the push dagger against the elbow joint. She gritted her teeth. Held on. Pulled back for all she was worth. Then, using an old trick she'd learnt from Caesar, she slackened her grip on Magpie's wrist. Only slightly. Only for a split-second. But enough to make her think she'd given up. To lull her momentarily. Then, without warning, Acid forced her arm back with as much vigour and rage as she could muster. Even with Magpie's head underwater, she heard the scream as the arm snapped at the elbow and she dropped the dagger. At the same time, Acid shoved her away and burst out of the water in a rush of briny spray. With the bats singing a song of bloodthirsty encouragement, she leapt at her old adversary and grabbed her around the neck with both hands. With legs spread either side of Magpie's flailing body she pushed her head under the water, down as far she could go.

"Die, bitch."

Amongst the foam and swirling seaweed she could see the assassin's cruel face leering up at her, those black shark eyes filled with the same hatred as always but with a desperation in them now. Fear too.

Well, good.

She deserved to feel afraid.

Biting her lip in grim concentration, Acid squeezed tight with both hands, shifting her weight to be better able to still the thrashing and keep a firm hold. Beneath her Magpie screamed silently from the depths, air bubbles rising and popping on the surface as she grabbed and punched with her one good arm, clawing at Acid's face and neck. A rogue fingernail tore down her cheek – opening up the torture wound from a few days earlier – but she didn't feel it. Didn't let up for a moment.

Revenge was the refrain and right now she was vengeance incarnate. This was for Louisa, her dear mum. But for herself too. For who she was, who she'd been, and for who she would become to survive whatever happened next.

She was vengeance.

She was justice.

She was Acid Vanilla.

And this ended now.

With an unyielding determination solidifying every muscle and sinew in her body she held Magpie down. The crazed assassin continued to claw wildly at her, fighting for survival. But then, finally, the thrashing stopped and her body went limp. A single bubble of air left her swollen lips and rose to the surface, and she was still.

Once certain the vile woman was dead, Acid rose to her feet, watching as the swirling sand and foam in the water settled once more and her own reflection appeared in the glassy surface, illuminated in the milky moonlight.

A real bloody mess, was how she'd have described herself.

Her hair was ragged and stuck to her skin with blood and saltwater. Her eyes and mouth were swollen, and the cut down her cheek was beginning to sting like hell as the adrenaline left her system and the bats faded into the background.

But she was breathing. She was alive.

And she'd done what she came here for.

Shifting her focus beneath her reflection, she saw the dead eyes staring up at her. "Louisa Vandella says fuck you," she spat. "And her daughter does too."

Leaving Magpie's broken body to bob to the surface (to be found by a dog walker or passing tourist in a few hours' time), she waded out of the rock pool and began the long walk back to the apartment.

FORTY-NINE

THE SUN WAS SOFTLY SETTING BEHIND THE JAGGED ROOFTOPS OF Soho, casting a pinkish-orange glow over the city streets. For once – for now – East London looked picturesque. Beautiful, even. And it was good to be home.

Acid turned from the window to see Danny leaning against the doorway. As their eyes met across the room, he threw up a conspiring eyebrow and gestured behind him. He wanted to talk to her alone, she already knew that. But she kept him waiting. Today was about Spook. About new chances and new fortunes.

"So, Acid – you like the new place?" Spook asked her, snuggling into the couch and smiling at her over a mug of steaming tea.

It was two days since Acid and Danny had arrived safely back in London, and for now peace reigned. Sonny had come good, as always, with a new passport (Sam Jones this time, much more standard, which Danny accepted without comment – although not really surprising to Acid, they were both drained of witty banter).

"I honestly think we can settle here for a while," Spook

continued, waving her arm across the room. "We can be happy here. What do you think?"

For effect Acid turned her attention once more to the decent-sized living area which led into an even bigger kitchen-diner. It was indeed a much nicer place than the depressing terrace which they'd been rotting in for the last year. The apartment had an affirmative lightness to it, it was airy and spacious, and it was newly decorated too, with an impressive couch that looked pretty comfortable, truth be told. But maybe that was why the bats were still niggling at Acid. Comfort wasn't what she needed right now. Comfort could very easily envelop a person. Make them soft and their determination flabby. She smiled back at Spook. For another time. Not for now.

"It's delightful," she told her.

The new place was above a dry cleaners, accessed through the front of the shop, and found for them by The Dullahan whilst Spook was convalescing above Dr Shi's practice a few blocks away – a convalescence that had put them back more than thirty grand. Yet it was clear Spook had received the best care. She was fit and healthy once more, and with a battle scar that she could be (and certainly was) proud of. Besides, Acid could afford it. Or she would be able to, as soon as Danny came good with the deal from the Fabergé eggs.

"Yes. The old geezer sure did well," she replied, catching her old rival's eye from across the room and winking slyly as he shook his head. "Central London too. We are being spoilt."

"It's a good price," The Dullahan said. "Plus, being somewhere busy, filled with life at all times, it'll be safer too. If the big man comes at ya again."

She held his gaze, letting him know the words had landed, but she didn't reply. The thought of Caesar still out there, still breathing air, sent a flurry of conflicting emotions spiralling through her mind. Beowulf Caesar. The last name on her kill list. The big one. She was going to find him. With the fire she now had burning inside of her, it was a forgone conclusion.

"Look at us all here," Spook giggled. "Like one big family."

Acid scoffed, taking in The Dullahan, dressed in a bright green Adidas tracksuit with the top zipped open to the waist and his emerald and sapphire encrusted shamrock pendant hanging over his gut. Then to Danny, his face patched up but with those baby-blues fixed on hers, smiling that cheeky smile of his, still willing her to come and talk with him. Finally she looked at her friend, little Spook Horowitz, comfy and safe on their new couch (teal velvet, wouldn't have been Acid's choice but it kind of worked). She noticed Acid looking and wrinkled her nose. *What?*

"If we're a family, we're a bloody weird one," she told her. "*Dysfunctional* does not do it justice."

"Aren't all families like that though, even the best ones?" Spook tilted her head to one side. "There's support here. That's what matters."

"All right, laddo, our car will be here soon," The Dullahan said, getting to his feet and shooing Danny out of the room. "I reckon we've got time for a swift pot of tea before then. Come on lad, help me."

When they were out of earshot, Acid turned back to Spook. "So you're feeling okay?"

"I am. And how about you? You seem different. To how you were before, I mean." She snorted, making a joke of it. "Because you're always *different* – to normal people – aren't you?"

She grinned but Acid remained stone-faced. What did they say about there being truth in humour?

"I want you to know, kid, you were right." She sighed. "I was a mess before. A real headcase. Sorry for putting you through that. I guess I've still got more going on than I like to admit. The way I understand it now, it was like I was in limbo, straddling two very different worlds and unsure how to step out of one and into the other – or if I even wanted to."

Spook's face fell, the smile fading as she sat forward on the couch. "And now? Do you want to? Can you?"

A shrug. "What if I don't need to? What if I can marry the two parts of me, somehow?"

"What does that even look like?"

Acid picked at the scab on her cheek. "I don't know. But for now I've got to keep hold of this fire. I have to keep moving forward with my mission." She held up her hand to stop Spook interjecting. "I know that's not what you want to hear, but that's the way it is. One more. Then I'll take some time out, I promise. To reflect. I'll see a professional, even, if that's what it takes. But I need you to support me in this. See - there's that word again."

Spook nodded, the mug of tea poised at her lips. "Sure. I get it."

"But I do believe I can find peace on the other side of this," she went on. "Who knows, stranger things have happened."

She had more to say but it could wait. Danny had reappeared, carrying a precariously balanced tray complete with a large teapot and a plate of biscuits. The sight of him in this domestic setting, knowing what they'd been through, what they'd shared (good and bad) over the last week or so, set her off laughing. And not her usual cynical scoff, but real demon-slaying sort of laughter. The sort that erupted from deep inside, from a part of her she'd long thought dead.

"Acid, before I go... can we...?" Danny gestured at the door once more, as he placed the tray down on the white coffee table in front of the couch. "I could do with having a few words. In private."

Shooting Spook a textbook eye-roll as she got to her feet, Acid followed the charming Irishman out into the hall and through into the larger of the two bedrooms. Except for a super-king-size bed, there was little furniture in the room, but it had been agreed Acid would take this one.

"What is it Danny?" she asked, closing the door behind her as he sat on the edge of the bed.

"Here." He patted the mattress next to him. "I want to say something to ya. Please."

She sat and rested her hands on her knees. Waiting. After a few seconds she glanced up, seeing Danny struggling for words. "What is it?"

He opened his mouth, but no words arrived. From his expression and the way he was flapping his hands about, she suspected she wasn't going to like what he had to say.

"Did you hear back from Carlos?" she asked, in an attempt to swerve the growing awkwardness.

"Oh aye, yeah. San Sebastian police are putting the whole thing down to a burglary gone wrong. Someone after Delgado's art. Most of the police were on his payroll anyhow, so I imagine they'll bury the investigation as quickly as possible."

"And Magpie?"

"Not heard anything, but if they tie her to him they'll cover that up too. I asked Carlos to check on the girls as well. They're all with Interpol. They'll be right."

Acid nodded. A good result. Though why didn't she feel one bit satisfied? She turned her attention back to Danny as he placed his hand on hers.

"Come to Antigua with me," he blurted.

"Excuse me?"

"Go on. I know my mammy will be there too, but she's no bother. We could have a good life, me and you. Think about it, all that money and our own tropical paradise. I—"

"What the bloody hell are you going on about?"

He shifted on the bed to look her in the eyes. "I love you, Acid," he said, speaking so fast it was hard to keep up. "I know that's heavy as all shite to hear. But it's hard for me to say as well. But I do. I know I do and—"

"No," she snapped, cutting him off dead. "You don't. You got carried away in the moment. In the excitement of it all. It happens. Heightened emotions and all that, one can confuse it for something else."

"I'm not confused, Acid. I do."

"You don't, Danny." She looked away out the window. "I'm not loveable."

"Please, don't tell me how I feel. I love ya. I know I do. Come with me. Please."

"Jesus. I've said no." She got to her feet and walked over to the window, looking down on the street below, but not focusing on anything in particular. "Forget about it. It's not happening."

Danny was quiet for some time, but she didn't turn from the window. She couldn't.

"Well, it was worth a try." He sighed. "I guess a part of me knew you'd say that. Not the marrying type, are ya?"

She smiled out the window, hiding it well. "No. I'm not."

Behind her she heard another deep sigh. "Shite. How am I ever going to find a girl who lives up to you, though? Someone who's cool as hell, and funny, and who I can properly talk to. Not to mention the fact you're a fecking knockout, with a killer body. Even with all those cuts and bruises. Ya see, all the usual women I meet are crazy."

She spun around, arms folded now. "I'm crazy."

"Aye, but you're good crazy. Amazing crazy. Most women are just weird and nagging and insecure."

"Do you ever wonder why?" she asked, her eyes widening. "Huh? What was it George Carlin said? Women are crazy, and men are arseholes. And the main reason—"

"Yeah – the main reason women are crazy is men are arseholes, I know the quote. I think he said men are stupid though, not arseholes."

"I prefer my version."

"I thought you might." He looked at her, eyebrows raised in defeat.

"All I'm saying is maybe next time you meet a girl, be nicer and she might not act so crazy."

He grinned joylessly. "You're breaking my heart here. Ya know that?"

"Am I? And how does that feel?"

"Awful. Like someone's kicked me in the nuts and the chest at the same time."

She let her arms fall to her sides and joined him on the bed. "Well, remember that feeling next time you're so ready to break some poor girl's heart."

"Shitting hell. Is that all this was?" he asked. "You teaching mankind a lesson one fool at a time?"

"No, it wasn't like that at all. I found you attractive and I needed a release. Plus, you are pretty terrific in bed." She nudged him with her shoulder. "But I don't do relationships."

He let out a deep sigh. "You're cold as ice, ya know that?"

"I have to be, sweetie. Safer that way. For everyone."

There was a knock on the door and The Dullahan put his head around. "Ya ready, laddo? The car's here for us."

Danny got to his feet and Acid did too. "I guess I'll be in touch then," he said. "Once the exchange has gone through and I've got your money."

"Thanks, and don't worry, you're going to be fine." She let her hand brush against his forearm for a second. "You're a good man, Danny. Better than you think."

"He's a fecking eejit!" The Dullahan exclaimed. "Come on, Lovejoy."

Acid followed the two men out the door and down the hall. "New driver, is it?" she asked.

"Aye, well the other one wasn't up to scratch, was he?"

"You can trust this one?"

"As much as you can trust any nefarious fellow trying to make a name for himself. But don't worry about me, I'm a wily one. It all turned out okay in the end, didn't it?"

"That's one way of looking at it," she replied. "And you'll let me know if you hear anything? About Caesar?"

"That I will. As always." He turned around. "Don't worry, lassie. You'll get him."

They were at the front door now. Acid leaned against the frame to watch as the two men left along the corridor that led through the dry cleaners and out onto Berwick Street. As she eased the door closed, she caught Danny's blue eyes as he looked back at her. She smiled and raised her hand in farewell.

Then she shut the door.

Because it was better this way, she hadn't been lying about that. Safer for them both. She already had two lifetimes of guilt weighing her down and she couldn't afford to put anyone else in the firing line. Couldn't afford to get distracted either.

Not now.

Like comfort, like contentment, love was the last thing she needed. Love made a person weak and stale and she couldn't – wouldn't – have that. Her sights were now firmly fixed on her mission, her energy restored by the fire of revenge burning in her belly. The old Acid Vanilla was back, the only person who could get this job done.

And she was ready.

Beowulf Caesar wouldn't know what hit him.

The end

GET YOUR FREE BOOK

Discover how Acid Vanilla transformed from a typical London teenager into the world's deadliest female assassin.

Get the Acid Vanilla Prequel Novel:
Making a Killer available FREE at:

www.matthewhattersley.com/mak

CAN YOU HELP?

Enjoyed this book? You can make a big difference

Honest reviews of my books help bring them to the attention of other readers. If you've enjoyed this book I would be very grateful if you could spend just five minutes leaving a review (it can be as short as you like) on the book's Amazon page.

ALSO BY MATTHEW HATTERSLEY

Have you read them all?

The Acid Vanilla series

The Watcher

Acid Vanilla is an elite assassin, struggling with her mental health. Spook Horowitz is a mild-mannered hacker who saw something she shouldn't. Acid needs a holiday. Spook needs Acid Vanilla to NOT be coming to kill her. But life rarely works out the way we want it to.

BUY IT HERE

Seven Bullets

Acid Vanilla was the deadliest assassin at Annihilation Pest Control. That was until she was tragically betrayed by her former colleagues. Now, fuelled by an insatiable desire for vengeance, Acid travels the globe to carry out her bloody retribution. After all, a girl needs a hobby...

BUY IT HERE

Making a Killer

How it all began. Discover Acid Vanilla's past, her meeting with

Caesar and how she became the deadliest female assassin in the world.

FREE TO DOWNLOAD HERE

Stand-alone novels

Double Bad Things

All undertaker Mikey wants is a quiet life and to write his comics. But then he's conned into hiding murders in closed-casket burials by a gang who are also trafficking young girls. Can a gentle giant whose only friends are a cosplay-obsessed teen and an imaginary alien really take down the gang and avoid arrest himself?

Double Bad Things is a dark and quirky crime thriller - for fans of Dexter and Six Feet Under.

BUY IT HERE

Cookies

Will Miles find love again after the worst six months of his life? The fortune cookies say yes. But they also say commit arson and murder, so maybe it's time to stop believing in them? If only he could...

"If you life Fight Club, you'll love Cookies." - TL Dyer, Author

BUY IT HERE

ABOUT THE AUTHOR

Over the last twenty years Matthew Hattersley has toured Europe in rock n roll bands, trained as a professional actor and founded a theatre and media company. He's also had a lot of dead end jobs...

Now he writes Neo-Noir Thrillers and Crime Fiction. He has also had his writing featured in The New York Observer & Huffington Post.

He lives with his wife and young daughter in Manchester, UK and doesn't feel that comfortable writing about himself in the third person.

COPYRIGHT

A Boom Boom Press ebook

First published in Great Britain in April 2021 by Boom Boom Press.

Ebook first published in 2021 by Boom Boom Press.

Copyright © Boom Boom Press 2015 - 2021

The moral right of Matthew Hattersley to be identified as the author of this work has been asserted by him in accordance with the copyright, Designs and Patents Act 1988.

All the characters in this book are fictitious, and any resemblance to actual persons living or dead is purely coincidental.

All rights reserved. No part of this publication may be reproduced, stored in a retrieval system or transmitted in any form or by any means, without the prior permission in writing of the publisher, nor to be otherwise circulated in any form of binding or cover other than that in which it is published without a similar condition, including this condition, being imposed on the subsequent purchaser.

Printed in Great Britain
by Amazon

17063640R00176